TAYLOR & ROSE

Secret Agents

VILLAINS IN VENICE

Also by Katherine Woodfine

Peril in Paris
Spies in St Petersburg
Secrets on the Shore (ebook)

'*Woodfine's crisp prose is instantly evocative,
and her quick-moving plots will appeal both to
newcomers and long-time devotees.*'
Guardian

The Sinclair's Mysteries

The Clockwork Sparrow
The Jewelled Moth
The Painted Dragon
The Midnight Peacock

'*Utterly enthralling*'
Abi Elphinstone

TAYLOR & ROSE
Secret Agents

VILLAINS IN VENICE

KATHERINE WOODFINE

Illustrated by Karl James Mountford

EGMONT

EGMONT

We bring stories to life

First published in Great Britain 2020
by Egmont UK Limited
2 Minster Court, London EC3R 7BB
www.egmontbooks.co.uk

Text copyright © 2020 Katherine Woodfine
Illustrations copyright © 2020 Karl James Mountford

The moral rights of the author and illustrator have been asserted

978 1 4052 9326 6
70061/001

A CIP catalogue record for this title is available
from the British Library

Typeset by Avon DataSet Ltd, Bidford on Avon, Warwickshire
Printed and bound in Great Britain by the CPI Group

For The Clan

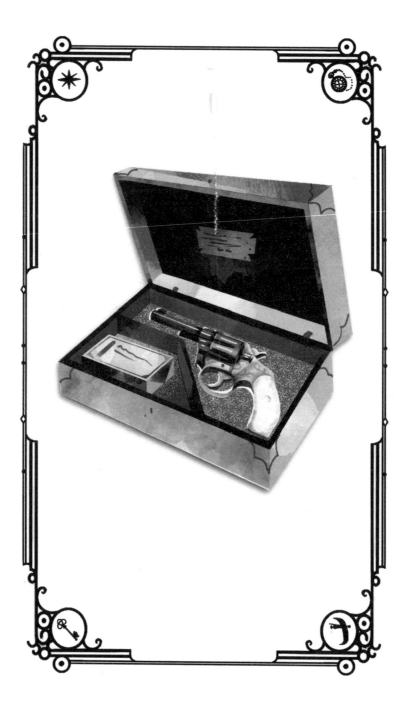

PART I

'. . . And so we are back in London again. After all our adventures, I must confess the city seems drab and dull. Nothing is the same as it was before and I find myself eager to resume our travels once more.

Once Papa's business here is complete, and before we return to Cairo, he has promised me a trip to one of the places I most long to see – Italy! So for the present I shall tolerate grey London, while dreaming of blue Italian skies . . .'

– From the diary of Alice Grayson

No. 2592   A NORTON NEWSPAPER   *One Half-Penny*

3rd February 1912

THE DAILY PICTURE

GREAT BRITAIN IN PERIL!

PRIME MINISTER RESPONDS TO GERMAN SPY THREAT

The Prime Minister has responded to growing concerns about German espionage taking place in Britain.

It is believed that there may be more than a hundred German spies at work in our naval ports and London - with the result that considerable information about the British military is now in German hands. Our sources report that details of naval artillery, plans of campaign, code books and wireless telegraphy keys are amongst the material that has already been gathered by these operatives.

'There is certainly no doubt that there are German spies in Britain, attempting to gather military intelligence,' stated Prime Minister Arthur Lockwood. 'But the public should be reassured that this is an issue the government takes very seriously. Measures are being taken by the War Office to ensure that enemy agents will be swiftly identified and arrested.'

Meanwhile in Germany, much has been made of the belief that Great Britain was ready to attack and destroy the German Naval fleet on several occasions last year (continued p4)

HAVE YOU ENCOUNTED A SPY?

If you have observed something suspicious let us know! The Daily Picture is offering a £10 reward for letters with information about suspected German spies: send to Mr W. James, Spy Editor, The Daily Picture, Norton Newspapers, Fleet Street, London EC4

CARNIVAL SPECTACULAR

TO TAKE PLACE IN VENICE!

A revival of the 18th century Carnival is to take place in Venice, Italy later this month, with many celebrated personages expected to attend. New York socialite Mrs V. Davenport will be the hostess of a spectacular gathering at an 15th century palazzo on the Grand Canal, with invited guests including Paris fashion designer César Chevalier, daredevil pilot Antonio Rossi, West End star Mrs Kitty Whitman, artist Max Kamensky, and newspaper magnate Sir Chester Norton. Entertainment will include a specially devised performance from the Ballets Russes, with refreshments to include traditional Italian delicacies – (continued p27)

— Italian troops blockade Red Sea Coast – p17
— South Pole Expedition: Latest Report – p19
— Fears of uprising in Albania – p23
— Circus of Marvels performs in Tokyo for the Emperor of Japan – p30

CHAPTER ONE

Charing Cross Road, London

It was sleeting in London as the young man slipped out of the office marked: *CLARKE & SONS SHIPPING AGENTS*, closing the door softly behind him. There was no one to see him and yet there was something furtive about the way he hurried down the stairs, tucking an envelope into his pocket as he did so.

Out in the street he looked swiftly around him before unfurling a black umbrella and walking purposefully in the direction of Charing Cross. It was a dingy February morning: motor-taxis and omnibuses swished through the grey slush on the road and a chilly, miserable-looking newsboy was selling copies of *The Daily Picture* from outside the brightly lit window of a hat shop while people well wrapped up in winter coats hurried past him towards the underground railway station.

The young man went by with the rest. He didn't glance at the newsboy, nor at any of the bright shop windows he passed, but instead kept on walking, his head down, his face concealed by the black umbrella.

He did not slow his pace until he reached the Charing Cross Road, where he turned to duck inside the door of a bookshop, pausing first to shake the sleet off his umbrella.

The bell jingled as he stepped through the door. Inside the shop was warm and snug: the light from the gas-lamps fuzzy, the windows fogged, the air rich with the smell of leather bindings and beeswax. He glanced around rapidly, taking in half a dozen people browsing the shelves that stretched from floor to ceiling. A lady in a fur-trimmed hat was flicking through the pages of a book by E. M. Forster, and an old man with a monocle was browsing the shelves of the poetry section. A cluster of schoolchildren was gathered around a stack of detective novels, while behind the counter, the bookseller was patiently listening to a gentleman explaining that he was looking for a book that he'd seen in the shop last year, although he couldn't remember either the title or the name of the author.

The young man went past them all, towards the back of the shop. In the dark corner marked 'Foreign Languages', he frowned at the shelves before locating a Russian phrasebook and flipping it open.

Across the shop, the gentleman at the counter was saying: 'I believe it had a *green* cover, although now I think about it, it may possibly have been *blue*,' while the bookseller listened wearily.

Nearby, one of the schoolboys was brandishing a copy of a newly published Montgomery Baxter detective story. 'You've simply *got* to read this,' he was exclaiming to one of his companions. 'The ending is awfully thrilling. I can't wait for the next book to find out what happens.'

'I bet I can guess,' said another of the boys with an air of great authority. Then in a very different voice: 'Oh, Jane, *you* can't buy it. Papa wouldn't like it!'

'I don't see why I shouldn't,' argued the girl beside him, tossing back her plaits. 'I've got half a crown of my birthday money to spend.'

'But look – why don't you get a school story instead? Or one of those books of fairy tales?' suggested the boy. He reached towards her and tried to take the copy of *Montgomery Baxter and the Lost Treasure* out of her hands, but she had no intention of handing it over and there was a scuffle. The Montgomery Baxter book fell to the floor with a thump, making the other customers look around disapprovingly and the bookseller frown over the top of his spectacles.

In that moment, unnoticed by anyone, the young man swiftly slid the envelope out of his pocket and inside the Russian phrasebook. A minute later the book was back in its place on the shelf and the young man had left the shop, pacing back along the street under his umbrella, the bell above the door dinging quietly behind him.

At the counter, the bookseller was trying to explain that they had rather a lot of books with green and blue covers, and could sir possibly remember anything else about the book, otherwise he was afraid he couldn't do much to help.

Meanwhile, the girl with plaits had picked up the Montgomery Baxter book. 'Murders and crimes and spies and all that sort of thing – they aren't *suitable* for girls,' her brother was blustering as the door opened again and another young man came in.

Properly speaking, he wasn't really a young man at all. He was probably only about sixteen, not much older than the schoolboys clustered around the display of detective stories. He wore a dark blue coat and cap and had a striped woollen scarf around his neck. He might have been an office boy, or perhaps a junior clerk. As he came into the shop, he caught sight of the book in the girl's hand and gave a little grin as he heard what her brother was saying, but then straightened his face almost at once as if remembering he was here on serious business. He went past the detective stories, past the fiction and poetry books, heading for the Foreign Languages section.

Once there, he ran a finger quickly along the spines until it settled on the Russian phrasebook. At the counter, the gentleman looking for the green or possibly blue book was tutting to himself and muttering that it was 'all very unsatisfactory' while the long-suffering bookseller wrapped *Montgomery Baxter and the Lost Treasure* for the girl with plaits. The young man fidgeted while he waited to be served, then handed over his money before tucking the Russian phrasebook into his pocket, now neatly wrapped in brown paper.

A minute or two later, he was following in the wake of the group of schoolchildren, out of the shop door and into the street, pulling his striped scarf more closely around him.

The sleet was falling faster and thicker now; a moment later, he had vanished into its blurry whiteness and disappeared.

CHAPTER TWO

Lyons Corner House, London

Not very far away from the Charing Cross Road, Sophie Taylor was sitting by herself at a table in the window of Lyons Corner House.

She did not notice the sleet outside the window. Neither was she paying any attention to the cup of tea that was rapidly cooling at her elbow, nor the bun waiting uneaten on a plate. Instead she leaned her forehead in her hands as she bent over the newspapers spread out on the table in front of her. She was frowning as she scrutinised the pages of the morning edition of *The Daily Picture*.

It did not make very reassuring reading. Threaded between the reports of an expedition to the South Pole and a review of a new play at the Fortune Theatre were several stories about conflict in Europe and beyond. There was unrest in the Balkans. Trouble in Morocco. Rumours of a rebellion in Albania. To someone else they might not have meant very much, but for Sophie they joined together to form a jagged pattern. She felt certain that they were all the doing of the *Fraternitas Draconum*, the sinister secret society who were working to try and start a terrible war.

Most people had never even heard of the *Fraternitas*. The other customers sitting in Lyons Corner House probably wouldn't have believed that such a group existed. Sophie glanced around, taking in the shoppers with parcels, talking and laughing and drinking tea. They all looked so contented and peaceful. They were not aware of the danger that she could see everywhere, hovering over them like a dark cloud.

For Sophie, the *Fraternitas* and their schemes were all too real. For a while now she'd been battling against their devious plots to spark off a horrifying war in Europe from which they intended to profit. She'd grappled with everything from shocking murders to Royal assassination attempts, and following in the footsteps of her parents, who had given their lives to the fight against the *Fraternitas*, she had formed a group here in London called the Loyal Order of Lions, who had vowed to work against them. And yet in spite of all her efforts, here the *Fraternitas* were, reaching right across Europe, seemingly stronger and more powerful than ever before.

Sophie sighed as she flicked back to the front page. As if that wasn't bad enough, there were the tensions growing between Britain and Germany. It was not news to her that there were German spies in Britain – after all, she'd

9

encountered them herself more than once. But a hundred of them? That was just nonsense. She knew the Prime Minister was trying to reassure people, but the front-page headline would only fuel everyone's fears and make things worse.

It had been three years since Sophie had found the missing Clockwork Sparrow and solved her first mystery. She'd been only fourteen then – a more-or-less-ordinary girl with a more-or-less ordinary job selling hats at Sinclair's department store. Now, she was going on for eighteen and she didn't think that anyone could describe her as 'ordinary' any longer. Nor was she a shopgirl: instead, she was one of the proprietors of Taylor & Rose, London's first young ladies' detective agency. What was more, she was also an agent of the government's Secret Service Bureau.

Four years ago, Sophie had been alone with no friends, family or money. She knew she had been lucky to get a job in any shop, never mind an elegant department store like Sinclair's. Now, she lived a life that most girls of her age couldn't even dream of: running her own business; travelling across Europe by boat, train and even aeroplane; carrying out secret missions for her country in Paris and most recently, St Petersburg. She'd taken on the infamous crime lord known as 'the Baron' and won. And yet as she sat in the window, flicking through the newspaper, she felt smaller and more powerless than ever before.

Under the table, Daisy whined and laid her head in

Sophie's lap. Dogs weren't allowed in Lyons Corner House but the kind-hearted waitress always looked the other way as long as Daisy stayed out of sight. The big Alsatian kept close to them all these days – sleeping curled up under Sophie's desk in the office, pattering after Billy every time he went over to the filing cabinet and, most heartbreaking of all, jumping up hopefully every time someone came to the door, wagging her tail as though *this* time it was certain to be Joe, coming back to them at last.

Sometimes Sophie let herself imagine it too. The soft sound of feet outside the door. Daisy bounding up and barking joyfully. The door swinging open and Joe strolling in, wearing his old jacket that smelled of the stables. He'd say 'Hullo, Soph,' just as though he'd seen her only yesterday. No one else ever called her 'Soph'. The thought gave her a sharp pain – jagged, like broken glass.

It had been three months since Sophie and Lil had returned from St Petersburg. Three months since they'd come back to London, excited to tell Billy and Joe about their adventures, but they'd found only Billy waiting for them, anxious and alone.

Ever since they'd solved the mystery of the Clockwork Sparrow, the four of them had been a team. There were others who worked with them, first and foremost Mei Lim, who was their receptionist and handled much of the important office work, from booking appointments to arranging payments. Then there was Tilly Black, who was

Taylor & Rose's technical expert. But at the centre of it all were Lil and Sophie, Billy and Joe. Even when she and Lil had begun travelling abroad on missions for the Bureau, they'd always known that Joe and Billy were in London, keeping things going. *Keeping the home fires burning*, she thought. After all, Taylor & Rose was a kind of home for all of them, and for her most especially. Because while Billy had his mum and Uncle Sid, and Lil had her older brother Jack, Sophie was all alone in the world. Taylor & Rose was her family. And she knew without them ever having discussed it that Joe had felt exactly the same.

Now, Joe was gone. In St Petersburg, Sophie and Lil had learned that there was a double agent at the Bureau – someone passing top-secret inside information to the *Fraternitas Draconum*. While they had been away, Joe had discovered the same thing. He'd seen documents being smuggled out of the Bureau and passed to a woman whom he'd followed to the offices of *The Daily Picture*. He'd gone out in search of the mysterious woman to try and find out more, but he had never come back.

They'd set out to look for him straight away of course. Sophie and Lil were no strangers to finding missing persons and they'd put their detective skills to work, recruiting all the other members of the Loyal Order of Lions to help them, and consulting their friends at Scotland Yard. They'd gone up and down Fleet Street, talking to everyone from street cleaners to shopkeepers. They'd spent days freezing themselves in the Embankment Gardens, watching the statue where Joe had seen the handover of the confidential information take place. They'd quizzed the staff of Sinclair's in case any of them might know something, and they'd talked to the people in the East End who knew Joe – not only Mei's family, but Mr and Mrs Perks from the Seven Stars Inn, and old Samuel in Limehouse who'd once taught Sophie to crack a safe. But as day after day went by without a single clue, Sophie had begun to feel a rising sense of dread. The *Fraternitas* were utterly ruthless, and if Joe had crossed their path she knew he would have found himself in the very gravest danger.

Billy had been beside himself. 'He told me he saw the double agent come out of the Bureau . . . he followed them . . . but he didn't know for sure who they were!' he'd fretted. 'I ought to have asked him more questions! I ought to have gone with him to the offices . . . if only I'd been there, then maybe . . .' His voice had trailed miserably away.

'You couldn't have known what was going to happen,' Lil had said, refusing to think the worst. 'Cheer up. I bet he'll turn up at any moment. You know Joe – he's so thorough. He's probably off following a lead.' But all the time Sophie's feeling of dread had been growing worse and worse.

In the end, it had been their old friend, Detective

Sergeant Thomas of Scotland Yard, who had brought the news she feared. He'd arrived at the Taylor & Rose offices carrying a navy-blue Sinclair's cap stained with something dark. Sophie had recognised it at once, even before Billy's horrified exclamation: 'That's Joe's!'

The cap had been found down an alleyway in Whitechapel. There had been reports of an altercation and a gunshot fired. By the time the local constable had arrived, he'd found only the cap, lying in a pool of blood.

'We saw the label marked *Sinclair's*, so we came straight here,' Sergeant Thomas had said, his voice quiet and grave. 'Betteredge said he believed this cap belonged to Joe. I'm very, very sorry.'

Sophie had had to grip the back of a chair to steady herself. They had been in danger so many times – in Paris, St Petersburg and here in London. And yet however frightening things had been, somehow they had always made it back to Sinclair's to talk about their adventures over tea and buns. Somehow she had believed they always would.

Dimly, she'd become aware that Mei was crying and Lil was saying in a loud voice that there had obviously been a mistake. The cap couldn't *possibly* be Joe's. He'd been investigating on Fleet Street, so what would he be doing in Whitechapel? Yes, he was missing, but he was probably just busy with an investigation. Perhaps he was following a suspect undercover? He was certain to be back soon,

14

probably with some important information for them all.

'Miss Rose – er – in the circumstances . . .' Sergeant Thomas had begun awkwardly. But Lil had cut him off before he could finish his sentence:

'Of *course* he isn't dead!' she'd exploded. 'That's ridiculous! You haven't found a body – all you've got is that stupid old cap!'

Billy had glanced at Sophie. His face had been very white and Sophie knew that he had been thinking the same thing she was. When people were murdered in the East End, they weren't left for the police to find. They'd found a body washed up in the river themselves once. It had been Joe who'd helped pull it out. A summer day – white frocks and straw hats and strawberries and cream – and then the horror of the body being dragged out of the water. It had all flashed back to her in that dreadful moment.

'Anyway, even if the cap *is* his, it doesn't prove anything!' Lil had argued. 'He might be injured! He might be hiding – lying low somewhere out of danger. But he isn't dead. He *can't* be.'

She had repeated the same thing again and again over the next few days. She'd refused to accept the official verdict: *missing, believed killed.* One cap didn't prove anything. Joe would come back, she'd insisted: she was certain of it. Sergeant Thomas was an idiot. Scotland Yard didn't know what they were talking about. But the days and then the weeks had limped by with no more news.

Somehow, they had to carry on. There were clients waiting for them: long-lost relatives to seek out, missing jewels to be located, blackmailers to catch in the act, stolen letters to be retrieved. There were accounts to balance and bills to pay, rather more of these than Sophie would have liked. Between all the travelling for the Bureau and the search for Joe, they were behind on their ordinary casework, and Taylor & Rose was beginning to struggle financially. Lil was too preoccupied with looking for Joe to notice or care, but Sophie knew that she must not let their business fail. One way or another, they'd stumbled through December. Christmas had come and gone, and now it was 1912 – a brand-new year.

Sitting at her table in Lyons Corner House, Sophie suddenly wished none of it had ever happened. She wished she'd never heard of the *Fraternitas Draconum*, the Secret Service Bureau, double agents or spies. She wished she was only a more-or-less-ordinary shopgirl, with nothing to think about except selling hats. But she knew she could never be that girl again.

Just then, the door opened and a young man in a striped scarf came in, bringing with him a gust of cold air. Billy Parker looked a great deal older and more serious than he used to as he came over to Sophie's table and dropped down in the chair opposite her.

'Did you get it?'

'Of course,' frowned Billy, looking a little insulted she'd even asked the question. 'Here.'

He handed over a small square package wrapped in brown paper, before reaching under the table to make a fuss of Daisy.

Sophie tore off the wrapping to reveal a Russian phrasebook. Tilting it so that there was no chance any of the other customers could see inside, she flipped it open to reveal a note in familiar inky scribble:

She closed the book with a snap, tucking it safely into her pocket. 'Thanks, Billy. Have some tea?'

'Yes please. Are you going to eat that bun?'

'You can have it.' She pushed it in his direction and he broke it in half, taking one piece and pushing the other half back towards her. For a few moments they sat in silence, chewing, trying not to look at the two empty chairs at the table.

After a while, Billy said: 'I s'pose I'd better go back to the office. I've got to write up that report on the Mountville case.'

'I'm going to the Bureau,' said Sophie. In spite of everything, she was glad of it. After all that had happened, her work for the Secret Service Bureau now felt more important than ever. What had happened to Joe made her all the more determined to do everything in her power to stop the *Fraternitas* for good.

It had stopped sleeting when she said goodbye to Billy and Daisy and went on her way to the Bureau. She could have taken a motor-taxi or at least an omnibus, but she decided to save the penny and walk to Lincoln's Inn, taking a grim pleasure in the icy wind against her cheeks. She walked fast and was soon crossing the courtyard towards the headquarters of the Secret Service Bureau.

It seemed a long time since she and Lil had first come here, full of curiosity, thrilled by the chance to work for the government. Now, it had become routine, and yet there was a wariness too. She could not forget that someone connected to this office was secretly working for the *Fraternitas*, and the same someone was no doubt behind what had happened to Joe in the East End.

The Chief's office looked just the same as it had on that first visit. The bookcase was still crammed with leather-bound books. The big map on the wall was still studded with pins and coloured flags. The desk was still stacked with papers and letters, pencils and blotters, diagrams and typed reports. The only thing that had changed was the music that was playing on the big gramophone in the corner: today, Sophie detected the strains of Vivaldi's 'Four Seasons'.

The Chief himself had not changed either. He was the same affable-looking old gentleman he had always been, humming in time to the music as he scrawled his signature in green ink at the bottom of a document and then set it carefully aside.

'Ah, Miss Taylor. Do come in and sit down. A most unpleasant day!'

As Sophie took a seat in the chair opposite him, amongst the papers on his desk her eye snagged on the same edition of *The Daily Picture* she'd read that morning, with the story about the German spies. What did the Chief make of that, she wondered?

'I won't keep you long. As a matter of fact, this is going to be rather a short meeting,' he was saying.

'Is it?' asked Sophie in surprise.

'Indeed it is!' The Chief sat back in his chair and smiled at her. 'I have some good news for you, Miss Taylor. You are, as they say, *off the hook*.'

Sophie only stared at him. She couldn't imagine what he meant.

'I shan't be needing your services for the moment,' said the Chief cheerfully. 'You and Miss Rose may consider yourselves released from the Secret Service Bureau.'

CHAPTER THREE

Secret Service Bureau HQ, London

'*Released* from the Bureau? Is – is there some sort of a problem?' Sophie faltered.

'A problem? Oh, my dear, my goodness, of course not!' exclaimed the Chief. 'You know how delighted I am with your work, and Miss Rose's too of course. It's simply that I don't expect to have a new assignment for you for the time being.'

Sophie felt astonished. Quite apart from anything else, now more than ever Taylor & Rose needed the generous fees they earned from the Bureau. And there had never been any shortage of work for them before, she thought: if anything, she'd heard the Chief say many times that there was *too much* work and not enough agents to cover it. What was going on?

'I don't have anything suitable, you see. No assignments that are the right *fit* for young ladies like yourselves,' the Chief was saying.

'But what about the *Fraternitas*?' asked Sophie.

'Ah! You may rest assured that things are moving forwards on that score. And of course I will keep you updated on any significant progress. But for now you've done your part, and done it very well I might add.' The Chief smiled again. 'You have worked hard. The last few months must have been exhausting. And tremendously difficult with – er – what happened to your young associate. Tragic business. Most unfortunate. If you'll permit me, Miss Taylor, might I suggest that this would be a good moment for you and Miss Rose to take a holiday?'

'A *holiday*?' Sophie repeated. What *was* the Chief up to?

'I know you are a hard worker, Miss Taylor. But even the best of us need a holiday every now and again, don't we? Rest and recuperation is important. And a change of scenery, perhaps. No sense in *overdoing it*, you know,' he finished in an unexpectedly firm voice, fixing her with a sharp, bright gaze.

'I suppose we could think about it,' she murmured.

'Very good, Miss Taylor. You do that,' said the Chief. 'Well, I'll be in touch when I need your services again. Thank you, my dear. Good afternoon!'

Sophie got to her feet. The Chief did not even glance at her as she left: he had already turned back to his documents and was once more humming under his breath.

Outside the Chief's door, Sophie found that the Bureau was unexpectedly busy. Normally, there was only Captain

Carruthers lounging back in his chair, studying a document, but today it seemed full of people. A messenger boy was at Carruthers' desk, waiting for him to sign for a stack of official-looking envelopes. Across the room, the tall, bronzed and handsome Captain Forsyth was deep in confidential conversation with a surly looking fellow in a dark raincoat whom Sophie knew by sight as another agent, Mr Brooks. They both looked over at her as she came out of the Chief's office and her cheeks flushed pink. The door had been open: had they heard she wasn't being given a new assignment? For them of course it would simply reinforce the idea that Sophie and Lil were lesser agents, and that working with female detectives was a waste of the Bureau's time.

She hurried past them, muttering only a quick, 'Good morning,' and barely making eye contact with Carruthers as she passed his desk. On their mission to St Petersburg he'd become something of a friend and normally she'd have stopped to chat with him, but now she was eager to get away.

Back at Sinclair's, Sophie went straight to the offices of Taylor & Rose, hurrying past the reception desk where Mei was on the telephone and passing the door of Billy's office without a pause. She knew they'd be waiting to hear what the Chief had said but she didn't feel like talking. Instead, she went into the office she shared with Lil, closing the door behind her and flopping down into her chair with a

23

long sigh.

The Russian phrasebook was still in her pocket. She took it out and opened it and read the note again. *Tonight at the usual place – 8 p.m.*. The words were reassuring.

It was three o'clock now and she certainly had enough work to keep her busy until then, she thought, eyeing the stacks of paper on her desk. But as she opened an account book she felt fidgety and unable to concentrate. Her mind was still running over the day's events: the newspaper stories. German spies. The *Fraternitas*. The meeting at the Bureau. Brooks and Forsyth, looking at her knowingly. *Tragic business. Most unfortunate.*

She knew she did not have time to be distracted. There was a great deal of work to be done – more than they could easily manage. They really needed to take on some more part-time help, she thought, but could they afford it? She frowned at the account book and then began jotting down some possible wording for a job advertisement. But after a moment she gave it up again. What she really needed was to talk it over with Lil – but Lil wasn't here.

She pushed the account book aside and instead turned her attention to a file of information about a new case that Billy had left for her. Before long she was so engrossed she did not even notice the light ebbing from the sky. Her head was still bent over the file when Billy put his head round the door to say he was taking Daisy out for her evening walk. She only said 'mmm' when Mei appeared a little later to say they were going home now and should she lock the office door? It was not until a quarter to eight that Sophie looked up and realised it was quite dark outside, and if she did not hurry she was going to be late.

Leaving the file on her desk, Sophie put on her hat and coat and slipped out of the now-empty office and down the back stairs. She'd once found the deserted store rather creepy at night, but now it seemed comforting and familiar. She sucked in a deep breath of the warm air, fragranced with rose and violet, and the spicy, heady aroma that made her think of rich furs and the cigars that Papa used to smoke after dinner.

Outside, the wind felt very cold against her face, smelling instead of motor-car fumes and bitter smoke. A cold rain was falling and she was glad of the shelter of her umbrella as she splashed through the puddles and out into the street.

Even on a gloomy February evening, Piccadilly Circus was full of lights, sparkling with the brightness of street lamps and motor-car headlights and illuminated advertisements for Bovril and Perrier. But Sophie turned quickly away from the glitter of shops and restaurants, hurrying across Regent Street towards the darker streets of Soho that lay beyond.

Here, the wide roads gave way to a twisty labyrinth of poorly lit streets lined with little shops, pubs and eating-houses. Sophie took a winding route along them, glancing up into a darkened window every now and again to check the street behind her. It had become a habit, but tonight more than usual she wanted to make sure she wasn't being followed.

She turned a corner, past a coffee merchant's, past an ironmonger's shop all shut up for the night, and then turned again, heading down a dark cobbled alleyway between two crooked buildings. Halfway down it was a doorway: once more, Sophie checked quickly around her to be sure she was alone before turning the handle and slipping through, closing the door behind her.

Once inside the dark shabby hall, she went swiftly up a steep narrow staircase, the stairs creaking beneath her feet. On the second-floor landing, lit only by a single flickering gas-lamp, she stopped and knocked sharply on a door. A moment later, it had opened a crack.

'Miss Taylor,' said a stern voice from inside. 'Come in. You're late.'

CHAPTER FOUR

A Secret Location, Soho, London

As the door closed on the dark stairwell, Sophie stepped into a small, snug sitting room, so different from what lay outside that it was hard to believe she was still in the same building. It was comfortably furnished with a blazing fire in the hearth and several cosy armchairs drawn up around it. A table was set with cups and a jug of cocoa and a plate of currant buns, and Sophie – who had missed her tea – heard her stomach rumble.

'Miss Taylor!' came a familiar voice from the depths of one of the large armchairs. 'Ignore my grandson's bad manners and come in and warm yourself, my dear. Sam, pour her a cup of cocoa, there's a good fellow.'

The Chief's feet were resting comfortably on a footstool before the fire while he puffed on his pipe. He gestured to the armchair beside him and Sophie sat down thankfully, shedding her damp coat, hat and umbrella, while Captain Carruthers, who as well as being the Chief's assistant was also his grandson, rather grumpily hung them up and poured her a cup of cocoa.

The three of them had been using this Soho room as a secret meeting place ever since November when she'd returned from St Petersburg and told the Chief about the double agent.

'If the Bureau truly has been infiltrated, then we cannot be too careful,' the Chief had said. 'We cannot count on any conversations at the office remaining confidential. We must have a safe place we can talk.'

No one else could know about their safe house, or the conversations that took place there. It was very important to make sure the double agent did not suspect they had been discovered. 'If they know we are suspicious, they will begin trying to cover their tracks,' the Chief had said. 'But if they don't . . . well, we may be able to find out who they are and *then* we can work them to our advantage.'

'You mean they might lead us to some of the members of the *Fraternitas*?' Carruthers had asked.

'Or we could use them to feed false information back to the *Fraternitas*,' suggested Sophie. 'To mislead them and disrupt their plans.'

'Indeed,' said the Chief, nodding to them both. 'But best of all we could persuade them to reconsider their loyalties. To return to our side and spy on the *Fraternitas* for *us*.'

'So the double agent would become . . . a triple agent?' Sophie had asked.

'Precisely!' said the Chief with a little smile, rubbing his hands together as though he relished the challenge.

In the days and weeks that had followed, Sophie and Lil had concentrated all their efforts on finding Joe and the mysterious woman, but all the while the Chief and Carruthers had been busy with investigations of their own, doing everything they could to identify the double agent that had been passing her secrets. It would not be easy, for they knew very little about him except what Joe had told Billy – he had watched a man whose face he had never seen clearly leaving the Bureau with some documents, which he had then hidden for a woman to collect.

Carruthers had set up a way for them to communicate secretly, via messages left inside books in the Charing Cross bookshop. But this was their first real meeting in weeks, and after what the Chief had said at the Bureau earlier that day, Sophie was more eager than ever to hear what he had to tell her.

'No Miss Rose this evening?' asked the Chief. 'She's still busy with your other cases, I suppose?'

'That's right,' said Sophie swiftly, her cheeks turning a little pink as she took a sip of her cocoa. It was not exactly a lie, but she felt uncomfortable saying it just the same, especially when Carruthers was looking at her through narrowed eyes as though he guessed exactly what was really going on.

'Well, you can brief her of course,' said the Chief,

nodding amiably. 'Thank you for cooperating with my little subterfuge earlier. I am sure you realise that I have no plans to *release you* just yet. You and Miss Rose are far too useful for that!' He gave a little chuckle and Sophie felt herself relax. She'd guessed that the scene in the Chief's office earlier had been a ruse, but she felt better now that it had been confirmed. 'But with any luck our double agent will have picked up the news on the grapevine, as it were, and will report back to the *Fraternitas* that you are taking a break. Which of course will leave you free from scrutiny for your real assignment. You may have guessed from my mentioning a holiday that I am sending you abroad . . .'

The Chief reached into a leather case at his side and drew out a battered-looking notebook. It looked like an ordinary exercise book but Sophie recognised it immediately. It had once belonged to a Bureau agent called Professor Blaxland and it contained vital information about a secret code that was concealed in a sequence of paintings by the Italian artist Benedetto Casselli. After Blaxland had been murdered by the *Fraternitas*, and the notebook had been stolen, Sophie had chased it across Europe to Russia, before finally returning it safely to the Bureau.

'As you know, we have been working hard to decipher the information in Blaxland's notebook,' the Chief explained now. 'You'll remember that Blaxland had discovered that Casselli's dragon paintings conceal clues to the location of a secret weapon, which he believed to date back to the sixteenth century. The nature of the weapon itself is still unknown, but it is undoubtedly powerful and very dangerous indeed.

'The *Fraternitas Draconum* want this weapon very much – they will stop at nothing to get it. But to do so they need the paintings, most of which are now safely in *our* possession.'

Sophie nodded. None of this was new information. She also knew that the spyglass she'd brought back from Russia had allowed the Chief and his experts to examine the paintings and discover the clues they contained. But what the Chief said next was news to her – and to Carruthers too, judging by his expression.

'With the help of the spyglass, we have discovered that each dragon painting contains a hidden clue – a short sequence of words and numbers. Blaxland's research indicates that the numbers are references to a seventeenth-century atlas created by the Italian cartographer Francisco Marino.'

'References? Like a grid reference?' interrupted Carruthers.

'Something of that kind, yes. But though we have access to the atlas – there is a copy in the British Museum – we have not yet been able to determine the location of the weapon. There is one painting still missing, so the clues are incomplete.'

the white dragon

the white dragon.

RED | BLUE

~~[scribbled out text]~~

?

N
R
S
B
E
L
R

ENEDETTO
CASSELLI
DRASONS

CLASSIFIED

THE WHITE DRAGON ✓

THE GREEN DRAGON ✓

THE RED DRAGON ✓ (LOCATED OCT '11)

2. THE BLUE DRAGON ✓

3. • DRAGON COURANT ✓ (LOCATED DEC '11)

4. • DRAGON COMBATANT ✓ (LOCATED JAN '12)

• DRAGON REGARDANT]

The Chief took a sheet of paper from the case and laid it before them both.

He prodded the final item on the list with the stem of his pipe. 'The *Dragon Regardant*, or as it is sometimes known, *The Black Dragon*.'

'Wasn't that the painting that was supposed to have been lost, or destroyed?' asked Carruthers.

'It was,' said the Chief. 'But according to the Professor's notes, that story was spread about by the *Fraternitas* to conceal the truth. In fact, they kept the painting hidden for centuries, passing it down from one generation to the next.'

'So where is it now?' asked Sophie.

The Chief smiled. 'As usual, Miss Taylor, you come to the point quickly. I have been working hard to try to discover the whereabouts of *The Black Dragon*. My sources now inform me that it forms part of a private art collection housed in Venice, Italy, and I want you and Miss Rose to go there and find it.

Sophie felt a sudden rush of exhilaration. This was something real, something she could actually *do* to help stop the *Fraternitas*. Finding the final dragon painting – the last piece of the puzzle that had occupied them for so long.

'You will find the painting in the Palazzo Stella, a palace overlooking the Grand Canal,' the Chief was saying. 'It belongs to one of the old Venetian families but I believe it has been let furnished to a tenant – a wealthy American.

You will need to find a way to gain admittance to the palazzo and examine the painting to obtain the final piece of the secret code.'

He reached into his case again and produced another familiar item – this time the velvet box containing the beautiful jewelled spyglass, which Sophie had brought back from St Petersburg. 'You'll need to take this with you.'

Carruthers was frowning. 'Is that a good idea? We can't risk the *Fraternitas* getting hold of it!'

'Having carried it safely across Europe before, I am quite sure Miss Taylor will take good care of it,' said the Chief crisply. 'Besides, remember that the spyglass is of no use without the paintings. And it will be far easier for Miss Taylor to get the final piece of the code *in situ*, rather than trying to remove the painting itself.'

'And once I have the code?' asked Sophie. 'What happens then?'

'There is a copy of Marino's map in Venice, at the State Archive. I suggest you go straight there to consult it. With the complete reference, you should be able to pinpoint the location of the weapon. We must not delay if we are to keep it out of the hands of the *Fraternitas*.'

Sophie nodded at once. While they still had no idea what exactly the weapon might be, she knew that it must not fall into the possession of the *Fraternitas*. Whatever it was, she knew that once they had it they would not hesitate to use it to help them spark off a terrible war in Europe.

They must get to it first.

And yet, since her time in St Petersburg, she had begun to wonder about the Chief's plans for the weapon too. Once they had tracked it down, would he turn it over to the British government so they could use it against their own enemies?

'What happens once we have found it?' she ventured to ask, not for the first time. She had made a promise that she would see the weapon destroyed so it could not cause harm to anyone, and she meant to keep it. But the Chief did not pay her question much attention.

'Let's not get too far ahead,' he said. 'Even once we know the location, it is likely that we will still need to crack the rest of the code. You will remember there are *words* as well as numbers hidden in the paintings, and rather cryptic they are too. The Professor had a few theories about what they might mean but nothing conclusive. Possibly they will make more sense once we know where the weapon can be found.'

The Chief held the spyglass out to her and Sophie reached to take it, but before he put it into her hands he gave her a serious look. 'I must warn you, Miss Taylor, this may not be an easy assignment. Though I have no doubt that finding the painting itself will be simple work for agents of your calibre, it is possible that for all our efforts to hoodwink them, the *Fraternitas* will still be watching. You know how much they want this weapon. They must realise we are close to finding it. So you and Miss Rose must be on your guard.'

'Couldn't I go with them and help?' suggested Carruthers.

But the Chief shook his head. 'I need you here, to keep up the search for the double agent. They are being extremely careful, but they will slip up eventually – I am sure of it – and no one else knows the workings of the Bureau like you do.' Carruthers flushed, trying to hide his pride, but the Chief had already turned back to Sophie. 'However, I *would* suggest you take some of your other young people along with you. There is safety in numbers, you know, and besides, it may help reinforce the idea that you are going on a little holiday, should our enemies be watching.'

Sophie nodded again and the Chief gave her an approving smile. 'I knew you would not be daunted. But I do want you to take some extra precautions just the same.'

Once again he reached into the case, this time pulling out a small wooden box and handing it to Sophie. She opened the lid and saw the gleam of silver and mother-of-pearl inside.

'It's . . . a revolver!' she said in surprise.

'A pocket pistol. Designed for ladies – perhaps a little daintier than a normal pistol, but just as effective.'

Sophie picked it up warily and weighed it in her hand. It was not the first time she had handled a firearm: Ada Pickering, the legendary New York detective who had trained her, had said it was important she knew how to shoot. But though Miss Pickering had taught her the basics, Sophie had never felt very comfortable with guns. Now, her thoughts flashed back to the East End alley: reports of a gunshot fired, Joe's blood-stained cap.

The Chief seemed to know how she was feeling. 'It's only a precaution,' he said reassuringly. 'Likely you won't have any need to use it. But in case you do, I've asked Brooks to give you a few lessons. He's our resident expert. Of course he doesn't know about your new assignment, but I've told him we're giving you a little extra training while you are *at leisure*, so to speak.'

Sophie nodded, though she didn't much like the idea of training with Brooks. Although she didn't know him well, she knew he disapproved of her and Lil. She knew too that he'd come to the Taylor & Rose offices while she'd been in St Petersburg, asking rude questions and making contemptuous remarks about young lady detectives. But the Chief was already moving on. 'You'll be travelling simply as ordinary holidaymakers – sightseeing, visiting museums, that kind of thing. Sam will make all the arrangements and provide you with a *dossier* on Venice. But for now, I need you to look at this.'

He took a folded sheet of paper from inside the Professor's notebook and held it out to her. For a minute Sophie didn't understand what she was looking at, but then she realised. 'It's the code!'

'Yes. You'll remember it was originally written in French – this is the English translation. I'm afraid I cannot let you take this with you to Venice. I'm not keeping a copy at the Bureau either. In fact, you and I will be the only two people who have seen the code in full.'

Sophie took the paper, noticing Carruthers looking a little annoyed and craning his neck slightly, as if hoping he might be able to take a quick glance at it too.

SEVEN STARS

GREEN LION, BLACK SUN

FIVE FINGERS

FOUR SERPENTS

WINGED HORSE AND MOON

TWO-HEADED DRAGON

11 5 7 18 12 155

'This information must not fall into the wrong hands. The only safe place for it is *in our heads*. So memorise it now, if you please.'

Sophie heard the fire crackle and suddenly felt nervous. It seemed a grave responsibility to be the only person besides the Chief who knew the code in full. Suppose she forgot something, or made a mistake? She felt Carruthers' eyes on her and the fire hot against her face and wished more than ever that Lil was here. With her talent for remembering lines and song lyrics and dance steps, she'd have found this easy. But there was no time to think about that now. Sophie fixed her full attention upon the paper:

She pictured each image as she went over them in her mind. *Seven stars* made her think of the inn near where the Lim family lived in Chinatown. *Green lion, black sun* – she remembered that from when they had first learned the dragon paintings contained hidden secrets. *Five fingers. Four serpents. Winged horse and moon. Two-headed dragon.* Could that somehow refer to the *Fraternitas Draconum* itself?

She repeated the sequence over and over to herself, until at last she felt as confident as she could that she would not forget it. She set the paper down and the Chief, who had been sitting staring into the fire smoking his pipe, looked up at her.

'You have it? You're sure?'

When she nodded, the Chief took the paper and threw

it swiftly into the fire.

The three of them sat and watched in silence as it flared up, burning brightly for a moment, before it fell away into grey ash and was gone.

CHAPTER FIVE

Bloomsbury, London

'A holiday! You want me to go with you on a *holiday*?'

Sophie let out a long sigh. She'd known as soon as she'd left the Chief the night before that she had to go and talk to Lil, but she'd also known that the conversation would not be easy. She'd been waiting for Lil to come home for hours, and now as she sat in the untidy sitting room that Lil shared with her older brother Jack, she knew it was going to be just as difficult as she'd feared.

'It's *not* a holiday,' she explained. 'That's just our cover story. The Chief wants us to go to Venice to track down the last dragon painting. If we can get to it, we'll have the final piece of the code, and we can find the secret weapon at last.'

Lil had only just come in and hadn't yet taken off her hat and coat. Now, she stood in the middle of the room and stared at Sophie for a long moment. 'I don't know how many more times I can say it,' she said. 'I don't know how to make you understand. I don't care about the code, or the weapon. I don't care about any of it.'

Jack had been sitting with Sophie while she waited for Lil to come home. She'd been glad of his cheerful company. The two of them were good friends: in fact, he'd sometimes given Sophie the idea that he'd like to be a little *more* than just friends, inviting her out with him, paying her compliments and even sketching portraits of her. One of these portraits had actually been shown in an exhibition once, which was flattering but also rather embarrassing. Jack was good fun but the truth was she didn't feel she had time for romance.

Now, Jack got to his feet. 'Come on, Lil. Sit down,' he said coaxingly. 'You've been out all day – you must be freezing. I've just made some tea and we've got some of those ginger cakes you like.'

But Lil just brushed him away. 'I don't want any cake.' That would have been strange enough, Sophie thought, for Lil was not one to refuse food and certainly never cake. But then Lil did not seem much like her usual self at the moment. She had always seemed to be glowing with health and energy: her hair gleaming, her cheeks pink, her eyes bright. She had always loved dressing stylishly, wearing bright colours and following the latest fashions from the trimming of her hat down to the heels of her buttoned boots. But now she was pale and looked tired, dressed in an old frock with a coat thrown over it any old how, her hair straggling and her boots soaked from tramping through the sleet.

'If we can get the weapon, we can stop the *Fraternitas* from using it,' Sophie tried to explain. 'The Chief says—'

'Bother the Chief,' said Lil shortly.

'But we have to—'

'Listen. The only thing I *have* to do is keep looking for Joe. I don't know why you don't understand that!'

'Why don't you at least let Sophie explain . . .' Jack interrupted, but Lil gave him an angry look and he subsided.

'It's no good trying to persuade me. I'm not going to Venice. I'm not doing any assignments for the Bureau. I'm staying here and looking for Joe. I won't give up on him. Just like I didn't give up on *you* when you went missing in St Petersburg,' she added pointedly. 'Now, if you don't mind, I'm going to get out of these wet things.'

She turned away and went into the bedroom. Sophie stared after her, feeling a little sick. She and Lil had sometimes disagreed before, but it had never been like this. Lil hardly spoke to her now, and she hadn't come to the Taylor & Rose office in weeks. The only thing she was interested in was finding Joe. She couldn't bring herself to accept that he was gone.

Sophie had lost a great deal in her life. She'd lost both her parents to the *Fraternitas Draconum*: her beloved papa murdered by the Baron in South Africa; her mother, Alice,

44

killed when Sophie was just a baby. She knew how it felt when people you loved vanished. She knew what it was like to be alone.

But nothing like this had ever happened to Lil. Until now, her life had been as bright and cheerful as one of the window displays at Sinclair's: brilliant lights, bonbons in coloured wrappings, pretty hats decorated with flowers and ribbons. What was more, there had always been a special connection between Lil and Joe, and on the way home from St Petersburg, Sophie had begun to suspect that their friendship might be changing into something deeper. It was no wonder that Lil wouldn't give up on the idea that he could still be alive somewhere if only she searched hard enough.

Just like I didn't give up on you . . . That stung. It was true that Lil had travelled all the way to Russia to look for Sophie when she thought she had gone missing. But couldn't Lil see that going after the *Fraternitas* was the only thing left that they *could* do for Joe now? Sophie felt quite sure that the double agent and the *Fraternitas* were responsible for whatever had happened to him in that East End alley. She was determined to do whatever she could to bring them to justice, and if that meant going to Venice, then to Venice she would go, with or without Lil.

But *safety in numbers*, the Chief had said. And much as she would like to, Sophie knew she couldn't ask Billy and Mei to go with her. Without them, things at Taylor & Rose would simply fall apart. But there were others who might go with her, she thought.

Now, she looked up at Jack. 'How would you feel about a trip to Venice?' she suggested. 'We can ask Leo as well,' she added.

'What – *really?*' said Jack, surprised and flattered.

It made perfect sense, Sophie thought. Jack was an art student, so of course he would want to go to Italy to see the museums and galleries. Venice was exactly the sort of romantic bohemian city beloved of artists and writers that he would choose to visit. And it would be even better if their friend Leo Fitzgerald, who studied with Jack at the Spencer Institute of Fine Art, came too. They could bring their sketchbooks and paintboxes, and even in the winter Venice was certain to be atmospheric and beautiful enough to appeal to two young artists. Leo knew a great deal about Benedetto Casselli's dragon paintings – in fact, it was she who had first noticed that the paintings concealed secret messages. Leo's special knowledge of the paintings could be very useful in her quest to find *The Black Dragon*, Sophie thought.

What was more, Jack and Leo were both sworn members of the Loyal Order of Lions and she knew they would do what they could to help her in her mission. They both understood how important it was to stop the *Fraternitas*, and Sophie guessed that Leo in particular would be keen to lend her support. After all, it was not so very long ago that they had learned that Leo's own godmother, Lady Tremayne, was secretly in league with the *Fraternitas*, and Sophie knew that this betrayal still stung.

Jack was looking more and more excited by the minute. 'Venice! I've always wanted to see it! And you know Leo and I will do whatever you need to help you find the painting. Oh, I say, we could go undercover!'

In spite of everything, Sophie had to smile, imagining Jack and Leo's efforts at going undercover. Like most of the art students at the Spencer the two of them were rather noticeable, dressing in unusual colours and daring styles – the exact opposite of a secret agent blending into the background. But then wasn't that the point? No one would suspect she was on a government mission if she was travelling with them!

'No need for anything like that,' she said quickly. 'All we have to do is act as though we're on a perfectly ordinary trip. With any luck, you won't have to do much except enjoy yourselves. I'll go and find the painting – hopefully it should be simple enough.' After everything she'd done, getting a quick look at one painting couldn't possibly be too difficult, she thought. 'Just think of it as a holiday,' she finished.

'Well, a holiday in Venice sounds perfectly marvellous,' said Jack. 'I'm sure Leo will think so too.' But Sophie noticed his eyes wandering uncertainly towards Lil's bedroom door.

'What about Lil?' she asked quietly.

Jack shook his head. 'I don't think you'll be able to persuade her to go. She won't think about anything except trying to find Joe.'

'Will she be all right here alone, do you think?' Sophie said in a low voice. She would never have asked such a question before. Lil had always been so independent, so sure of herself, so full of energy. Someone who thought nothing of going undercover in a Royal castle, posing as a debutante at London's high society balls, stowing away on a train to Russia, or performing with a circus. But things were different now.

'I'll ask Tilly and the others to keep an eye on her,' said Jack. 'And perhaps Billy could drop in sometimes and see how she's getting on?'

Sophie nodded. She knew that he would, but even so it felt all wrong that she was about to go off on another mission, leaving Lil alone to grapple with a hopeless investigation. And while she would be glad to have Jack and Leo with her, it wouldn't be the same as going to Venice with Lil. For a moment, she thought of their first case for the Bureau – the two of them setting out together on the train, suitcases in hand, full of excitement about this new kind of adventure – and felt a wave of sadness. Whatever else might happen, things could never be quite like that again.

For a little while she waited, but Lil's bedroom door

remained closed so at last she said goodbye to Jack and went down into the street to hail a taxi. The driver gave her a surprised look when she asked him to take her to the shooting range at Vauxhall: he couldn't have had the slightest suspicion that the dainty young lady sitting in the back seat of his motor was in fact a secret agent with a pistol in her pocket. In the past, the thought would have made Sophie laugh to herself, but now she felt too sombre even to smile.

At the shooting range she found Brooks waiting for her. He looked about as happy to be there as Sophie was herself, wearing an impatient look as though he couldn't wait to go on his way. He didn't bother with any pleasantries but plunged straight in, quizzing her about what she already knew about firearms. After showing her how to load the gun, he set about making her practise, criticising her stance and correcting her aim until she was consistently hitting the bull's eye on the paper target.

'That'll do for today,' he said gruffly when Sophie's arm felt stiff and sore and her ears rang from the sound of gunshots. 'Back here again, same time tomorrow. We've got a lot to do.'

Of course, shooting practice was not the only thing Sophie had to do before she left for Venice. There was work to be done at Taylor & Rose, but what was more she wanted to make sure she gave the impression she really was taking a holiday. So while of course she talked over the assignment secretly with Billy and Mei, she was careful to tell everyone else her cover story. In the Ladies' Fashions Department at Sinclair's she told the shopgirls that she needed a new frock for a trip abroad, and in the Book Department she asked for the latest edition of the *Baedeker's Guide to Northern Italy.*

In between, she went quietly to the shooting range each day to meet Brooks. While the lessons were not enjoyable, Sophie had to admit Brooks knew what he was doing. Before long, she could load the pistol, clean it and shoot with at least reasonable accuracy. 'Acceptable,' said Brooks curtly, which Sophie guessed was as close as she was going to get to any kind of praise. But the sour look on his face made it quite clear that he still didn't think much of young lady secret agents, and he certainly didn't think it was worth his time teaching them to shoot.

Back home, she finished her packing. It was an easy task: on previous assignments, she'd had to think carefully to make sure that every item of her luggage, from her hat-pins to her handkerchiefs, were just right for the person she was pretending to be. But this time she was travelling simply as herself. Her frocks were neatly folded in her suitcase; she'd packed an umbrella, thick stockings and stout boots in case of bad weather. Beside it was a battered leather attaché case, covered all over with luggage labels. It held a Box Brownie camera, her *Baedeker's Guide* and a few other supplies that any young lady traveller might need on her journey – some hair-pins, a comb, a small bottle of *eau de cologne.* But underneath, in the hidden compartment of the attaché case, were the true necessities of her trip: the spyglass in its velvet box, a map and briefing on Venice supplied by Carruthers, and the little pearl-handled pistol.

Last of all she added an old blue notebook, faded and battered with reading. On the cover was handwritten in black ink: *Alice Grayson – Diary 1884.* It was the volume of Sophie's mother's diaries that dealt with her travels in Italy as a young girl. Even though Alice had died when Sophie was just a baby, she felt she had got to know her through her diaries. Having her mother's diary with her always felt rather like the company of a friend.

She closed the attaché case and then went quickly over to her writing desk. Taking out a sheet of paper and a pen, she began scribbling a note. She had to try one last time to persuade Lil to join her.

The next morning, after a final visit to the Taylor & Rose office, Sophie set out for the railway station. As she crossed the busy station concourse, she glanced around her, wondering whether in spite of all her efforts, the *Fraternitas* might have their spies watching.

Jack and Leo were waiting for her by the news stand, looking rather excited. They certainly didn't look a bit like detectives or secret agents, which would be a jolly good thing if anyone *was* spying on her. As usual, Jack's dark hair was flopping into his eyes; he had a satchel slung over his shoulder and the cuffs of his tweed coat were spattered with paint.

Dear Lil –

Do change your mind and come with me to Venice. I know you don't want to give up on Joe. But the Fraternitas are to blame for ~~his death~~ what happend to him. We can't let them get what they want – We can't let them win. ~~I wish. I'm sorry that~~

I'm leaving on the boat-train at 10 O'clock tomorrow morning. Meet me at the station under the clock – and we can do this together, for Joe's sake.

Love,
Sophie

Meanwhile, Leo's hair was cut daringly short in the manner of the young lady art students at the Spencer; she wore a beret, a long flame-coloured scarf and what looked like a man's overcoat missing several buttons. She walked with a limp, leaning on a handsome mahogany cane with a handle carved into the shape of a lion's head.

'I say – here we all are!' exclaimed Jack in a loud, enthusiastic voice. They were playing their parts to perfection, Sophie thought. 'Ready for a holiday?'

'Absolutely!' she said, smiling blithely back at him.

In keeping with their role of tourists, they lingered to choose some reading matter for the journey – *Tit-Bits* and *The Strand Magazine*, and the morning's edition of *The Daily Picture*. They bought a luncheon basket of provisions and several packets of chocolate. All the time, Sophie kept glancing over at the station clock, just in case she saw Lil's familiar tall figure waiting there for her. But the people standing under the clock were all strangers, each of them waiting for someone else.

'Come on,' said Jack as she lingered for a few more moments. 'If we don't get a move on, we'll miss the train. Want me to grab that case for you, Leo?'

Sophie turned to follow them, but as they went out on to the smoky platform she could not help looking back over her shoulder at the station clock one last time before they hurried away.

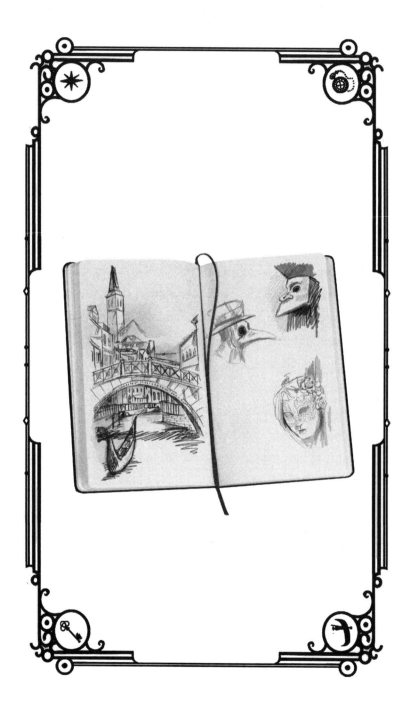

PART II

'We arrived in Venice from the sea, to find it wreathed in mist . . .
What a fascinating place it seems to be – shimmering jade-green
canals, twisting alleyways and secret squares.

There is so much to see and marvel at. I cannot shake the
feeling that Venice is somewhere that all manner of mysterious
things could happen.'

– From the diary of Alice Grayson

CHAPTER SIX

Fleet Street, London

Lil shivered as she paced along Fleet Street, her hands buried deep in her pockets. She must have walked up and down this street hundreds of times in the past few weeks. Everything was so familiar: the chemist's, the stationer's, the café with the striped awning; the motorbuses rumbling by, carrying passengers from the West End towards the East. The smell of paper and ink that wafted from the printing presses; the whirring and clanking of cylinders and belts and gears; and above it all the chiming of the bells of St Dunstan's and St Bride's.

The people were familiar to her too: the newsboy selling papers on the corner, the shoe cleaners, the waitresses in the café with their frilly aprons. She knew *them* especially well after all the hours she'd spent sitting at a little table in the steamy window, making one cup of coffee last as long as she could. But most of all she was interested in the staff of *The Daily Picture* – the reporters and filing clerks, the typewriter girls and telephonists, the printers' boys in smocks smudged with ink dust, all of whom she saw streaming in and out of the big red-brick building every day.

She knew their faces now and she knew their daily routines. She knew when the office doors were unlocked in the morning and when the clerks and telephonists arrived. She knew where the typewriter girls went for their luncheon, and the pubs the young reporters visited to gossip with their rivals at the *Post* and the *Gazette*. She knew when the inky-fingered printers left after their long night shift and when the delivery vans arrived in the morning to carry the finished papers out across the city.

Yet in spite of everything she knew about this little stretch of Fleet Street, she was no closer to knowing anything that really mattered. Who was the woman Joe had seen? And the question that she asked herself a hundred times a day: *what* had happened to him?

She'd gone over it a million times – at first with Sophie and the others and then later by herself. Joe had discovered that someone at the Bureau was passing information to a woman, whom he'd followed back to the offices of *The Daily Picture*. He'd gone to stake out the offices and try and find out more, but then he'd just disappeared. The only clue was his cap, which had been found in an alley out in Limehouse.

Now, as she walked, Lil found herself wondering all

over again how Joe could have ended up in the East End. She knew he didn't like going there. It was too much of a reminder of his old life, when he'd been part of the gang known as 'the Baron's Boys'. She was certain it wasn't somewhere he'd have chosen to go. Could he have been discovered and taken there against his will? Or maybe he'd followed the woman there?

It always came back to the woman from *The Daily Picture*. But Lil still hadn't the least idea who she was. All she knew was that there were dozens of women coming in and out of the big office every day. Even now she could see two girls in smart hats hurrying inside out of the cold; a professional-looking older woman striding in behind them, carrying a briefcase; whilst on the pavement, a fashionable lady in a fox fur was being helped out of a motor car by her driver before she swept through the doors. Any of them could have been the woman Joe had seen. Lil didn't know how old she was, or what colour was her hair, or whether she wore spectacles, or anything like that. All Joe had told Billy was that she had been rather smart and dressed in an expensive-looking suit.

It was so jolly frustrating, Lil thought. And the stupidest thing about it all was that Joe himself would have been so much better at this investigation than she was. *Surveillance* was not really in Lil's line. Action was what she liked, not watching and waiting in the shadows. Joe, on the other hand, had seemingly limitless patience and was an expert at keeping out of sight. Now, she imagined she could hear his voice in her ear, encouraging her, just like he always had. *Chin up. Keep going. Take it slowly. Don't give up.*

Joe never gave up. And although he didn't make a fuss about it, he always did the right thing. He'd been the only one who'd understood when she'd decided she must go to St Petersburg to find Sophie. And just look at how he'd managed to track down a dangerous double agent all by himself! He might be quiet but he was brave and loyal. He'd do anything for her – he'd proved that over and over again.

Lil tied herself up in knots thinking of all the things Joe had done for her. Sometimes the big things, like when he'd given himself up to his old enemies the Baron's Boys to try and save her. But more often than not it was the small, ordinary things she thought of. Joe shyly inviting her to go walking with him along the river. Joe turning up on her doorstep in his best suit, carrying a bunch of flowers. The very last time she'd seen him he'd insisted on accompanying her to the train station. She thought of how he'd said goodbye to her on the station platform and that moment when she thought he was going to kiss her. She rubbed her cold hand across her face. Horrid bitter wind, getting in her eyes.

The worst thing about that memory was he'd tried to persuade her that he should come with her to help find Sophie. And Lil had told him not to! If only she'd said *yes,* he would have been on the other side of Europe with her, instead of here on Fleet Street on the trail of a double agent. How he'd have enjoyed travelling with the Circus of Marvels! With his gift for working with animals, they'd probably have given him a job straight away.

For a moment, Lil let herself imagine the other life that she and Joe could have had. Travelling together with the circus – sleeping in train carriages, staying in foreign cities, staying up late after performances playing cards with her friends Hanna and Ravi. Lil could have worked as a dancer or learned acrobatics. Gosh, she'd even have helped Cecil with sewing the costumes, if she had to! It would have been such fun. And all this – London, Fleet Street, *The Daily Picture*, the Secret Service Bureau – would have been quite forgotten, as though it had never existed at all.

A rush of anger surged through her. Even thinking of the Bureau made Lil feel furious. This was all their fault! If she and Sophie had never started working for them, none of this would have happened. She'd been so stupidly proud and excited to be a secret agent, swanning off on important Bureau missions: tracking down spies and secret messages, travelling across Europe, going undercover. She'd felt like the heroine of a spy yarn. And all the time Joe had stayed behind in London, quietly working and helping behind the scenes. But because of what they had been doing – what *she* had been doing – he had fallen into some unknown danger. And now he was gone and the Bureau didn't even seem to care.

Of course the Chief had said he was terribly sorry about what had happened. He'd *said* all the right kinds of things – but he hadn't actually done a single thing to help. The only thing the Bureau were interested in was finding out who the double agent was, in order to protect themselves and their all-important secrets.

She couldn't understand how Sophie could bear to carry on working for them. Not to mention going back to Taylor & Rose as though everything was normal! And Billy and the others were just as bad. Lil couldn't stand to be at the office, seeing them going about their daily business: Sophie meeting a client to talk about a new case, Mei answering the telephone, Tilly tinkering in the little back room she used for her experiments and inventions.

Lil had been avoiding them all. She'd been avoiding her brother too, which would normally have been easy. Jack kept odd hours, getting up late and staying up until after midnight working in his studio, or going out to the Café Royal with his art-school friends. But lately he'd taken to spending his evenings in their little sitting room, as though he wanted to keep her company. She couldn't stand him being gentle and kind to her – she'd have preferred it if he was bossy and irritating like he usually was. She knew he didn't understand – if he had, he wouldn't have rushed off to Venice with Sophie, as though heading out on some marvellous adventure.

Lil sighed, her breath puffing out like a cloud in the cold air. Of course she knew that Sophie was trying to do the right thing. In her pocket, her fingers closed on the note that Sophie had sent and gripped it hard. She was glad to have it there, even though she hadn't sent a reply. She hadn't known what to say. Lil never would have imagined that she wouldn't know what to say to *Sophie* of all people.

In all her life, Lil had never felt so alone.

She came to a halt outside the café and blew on her cold fingers, wondering if she ought to go inside. She felt frozen to the core and knew it was too chilly to hang about in the street for much longer, but the very thought of another dispiriting hour or two of watching from the window was unbearable.

Lil sighed. Surely there must be something else she could do? Something she hadn't yet thought of? For a moment she imagined brazenly striding into the office of the newspaper to ask questions – but what on earth was she supposed to say? 'Excuse me, is there a woman here who's involved with a secret society called the *Fraternitas Draconum*?' 'Could you tell me who on the staff is receiving secret government information from an undercover source?'

Could she disguise herself and bluff her way inside to investigate from within, she wondered? Get a job as a telephonist or typewriter girl, dress as a cleaning lady, pose as someone's niece or long-lost grand-daughter? Yet somehow Lil couldn't summon her usual enthusiasm for dressing-up and playing a part. This mattered too much. She couldn't afford just to leap in wildly.

Lil's shoulders slumped and she turned to go inside the café. But just as she did so, she caught sight of a familiar figure moving along the street and stopped, frowning. For a moment she struggled to place him, and then she remembered. It was Charlie Walters, the photographer. She'd met him first at Sinclair's and then again a few months ago, on the boat to Hamburg. He'd been headed to St Petersburg to photograph the Circus of Marvels and unbeknown to him she'd been on her way there too. Now, she remembered that he worked for *The Daily Picture*, and judging by the big portfolio he carried he was dropping off some photographs. Seeing him gave her a sudden idea.

Lil had always acted quickly. Now, she almost darted forwards to call out Walters' name, but then she checked herself. *Take it slow*, said Joe in her head. *No need to rush.* Apart from anything else, Walters would probably not recognise her. She knew she did not look much like the Lilian Rose he knew: the traveller, the chorus girl, the up-and-coming theatre star.

Instead, she walked briskly away from the café and the offices of *The Daily Picture*. She was going to play a part after all, she decided. She would dress herself up like the Lil she'd been before: put on a stylish hat and a smile and go and tackle Walters.

She felt a surge of exhilaration at the thought of taking action at last and forgot all about the cold as she marched towards home. At last, she had the beginnings of a plan.

CHAPTER SEVEN

Venice, Italy

S ophie peeked out from between the lace curtains. Outside, Venice lay waiting for her, veiled in fog.

The dining-room window overlooked the canal, but from here she couldn't see much more than the shadowy shapes of bridges and the outlines of buildings through the mist. This was certainly not the Venice she'd read about in her mother's diaries, which had been full of descriptions of sunlight and shimmering green water, but the murky city was intriguing just the same.

'What perfectly dreadful weather!' came a fretful voice from behind her.

'So damp and unpleasant!' tutted another.

'I can feel the draught from the window from here,' said a third in a distinctly accusing tone.

Reluctantly, Sophie let the curtains fall back over the window, hiding the view of the canal beyond, and turned back to contemplate the dining room of the

Pension Mancini.

Over the last year or so, she'd become a seasoned traveller. She'd come to feel just as much at home in an elegant suite at one of the finest Paris hotels as she did in a shabby little attic room in the home of a kindly Russian family. She was perfectly comfortable with staying in peculiar places, but she had to admit she was not very enthusiastic about the Pension Mancini.

Really, they might not even be in Italy at all, she thought as she took her seat between Jack and Leo at the breakfast table, which had been spread with a white cloth and set with silverware. For one thing, all the people around them were English. There were the three elderly ladies wearing shawls, complaining vigorously about the cold and the need for woollen stockings and hot-water bottles. There was a red-faced old gentleman tucking into toast and jam. A pale young man was flicking through a volume of Lord Byron's poetry, and beside him a tall lady in purple – his mother, Sophie guessed – was examining an English newspaper through a pair of gold-rimmed spectacles. She looked very much like one of the well-to-do ladies who took afternoon tea at the Marble Court Restaurant at Sinclair's.

The décor was thoroughly English too. There was a good deal of heavy wooden furniture, well-stuffed crimson armchairs and lace doilies. There was even a picture of the King hanging in pride of place on the wall. As for the breakfast table, it was set with teapots and milk jugs and pots of jam as bland and ordinary as in any run-of-the-mill London boarding house.

They'd arrived in Venice late the previous night, getting only a few tantalising glimpses of the city in the dark. The journey had been easy, though after travelling across Europe in her friend Captain Nakamura's aeroplane on her last mission for the Bureau, Sophie had found taking the boat and train like an ordinary tourist rather dull. On the other hand, Jack and Leo, neither of whom had travelled abroad much before, had been fascinated by everything – from the stale sandwiches and dishwater tea in railway station refreshment rooms, to the Italian-speaking customs officials. Jack had been full of enthusiasm about it all, and even Leo, who was usually a quiet, reserved sort of person, had been bright-eyed and excitable, talking about all the galleries and museums she hoped to visit in Venice.

But Sophie had not felt so enthusiastic. As she'd sat gazing out of the window of the train that would carry them to Venice, she'd still been thinking about Lil. The last time she'd taken a journey like this, they'd stood side by side on the deck of a boat, watching St Petersburg disappearing into the distance. That night, they'd stayed up for hours talking: they'd had so much to catch up on after being apart for months. It had felt wonderful to be together again. But now here she was, watching the rain lash against the windows of the train, without

Lil once more.

She'd wondered then if she was doing the right thing. She knew that nothing she did would help Joe now, but she could help *Lil*, couldn't she? After all, Lil had always been there for *her* – from the very first days of their friendship when she'd dived in to help Sophie find out the truth about the Clockwork Sparrow and prove her own innocence, to travelling across Europe to search for her in St Petersburg. Lil was intensely loyal – it was something that she and Joe had always had in common, no matter how different they might have been in other ways.

Sophie hated the thought of not being there for Lil when Lil needed her. But this was what it meant to work for your country, wasn't it? Lil needed her, but the Bureau needed her more. Stopping the *Fraternitas* could help thousands, maybe hundreds of thousands of people, all over Europe. She thought she was at last beginning to understand what had made Papa leave her behind to go off on his final mission to South Africa in search of the Baron, knowing that he might never return.

When they'd at last arrived in Venice, they'd gone straight to the Pension Mancini, where Carruthers had arranged rooms. Sophie had half hoped he'd booked somewhere like the Grand Hotel Continental, the elegant Paris hotel where she'd stayed the previous year. But of course while a place like that had been just right for the wealthy heiress she'd been impersonating then, it wouldn't be right for this assignment. The Pension Mancini on the other hand was exactly the kind of small, genteel hotel where young ladies like herself and Lil might stay, especially if they were travelling alone.

And so she found herself here in the dining room, surrounded by polite English conversation and hushed voices, the tinkling of teacups, spoons and knives. As they took their seats at the table, she was conscious that the elderly ladies were looking at them warily, eyeing Jack's rather long hair and paint-spattered cuffs and frowning at Leo in her gentleman's shirt and pocket watch.

She saw that Jack was noticing this too and had at once flashed the ladies his most charming smile. 'Good morning!' he said courteously.

There was a moment's pause while the ladies bristled at being addressed by an unknown young man. Then: 'Good morning,' said one of them in a very prim voice.

Just then, the door opened and a fair girl of about Sophie's own age came hurrying in, still fiddling with the buttons on the cuffs of her frock. It was rather a nice frock, Sophie thought, chosen by someone with a good eye for colour – a delicate blue-grey with a rose-pink silk sash. 'I'm sorry, Great-aunt Caroline,' she muttered as she slipped into a seat beside the prim lady. 'I overslept.'

'Really, Ella! You *must* learn to be punctual!' her great-aunt tutted. 'A *lady* is never late!' Ella said nothing but Sophie thought she looked a little weary, as though she'd heard this many times before. She slumped down into her chair, but as she did so she noticed Jack, Leo and Sophie sitting at the table. Sophie noticed her sitting up a little straighter.

Signora Mancini, the dour-faced landlady – an Englishwoman who had married an Italian – came clumping through into the room with a jug of coffee to fill their cups. Close at her heels was a small maidservant, carefully balancing a large tureen of steaming porridge. She placed it on the table close to Leo, who eyed the greyish contents rather uncertainly.

'I'd steer clear of that, if I were you, young lady,' said the red-faced old gentleman in a whisper, so that Signora Mancini wouldn't hear. 'Quite inedible. Try the bread. It's really not too bad.'

'Oh – er – thank you,' said Leo.

The old gentleman smiled at her and introduced himself as Dr Beagle.

'I'm Leonora Fitzgerald,' said Leo shyly. 'These are my friends – Jack Rose and Sophie Taylor.'

Before Dr Beagle could say another word, the prim lady had leaned across him to take a closer look at Leo. '*Fitzgerald*, did you say? Good heavens, of course! The likeness is unmistakable! You must be Sir Horace's daughter!'

Leo flushed red. She did not get on particularly well with her wealthy, aristocratic father and disliked the idea of resembling him. And she certainly did want to meet any of his friends. But the prim lady did not notice her embarrassment. 'Of course *I* have known Sir Horace Fitzgerald for many years,' she said in a loud voice – loud enough to be heard by everyone at the table. She turned back to Leo. 'My name is Knight – Mrs Caroline Knight. How delightful to make your acquaintance, my dear Miss Fitzgerald. I knew your mother *terribly* well when she was a girl. Tell me, how *is* dear Lotty?'

'Um – actually my mother's name is Lucy,' said Leo, but if Mrs Knight heard her, she showed no sign of it. She had already turned her attention to Sophie, staring at her intently from piercing pale blue eyes. 'And you are Miss Taylor? Well, I suppose you must be one of the Yorkshire Taylors? You have quite the look of Millicent Taylor about you. Of course it has been many years since I was a guest at Hatherley Manor, but I daresay the gardens are as splendid as ever.'

Sophie had never heard of either Millicent Taylor or Hatherley Manor, but before she could reply, Mrs Knight had moved on to Jack, her pale eyes now flicking over him with great interest. 'And Mr Rose, did you say? How do you do? *This* is my great-niece, Ella,' she added with a flourish. Sophie realised that his proximity to the aristocratic Miss Leonora Fitzgerald had changed everything. It didn't matter now if Jack had paint on his shirtsleeves: Mrs Knight was certain he must be an eligible young gentleman.

'Say *how do you do*, Ella,' Mrs Knight prompted her,

while Ella's cheeks flooded with pink. But before she could speak, Mrs Knight ran on: 'Do forgive her, Mr Rose. She's only just left school and is in need of *polishing*. Her dear father asked me to take her to see a little something of Europe. So important for young ladies to travel, don't you agree? And how *wonderful* for her to have some other young people here. I suppose you are here to see all the sights?'

'That's right,' said Jack cheerfully. 'Leo and I are studying at the Spencer Institute of Fine Art and we're tremendously interested in Italian painting.'

'At the Spencer?' Dr Beagle interjected, surprised and interested. 'Are you indeed? Then you will know my old friend Professor Jarvis.'

Leo's face suddenly brightened. 'Oh! I thought I recognised your name!' she said excitedly. '*Dr Septimus Beagle* – I've read all your books!'

'Have you, my dear?' asked Dr Beagle, looking pleased. 'Well! That is *most* gratifying.'

'Dr Beagle is an art historian,' Leo explained to Sophie. 'He's an expert on Italian Renaissance painters, like Benedetto Casselli, for example,' she added with a twitch of her eyebrows.

But Mrs Knight had already pushed her way back into the conversation. 'Yes, well, I am very pleased to meet you, Miss Fitzgerald. This little hotel came recommended to me by my friend Mrs Balfour, but just the same I was unsure if it was really a suitable place for Ella. It is so important for a young girl to meet the right *kind* of people, don't you agree? But now that I see you are here, I am *perfectly* satisfied.'

To Leo's alarm, Mrs Knight leaned across the table and patted her hand, before launching into a long and complicated story that seemed to relate in some way to the Fitzgerald family, though it was hard to say exactly how. Mostly, Sophie thought, it seemed to be an opportunity for Mrs Knight to mention the names of at least a dozen important society people. She couldn't possibly have known that nothing was less likely to impress Leo, who sat looking trapped and uncomfortable.

Meanwhile, Dr Beagle was smiling at Sophie. 'Are you a student of art too?' he asked.

'No, I'm afraid not,' said Sophie.

'Ah – then literature perhaps? Or history?'

'Actually, I'm not a student at all. I work at Sinclair's department store,' she explained, thinking that the guests here did not seem the kind of people who would approve of young lady detectives. Yet as she spoke, she felt an unexpected pinch of regret. It wasn't because people looked down on young girls who worked for a living – she was quite used to that. But she had sometimes wondered what it might be like to have the chance to study something she loved, as Jack and Leo did.

If Dr Beagle was the sort of person who looked down on shopgirls, he was much too well mannered to show it. 'A most magnificent store,' he said politely. 'And Mr Sinclair is a great supporter of the arts, I know, with a fine collection of paintings of his own.' He wiped his mouth with his napkin and turned to include Jack in the conversation. 'Do you know, that puts me in mind of an odd story I heard, about Benedetto Casselli, who as Miss Fitzgerald says is one of the artists who interests me. A few years ago, a rare Casselli painting was included in an exhibition at Sinclair's. But then the painting suddenly vanished and no one could understand *how*. Well, it turned out that the curator of the exhibition – Mr Randolph Lyle, a terribly well-known art collector – was the one behind the theft all along! What was more, he also turned out to be in possession of *another* Casselli painting that he had stolen from an art gallery some months before. Very shocking, what!'

'Very,' murmured Sophie in agreement, trying not to look at Jack. She wondered what Dr Beagle would say if he knew that *they* were the ones who had solved that mystery – and rescued both of the paintings from Mr Lyle's apartment? For a brief moment her thoughts carried her back to London, more than two years earlier. It had been her first encounter with Casselli's dragon paintings, not to mention the *Fraternitas* themselves. She remembered how Joe had helped her to eavesdrop on one of their secret meetings and felt the same horrible jolt she experienced every time she remembered he was gone.

'I believe the London art world was in quite an uproar

75

about it,' Dr Beagle was saying. 'Of course, I missed the furore myself – I was here in Venice at the time, working on a new book. I spend several months of each year here, you see.'

'Then you'll be just the person to tell us which galleries and museums to visit,' Jack said at once.

Dr Beagle looked pleased by this. 'Of course. It would be my pleasure!' he said with a courtly bow of the head.

'. . . and dear Lady Fitzmaurice was *quite* delighted by the whole affair,' Mrs Knight was saying to Leo, her voice growing louder. 'And then the Countess of Alconbourgh said . . .'

As if taking pity on Leo, who was looking more and more miserable by the minute, the tall lady with the spectacles suddenly put down her newspaper and spoke up from along the table, cutting directly across Mrs Knight's flow of conversation. 'Do tell us, Dr Beagle – how was your excursion to Burano yesterday?' she asked in a brisk voice.

Dr Beagle smiled, as if he understood what she was doing. 'Perfectly charming, Mrs Wentworth. Just as I remembered it.'

Mrs Knight bristled, looking irritated by this interruption. 'Well! When *we* went to Burano last week—' she began.

'I must say it was pleasant to get out of the city,' went on Dr Beagle brightly, as if she hadn't spoken. 'I have never known Venice to be quite so busy at this time of the year.'

'That is because of Mrs Davenport, I suppose,' said Mrs Wentworth. 'Archie and I took a gondola down the Grand Canal yesterday afternoon and passed the Palazzo Stella. There were dozens of boats going in and out, weren't there, Archie?'

The pale young man said only 'mmmm' without taking his eyes from his book, but Sophie's ears pricked up at once. The Palazzo Stella was the name of the building where the Chief had told her *The Black Dragon* could be found.

'This *Carnevale* is obviously going to be quite an occasion,' Mrs Wentworth went on.

'I say – is there going to be a carnival?' asked Jack with interest.

'Yes indeed! It is carnival season, you know. And this year an American lady – a Mrs Davenport – has rented a wonderful old palazzo on the Grand Canal,' explained Mrs Wentworth. 'She's planning to hold a rather extravagant party there, inspired by the old Venice *Carnevale* of the eighteenth century. Masks, traditional costumes, all that kind of thing.'

'It's caused quite a stir,' agreed Dr Beagle. 'Everyone seems to be talking of it.'

'Mrs Davenport is a very *unusual* person,' Mrs Wentworth went on, frowning as though she was not quite sure what to make of her.

Ella spoke up unexpectedly. 'She wears the most

wonderful clothes!' she sighed. 'We saw her outside Florian's and she had on a simply extraordinary embroidered velvet cape and a black lace veil – she always wears a veil over her face. And then yesterday we saw her out in her private gondola – it's all trimmed with gold decorations, and she was wearing a gold dress with a gold parasol to match. She was with some of her friends – she has all kinds of people staying with her. Designers, actors, artists . . .'

'Ella! That's quite enough,' tutted Mrs Knight. 'You mustn't *chatter* so!'

But Jack's eyes had already lit up. 'Artists?' he repeated eagerly.

Sophie was listening keenly too, though her interest was rather different. If there was to be a party at the Palazzo Stella, with lots of guests arriving in masks and costumes, she thought it could be exactly the opportunity she needed to sneak inside.

'Yes, Sergei Diaghilev himself is staying there. Apparently his *Ballets Russes* are going to perform at the party. And César Chevalier, the Paris fashion designer is there too. He's made a special costume for Mrs Davenport to wear.' At this, Ella gave a little sigh, as though she could imagine nothing more blissful. 'She's from New York and very much part of the artistic set out there,' Mrs Wentworth added.

'Hmph!' interrupted Mrs Knight, clearly wanting to be

at the centre of the conversation once more. '*That* Mrs Davenport is no more from New York than I am! When we saw her outside Florian's, the wind blew back that silly veil she wears – a very affected habit if you ask *me* – and I knew her at once as Jennie Hardcastle's youngest girl. Why, I must have seen her a dozen times at the Hampton-Laceys! I did hear she had been widowed and gone to New York . . . I suppose she must have married this *Davenport* fellow out there, whoever *he* may be,' she sniffed.

Beside her, Ella opened her mouth as if she was going to say something else, but before she could get as much as a word out, Mrs Knight began to scold again. 'You must stop *interrupting*, Ella. It's *very rude*,' she instructed, before plunging into another long story about something that had once happened at a ball at the Hampton-Laceys.

There was no chance for anyone else to say anything, and Sophie could learn no more about the Palazzo Stella. Between Mrs Knight's conversation, the inedible porridge and the stuffy atmosphere of the dining room, she felt glad when breakfast was over and they could escape. As she, Jack and Leo hurried into their hats and coats and went out together into the damp, foggy air, Sophie saw Ella standing in the window looking rather wistfully after them, before she was called back inside by Mrs Knight.

But as the door closed behind them, Sophie forgot about the Pension Mancini and its guests. All at once, she felt a surge of excitement. Here she was, in a brand-new

79

city. She took in a great, deep breath of salty air, listening to the unfamiliar sounds: the distant clang of bells, the clatter of their boots on the cobbles, the voices of a group of Italian women with baskets over their arms, the beating of wings as a cluster of pigeons took flight.

The fog was beginning to clear as they walked along a street, then up some steps and over a little bridge, crossing a canal. She was beginning to glimpse the city she'd read about in her mother's diaries: the narrow streets, the old houses with their red-tiled roofs and dark green shutters. Jack and Leo had already fallen behind her, dawdling to admire the colours and textures of crumbling brick, faded stucco and wet stone, but Sophie went ahead, following the signs that pointed to San Marco, enjoying the chance to explore.

She went past a church and through another little square, and then all at once, she emerged on the edge of an expanse of green water, alive with steam-ferries and motor-launches, rowing boats and gondolas. A sudden gleam of sunlight sparkled across the water, and she felt suddenly light and free – glad to be far from London and everything that had happened in the past months. The bells clanged and birds swooped and soared above her head as the gondoliers called out to each other in Italian, and Venice seemed starred with possibilities.

'The Grand Canal!' exclaimed Leo as she and Jack came ambling up.

'I say – that's more like it!' said Jack appreciatively. 'Gosh – I don't think much of our hotel, Sophie. I thought Venice was supposed to be full of romance and drama and intrigue. But that place is about as dull as one of Mother's tea parties!'

Sophie laughed. 'Don't worry. We won't have to spend much time there. We've got all this to explore.'

'Isn't it marvellous?' said Leo, who looked as though she was itching to get out her paints already. 'And I can hardly believe we've met Dr Beagle!'

'Is he really an expert on Benedetto Casselli?' asked Sophie. 'Do you suppose he might know anything about *The Black Dragon*?'

Leo shrugged. 'It says in his book about Casselli that the painting was lost centuries ago. I think that's what all the art historians believe.'

'Still, you never know, he might tell us something useful,' said Jack. 'He seems like a decent sort of fellow. But that Mrs Knight! What an awful snob! She was very determined to impress *you*,' he added, giving Leo's shoulder a nudge. 'The daughter of Sir Horace, and all that.'

'*Don't*,' said Leo, flushing red. 'It's perfectly ghastly.'

'Just wait until she finds out that I'm only a penniless art student and Sophie's a young lady detective,' Jack went on. 'She won't be nearly so keen on us then. Oh, I say – this must be San Marco!'

While they'd been talking, they'd strolled onwards,

crossing a bridge and going along several more winding streets. Now, they found themselves standing at the edge of an enormous open square. At one end of it was the magnificent building that Sophie knew from her *Baedeker* was the Basilica di San Marco, Venice's most famous church: a perfect fairy tale of turrets and domes, spires and statuary, crowned with a sprinkling of stars and a golden lion. Beside it, reaching upwards into the grey sky was the campanile – a tall, pointed tower built of red brick. Although it was early, the square was already bustling with people: American tourists listening to a gentleman talking about Italian architecture; artists with easels; a group of nuns all in black; and waiters setting out tables and chairs in front of a café.

'Let's go in there,' said Jack, looking at the café. 'That breakfast was awful, and I'm jolly hungry. Before we do anything else, we must have something decent to eat.'

Sitting inside the little café was like being inside a jewel box richly decorated with lavish painted ceilings and gleaming gilt. Over cups of hot chocolate and sweet pastries, they discussed their plans for the day. Leo was keen to take a gondola ride along the Grand Canal, which Sophie agreed to at once. Not only did it seem exactly the kind of the thing that three perfectly ordinary English tourists would do on their first day in Venice, it would give her the chance to take a closer look at the Palazzo Stella from the water.

Fortified by their second breakfast, they returned to the edge of the water, where a row of glossy black gondolas were moored to tall striped poles. Jack quickly got the attention of a young gondolier with a moustache and a bright red neckerchief, and Sophie watched, marvelling at his confidence. He'd never been to Italy before, he spoke no Italian and had not the first idea how the gondolas worked, and yet here he was, chatting away to the gondolier, clapping him on the shoulder like he was an old pal. He was so like Lil, she thought with a sudden pang of missing her best friend more than ever. They were both so good at making friends with everyone they met; she didn't think either of them had the slightest idea what it was like to feel shy or unsure.

Leo was quite different – not shy exactly, Sophie thought, but certainly reserved, and often a little uncomfortable with new people. Now, she gave Sophie a quick rueful smile as if she knew exactly what she was thinking, while Jack turned to them both and announced: 'This is Paolo! Paolo, these are my friends – Sophie and Leo. Paolo is going to take us out in his gondola and show us all the sights.'

It was fun to clamber down into the long narrow gondola, which rocked gently to and fro on the water as they all took their seats. Sophie enjoyed the feeling of fresh cold air against her face as Paolo sculled expertly out into the canal, weaving between the other boats. He spoke

English well, and pointed out the sights to them as they passed by, gesturing to the church of Santa Maria della Salute, Venice's famous art gallery the Accademia, and a whole string of Venetian palazzos with tall windows and grand balconies. Jack and Leo were soon debating which were Gothic and which Romanesque, which Baroque and which Rococo, but though Sophie admired them, there was only one that she really wanted to see.

'Which is the Palazzo Stella?' she asked Paolo.

'Aha! You wish to see where Signora Davenport is holding her *Carnevale*?' Paolo asked at once. 'It is just over there –' and he gestured across the water to a large, square building.

Sophie stared at the rows of pointed windows, the columns and balustrades, and the waterfront terrace with stone steps leading up to a large, arched doorway. 'The Palazzo Stella is one of the oldest on the Grand Canal,' Paolo explained. 'It was built hundreds of years ago for one of Venice's most powerful families. Today it is let out to wealthy visitors, like Signora Davenport. See – the preparations for the party are beginning.'

He pointed to the waterfront terrace. Sophie had already noticed that several boats were moored up outside, and now she saw that people were busy unloading them. Two men were lifting out what looked like cases of wine, while another carried a large hamper. As they watched, a gondola drew up and a young woman in a white apron got out, carrying a basket of expensive hothouse flowers, which she carried briskly up the steps towards the house.

'This party seems like it's going to be a splendid affair,' said Jack. 'I must say, I'd rather like to go to it myself!'

Paolo laughed. 'No doubt! But this party is for Signora Davenport's invited guests only. *Very* important people, very rich people, from all over Europe. She has employed local men to stand guard at the entrance, with instructions to admit only those with invitations. My cousin Mateo is one of them. He says the party is to be very . . . what is the English word . . . ? *Exclusive*. So unless you happen to be a personal friend of Signora Davenport . . .' He laughed again and shrugged, as if to say Jack would have no chance. 'But do not worry. There will be much more to see in the streets too. At carnival time all of Venice is like a party. There will be people in masks and costumes – music – fireworks . . . And now, if you look ahead, you will see the famous Ponte del Rialto – the Rialto Bridge – approaching . . .'

But Sophie was still looking back at the Palazzo Stella, her brow furrowed with thought. It sounded like getting inside during the party was not going to be as easy as she had hoped. But perhaps that did not matter? As she watched the palazzo grow smaller behind them, she thought she might have the beginnings of a plan.

CHAPTER EIGHT

London

'**H**ow delightful to see you here, Miss Rose!' exclaimed Charlie Walters. 'A quite unexpected surprise!'

'Unexpected? Why – what do you mean?' asked Lil innocently. 'You invited me to come to take some portrait photographs when we met on the boat to Hamburg at the end of last year.'

She'd presented herself at his door earlier that afternoon, looking every inch a young lady of fashion. She wore a smart green coat with shiny black buttons; her dark hair had been carefully arranged; and her hat had been pinned at a dashing angle. She wore green gloves, tinkling jet earrings and had even added a touch of rouge to her pale cheeks.

Charlie Walters had wasted no time in ushering her into his studio, where he had posed her against a background painted with a springtime scene of blossoming trees, blue skies and fluffy clouds – quite different from the grey February day Lil could see outside the studio windows.

'I did indeed,' acknowledged Mr Walters, peering at her through the camera lens. 'But that was a while ago, and since then I found out a bit more about what you'd been up to! *Taylor & Rose Detectives*, eh? Bit of a change from when we first met! You were performing in the chorus at the Fortune back then. But now – well, by all accounts you're one of London's foremost young lady detectives.' He grinned and gave her a little bow.

'Not so very much of a change,' said Lil, forcing herself to laugh. 'Acting skills are rather handy when it comes to undercover detective work.'

'I s'pose you were off to solve a case when we met on the boat,' went on Walters as if the very idea of it was amusing. 'What was it? Chasing a runaway debutante? Or tracking down a misbehaving husband?' He gave another little chuckle.

Lil kept smiling blithely, though her cheeks were beginning to ache. 'Something like that. And you – you were going to . . . St Petersburg, wasn't it?' Walters might think he was so jolly clever, but he'd never cottoned on that she'd been in the same place at the same time, and had even performed in the circus ring before his very eyes.

'That's right. And what an adventure it was!' exclaimed the photographer. 'I was there to photograph the Circus of Marvels for *The Daily Picture*. Their reporter, Miss Russell and I, we travelled right across Europe with them. Got to know all the circus folk. And then when we got to Russia – well, you'll have seen it in the papers, I'm sure! A bunch of young revolutionaries attacked the Tsar and his family at the gala performance in St Petersburg. Miss Russell and I were right in the thick of it! You can't even imagine!'

Lil widened her eyes as though shocked and amazed at the very thought – though as a matter of fact she didn't need to imagine it. She had been performing with the circus on the night of the attack and she knew that neither Walters nor Miss Russell had been in the building at the time. Instead, they'd been safe in their comfortable hotel – though that hadn't prevented Miss Russell from writing an 'eyewitness' account of the whole affair for *The Daily Picture*, just as if she'd been on the spot and had seen it all for herself.

'That's the thing about my line of work,' said Walters proudly. 'You never know where you'll be from one day to the next. Mixed up in something dangerous like that one day, and taking portraits of a beautiful young lady like yourself the next,' he added, flashing her what he obviously intended to be a charming smile.

'Do you do a lot of work for *The Daily Picture*?' asked Lil, hoping to lead the conversation in a more useful direction.

'A fair bit,' said Walters, squinting through the camera lens. 'Right – we're almost there. Turn your head a little to the left? Perfect. *The Daily Picture* is a decent rag . . . I do some work for them, and also for some of the other papers and magazines in the Norton Newspapers group.'

'And do you often work with Miss Russell?' Lil asked. 'It's splendid to see a young lady journalist like her. I wouldn't have thought there were many women working in a newspaper office!'

'Huh!' snorted Walters. 'That's where you're wrong. *The Daily Picture* is full of them! But they're mostly secretaries and that sort of thing. There are a few lady reporters but they generally write about fashion or society news – who's getting married, who's attending which parties, the season's loveliest debutantes – you know the type of thing. But Miss Russell is one of Sir Chester Norton's bright sparks. I should introduce you . . . you'd like her. And do you know, she'd be interested in *your* story, I'm sure of it.' Walters paused for a moment and snapped his fingers as though he'd just had an idea. 'I say! I bet she'd love to write a feature piece all about you and your agency. *From dancer to detective* . . . or maybe it should be *From stage to sleuth?* That would be quite a headline, wouldn't it?'

Lil had no desire to be a headline. Once, she'd rather enjoyed having her photograph in the newspapers, but those days seemed a long time ago. On the other hand, she wasn't getting much useful information from Walters, and the chance to meet Miss Russell might take her a little closer to *The Daily Picture*. 'Oh, I can't imagine anyone would want to read anything about *me*,' she improvised, with a flutter of her eyelashes.

Mr Walters gave her his most flattering smile. 'Now, that's where you're quite wrong, Miss Rose. London's leading lady detective? Why, people would love it! That's the sort of thing that sells papers. And I could take some portrait photos to go with it. We could have you in disguise! Or posing with a magnifying glass . . . or, I say, what about a *revolver?*'

'My goodness!' said Lil with a laugh, thinking how appalled Sophie would be by the idea of a sensational newspaper story accompanied by racy portraits. She had always hated the idea that people saw Taylor & Rose as a fashionable curiosity, rather than a legitimate detective agency that just happened to be run by two young women.

But Sophie was away in Venice, Lil reminded herself, and this could be a chance to get to know Miss Russell, who would likely be far more useful than Charlie Walters when it came to inside information about the other staff of *The Daily Picture*. What's more, if Lil agreed to an interview, perhaps she'd even get the chance to visit the offices herself? Once she was inside, she could try to track down the mysterious woman and at last she might be able to discover the truth about what had become of Joe.

'Terrific for business too, of course,' Walters was saying. 'I'll bet Sinclair would be keen. Now, there's a fellow with an eye for publicity! Tell you what – I'll put through a call to Miss Russell at the office right away and see if she can join us for tea.'

Lil felt certain that Miss Russell would be far too busy to drop everything and come round to Charlie Walters' studio. But, sure enough, by the time Walters had finished taking his photographs, there was a brisk tap on the studio door and Miss Russell herself appeared.

Lil shook her hand courteously as Walters introduced them. Miss Russell didn't look to be much older than Lil herself; she was dressed in a plain dark coat and hat adorned with nothing more than a ribbon band, which she immediately took off and tossed over a chair. Underneath, she wore a simple skirt and blouse, making Lil feel rather a peacock in her fashionable frock and tinkling earrings. She'd actually glimpsed the young reporter a few times before – once on the airfield in Paris, where they'd saved the Crown Prince of Arnovia from being kidnapped, and again in St Petersburg – though Miss Russell did not seem to remember her from either. She did however give Lil a sharp look as she shook her hand, as though she was getting the measure of her.

'It's a good idea, Charlie,' she agreed as Walters enthusiastically explained his plan for the feature interview. Unlike the photographer, she did not seem at all inclined to flatter, but simply eyed Lil with the same curious, questioning look as she poured tea from the chipped pot. 'But I'd have to write it up before we leave.'

'We're off on another assignment in a couple of days,' explained Walters. 'More travelling! It's a real perk of the job you know, Miss Rose.'

'Though I imagine you get a fair bit of that in *your* line of work too,' said Miss Russell. 'As it happens, I met your partner Miss Taylor in Paris last year.'

'Oh, really – did you?' asked Lil as if this was new information. In fact she knew that Miss Russell had got Sophie into a rather sticky situation at the *La Lune Bleue* nightclub, which had almost threatened to ruin the whole case.

'Will Miss Taylor be joining us for the interview?' asked Miss Russell through narrowed eyes.

'Unfortunately she's away at the moment,' said Lil breezily. 'Otherwise I'm sure she'd have been delighted.'

'Hmmm,' said Miss Russell, not sounding very convinced. 'Well, I'd like to get the interview done now if that suits? I've got rather a lot to do before we leave.'

Now? For a moment, Lil was startled. But she knew she should not appear ruffled. 'Of course – that's fine,' she said, smiling warmly.

Miss Russell gave a businesslike nod and got to her feet. 'Excellent. Well, thanks for the tea, Charlie. If you can get those pictures developed as soon as possible, that would be a help. Come along, Miss Rose.'

Outside on the street, Miss Russell hailed a motor-taxi. 'Sinclair's department store,' she instructed the driver curtly.

'Oh – aren't we going to your office?' asked Lil in surprise.

'I always do my interviews in my subject's own environment,' said Miss Russell, as the motor car rumbled towards Piccadilly. 'It adds background.'

'I see,' said Lil, disappointed and suddenly a little anxious. She'd thought this would be her chance to get inside the offices of *The Daily Picture* and finally track down the mysterious woman Joe had been watching. What's more, it had been weeks since she'd set foot in the offices of Taylor & Rose, and now she'd have to turn up with Miss Russell in tow. Whatever would Billy and Mei make of that?

At Sinclair's, Miss Russell strode up the steps and through the great doors with the confidence of Mr Sinclair himself. She did not look in the least bit intimidated by the glistening chandeliers, the marble entrance hall or the richly dressed customers. 'Afternoon, Alf,' she said to one of the doormen, who nodded and touched his hat in return. Seeing Lil's surprise, she explained: 'I'm here a great deal. Mr Sinclair's Press Club Room is tremendously convenient for us journalists. First floor, if you please,' she added to the operator as they went together into the lift.

It seemed rather strange to be approaching the glass door with its elegant gold letters reading *Taylor & Rose Detectives*. It was all so familiar, and yet a little like something from a dream. Lil could hardly believe that she wouldn't find Joe somewhere inside – probably sitting by Billy's desk with Daisy snoozing on his feet, chatting over one of their cases or sharing news from the stable yard over tea and buns. For a moment she faltered, but with Miss Russell at her side, she forced herself to sweep over the threshold.

Inside, the reception area looked smart and elegant. A bouquet of roses stood on the table beside a stack of illustrated fashion papers, which waiting clients could browse while sipping tea from a china cup and nibbling delicacies from the Sinclair's Confectionery Department. Behind the desk, Mei and Billy were sitting together, going through some letters. Now, they both looked up in surprise.

'*Lil!*' exclaimed Billy, and then seeing Miss Russell, wondering if she was perhaps a new client, tried to smooth over his surprise. 'Er – good afternoon. We weren't expecting to see you today.'

'Miss Russell, this is our office manager, Mr Parker,' said Lil, conscious that her cheeks were turning red. 'And this is Miss Lim, our receptionist.'

'How do you do?' said Miss Russell, looking Billy and Mei up and down. 'Goodness, you're all very *young* aren't you?' she added – rather cheekily, Lil thought, given that Miss Russell herself couldn't have been more than a year or two older than she was.

'Miss Lim? Is that a Chinese name?' Miss Russell asked.

'As a matter of fact it is,' said Mei, lifting her chin as though she wasn't sure what that had to do with anything. 'My father's family are from China.'

Hearing Mei's East End accent, Miss Russell looked

more surprised than ever, but before she could say anything else, Tilly emerged from the back office, obviously interested to see what was going on. As usual she was wearing a large, rather dirty apron over her frock, and had a pair of old motoring goggles perched on her curly black hair. Daisy pattered close at her heels and when she saw Lil she bounded over, giving little yelps of welcome.

'And this is Miss Black, our technical expert,' said Lil, bending down to make a fuss of Daisy.

'Well! You are quite an *unusual* bunch,' said Miss Russell, eyeing Tilly with great interest and then reaching in her pocket for her notebook as if she planned to start writing things down straight away.

Tilly frowned. 'Who are you?' she asked abruptly.

'This is Miss Russell,' said Lil, more embarrassed than ever. The others were all goggling at her and she knew they were wondering what on earth was going on. 'She's a journalist. She's writing a piece about us for *The Daily Picture*,' she added, eyeing Billy, willing him to understand what she was doing.

'Oh . . . !' was all he managed to say.

'And Miss Taylor is away at the moment, is she?' asked Miss Russell, looking around as though she thought Sophie might be about to appear. 'On a case, I suppose?'

'Actually she's taking a holiday,' said Mei blandly.

'A holiday?' Miss Russell sniffed, as though she disapproved of the very idea of such a thing.

'Er – let's go into my office,' said Lil hurriedly. 'Mei, would you bring us some tea?'

She ushered Miss Russell quickly away from the others and into the office she and Sophie shared, Daisy following behind her. She saw that Sophie had left her desk as tidy as ever: there was only a neat stack of mail, next to a Cook's continental railway timetable, the only clue to where she had gone. Opposite, Lil's own desk was just as she had left it – a mess of papers and letters, some case notes muddled together, with some pages torn out of *La Mode Illustrée*, a couple of telegrams, some newspaper clippings, old publicity photographs and theatre programmes pinned up on the wall. Everything was covered with a film of dust, as though no one had liked to touch anything.

Miss Russell was staring around curiously. Now, she settled herself down in a chair and got out her notebook and pen. 'This is all tremendously interesting, Miss Rose,' she said with great satisfaction, looking around – from the untidy desk to the dog at Lil's feet. 'I feel like we're going to have plenty to talk about. Now . . . where shall we begin?'

CHAPTER NINE

Pension Mancini, Venice

It wasn't until the evening that Sophie, Jack and Leo returned to the Pension Mancini – weary and rather cold, but content. They'd had a busy day and Sophie felt quite satisfied that they'd behaved exactly like three young people enjoying all the sights of Venice.

After their gondola ride, they'd gone inside the Basilica di San Marco to admire the magnificent gold mosaics. They'd walked up to the Rialto market, where they'd looked at the stalls heaped with colourful produce and rows of shimmering fish, and they'd taken refuge from the cold in a café, where they'd stood at a tall counter drinking tiny cups of coffee and eating cream-filled buns covered in chocolate and nuts. They'd taken a tour of the Doge's Palace, where they'd seen the attic prison from which Casanova escaped, and where Jack and Leo had exclaimed over paintings by artists like Titian and Tintoretto. Finally, they'd eaten dinner in a cosy little restaurant lit by flickering candles.

Sophie hadn't spent a day like it in a long time. Every now and again – sipping coffee and watching the people, taking snapshots of Jack and Leo with her Brownie camera, getting lost in the labyrinth of twisty streets and alleyways and then realising they had the map upside down – she'd been able to forget, just for a few moments, why she was there. But she couldn't fail to think of her assignment for long, and back at the Pension Mancini that evening, she hurried straight up the narrow stairs to the top-floor bedroom she was sharing with Leo.

The spyglass and pistol were too important to leave behind, so she'd carried them with her in her pockets. But she'd deliberately left the empty attaché case behind in her room, with a single hair carefully positioned over the handle. She knew that if anyone had been snooping around the room and had tried to open the attaché case, the hair would have been dislodged. But while it was obvious that the room had been cleaned by Signora Mancini's maid – the pillows had been straightened and the towels folded neatly – the attaché case was exactly as she had left it, the hair still in place.

Relieved, she went back down to the parlour, where the guests were drinking coffee after dinner. On one side of the room, Mrs Knight was part of a group playing bridge, whilst Ella, wearing a pretty indigo-blue frock, sat beside them looking thoroughly bored. On the other, Jack and Leo were sitting with Dr Beagle, apparently deep in conversation.

'Dr Beagle is telling us about the history of Venice,' said Leo as Sophie sat down beside them. 'It's tremendously interesting. Please – do go on.'

Dr Beagle looked pleased by this. 'Well, I was just saying, Miss Taylor, that the unique position of Venice makes it extremely vulnerable to *flooding*. Over the years, the waters have risen considerably and some buildings have begun to crumble into the lagoon . . .'

Sophie nodded as though she was listening attentively, but in fact she allowed Dr Beagle's voice to fade away. She wanted to think over her plan for getting inside the Palazzo Stella. She thought she knew how it could work: she'd need to buy some supplies, but of course she had plenty of money from the Bureau to cover any necessary expenses. And thanks to her mother's old diary, she had a good idea of exactly where she could get them.

'. . . and the *winged lion* is the symbol of St Mark, the patron saint of Venice. You will see it everywhere in the city – on buildings, on flags and of course on a column in the Piazza San Marco. On the other column you will see what many people mistakenly think is a *crocodile* but is in fact a *dragon*. The dragon is a symbol associated with St Theodore, another most important saint here in Venice . . .'

She'd do it tomorrow, Sophie decided. It had been fun spending the day enjoying Venice like a tourist, but it was time to get on with the real business at hand.

Leo caught her eye, almost as though she knew what

Sophie was thinking. 'We went past the Palazzo Stella on our gondola ride this morning,' Leo said to Dr Beagle. 'What a magnificent place it is! Have you ever seen inside it?'

The old gentleman looked regretful. 'Alas, no. It is privately owned and to my knowledge has never been open to the general public, though I understand there are some fine old paintings there. I am sure it will be a magnificent setting for a *Carnevale* celebration!'

'Tell us a bit more about the Venice *Carnevale*,' said Jack eagerly. 'What's the history of it?'

'Well, traditionally it was a time when the people of Venice would set aside their work to enjoy dancing, plays and feasting,' Dr Beagle explained. 'They wore masks, which allowed them to leave behind their ordinary identities and behave however they wished. It was often a time for mischief and mayhem. Soon Venice's *Carnevale* became famous and people came from all over Europe to see it. But at the end of the eighteenth century it was outlawed by the Holy Roman Emperor and the wearing of masks was forbidden. For a long time there was no Venice *Carnevale*, but little by little, unofficial celebrations have begun to take place once more.'

'Like Mrs Davenport's party?' said Jack. 'Do you know much about what she's planning?'

But Dr Beagle just shook his head vaguely. Sophie saw that he was much more interested in the Venice of long ago than the Venice of today. 'Now, the masks traditionally worn at *Carnevale* are most interesting,' he went on. 'The *Bauta* is a white mask, worn with a black tricorn hat and black cloak, which conceals the wearer's face completely. It was once worn at secret gatherings and political meetings. Then there is the *Medico della Peste*, the Plague Doctor mask. It has a long beak, mimicking the masks that doctors used to wear when they treated plague victims here in Venice. The beak was stuffed with herbs as it was believed this would prevent the doctors from catching the disease –' Dr Beagle fell silent, and Sophie saw that Mrs Knight was sweeping across the room towards them with Ella following reluctantly in her wake.

'Good evening, Miss Fitzgerald,' she began, ignoring Dr Beagle and beaming at Leo, showing every sign of sitting down in the armchair beside her. 'I do hope you have had a pleasant day!'

Dr Beagle got quickly to his feet. 'Well, I must be going to bed. It has been very enjoyable talking to you young people,' he said hurriedly. 'Goodnight to you all.' With a courteous little bow, he shuffled from the room.

Mrs Knight did not seem to have noticed his departure. 'I'm sure you won't mind if Ella joins you,' she twittered, beaming at Leo, while behind her Ella looked mortified.

'Oh, of course,' said Jack at once, moving over. Ella's cheeks turned even redder while Mrs Knight simpered with pleasure. 'Sit down, Ella!' she instructed. 'Well, I'll leave you to talk . . .'

She swished back across the room, returning to her seat with the other ladies, though Sophie could already see her turning back to peer at them, her eyes glittering with interest.

'I'm awfully sorry,' said Ella awkwardly. 'I didn't want to barge in on you like this. It's just my great-aunt, she's – well – she's . . .'

'Absolutely unbearable?' chipped in Jack. Leo looked aghast but Ella laughed at once.

'That about covers it,' she said. Seeing Leo's shocked face she explained: 'Don't worry – I'm not in the least bit offended. I'd barely spent any time with Great-aunt Caroline until we came to Italy. I'd only seen her at family parties and so on. I have simply dozens of great-aunts,' she said with a sigh. 'Anyway, Great-aunt Caroline somehow managed to persuade Papa that she was exactly the right person to be my chaperone for this trip. I wanted to see all kinds of exciting things and have some real adventures, but all my great-aunt cares about is doing things that are "suitable". And getting me ready for my court presentation in the summer of course. I'm to be a debutante, you see,' she finished with a small shrug.

'How *ghastly*,' said Leo with a sympathetic shudder.

'Oh, I don't really mind too much,' said Ella philosophically. 'Not that I really *want* to be presented at Court – but just think of all the wonderful clothes I'll be able to see! That's what I really want to do – I want to be a *couturier*, making glorious outfits. Like Henrietta Beauville or César Chevalier, or someone like that.'

'What a marvellous idea,' said Jack enthusiastically. Sophie noticed that he was looking at Ella rather admiringly and Ella seemed to notice this too, for she blushed as she went on.

'Oh, I'll never be allowed to, of course. Great-aunt Caroline says I shouldn't even sew any of my *own* clothes.' She imitated her great-aunt's voice. '"*Embroidery* is a perfectly ladylike occupation, but it would seem most peculiar to *make your own gowns*, instead of going to the dressmaker like everyone else. Why, people might think that you can't afford it!"'

'Goodness knows, they don't like you doing anything *peculiar*,' said Leo with feeling.

Across the room, Sophie could see Mrs Knight watching them all. Seeing Ella talking with Jack and Leo, she looked pleased, and when the two ladies she was talking with said 'goodnight', she got up as though she meant to come back and join them herself.

'Oh – er – I suppose we ought to go up to bed,' said Leo hurriedly, who had evidently noticed this too. 'I mean, we want to get up early tomorrow so we can beat the crowds at the Accademia.'

'You don't have to explain. I'd do just the same if I was you,' said Ella with a little groan, sitting back despondently as Mrs Knight approached.

'Goodnight,' Sophie, Jack and Leo chorused politely, before making their escape.

Upstairs, they took refuge in the bedroom Sophie and Leo were sharing. Jack winced at the riot of pink and crimson; roses on the curtains, roses on the eiderdowns, and yet more roses on the wallpaper.

'Phew!' said Leo, dropping down on her bed. 'Thank goodness we got away!'

Jack flopped down beside her. 'I do feel sorry for Ella, though. She seems like a jolly nice girl.'

'Hmm, yes. Pretty too,' said Leo with a little grin and Jack went red. 'But however nice she might be, I can't stand any more conversation with Mrs Knight. Anyway, Sophie, now we're alone, do tell us about your plan. Are you going to try and use the *Carnevale* to get inside the palazzo?'

'And what can we do to help?' added Jack eagerly. 'I was thinking – perhaps we could disguise ourselves in costumes and masks? We could create a diversion while you sneak inside!'

Sophie smiled, thinking how much Jack sounded like his sister. Lil was usually the one who created diversions – sometimes rather *too* enthusiastically. If Lil had been there, Sophie knew she'd have relished the chance to dress up in an elaborate costume and talk her way into Mrs Davenport's exclusive party, posing as a society lady or a dancer with the *Ballet Russes*, or using her London theatre connections to acquire an invitation. Sophie could picture her, extravagantly masked and cloaked, sweeping into the grand palazzo amongst all the important guests.

But Lil *wasn't* there, she reminded herself. Sophie knew she would have to do this in her own way.

'Actually, I think it will be easier if I use the party preparations as my cover, rather than trying to sneak into the party itself,' she said now. 'Remember all those people we saw delivering supplies this morning?'

'I say – that's an awfully good idea!' exclaimed Jack. 'We could pretend to be delivering something and use that as our way of getting inside! Just like the time we helped you and Lil get into Mr Lyle's apartment to find the stolen dragon paintings!'

But Sophie shook her head. 'It's better if I go alone.' Realising that Jack was about to argue, she went on: 'Just in case anyone is watching, we have to keep up the impression that we're here on a perfectly ordinary sightseeing trip. So I need you two to go and see more of the sights tomorrow, while I sneak into the palazzo.'

Leo frowned at once. 'But Sophie, if someone *was* watching us, wouldn't they see at once that you weren't with us, and wonder where you were?'

'I thought of that. Why don't you invite Ella to go with you?' Sophie suggested. 'She's about my height and fair-haired. Bundled up in a hat and coat, someone watching might easily think she was me.'

'That's a good idea. But do you think Mrs Knight would let her go out with us?' asked Leo.

Jack snorted. 'Of course she would! She'd let Ella go anywhere with *you* – Sir Horace's daughter! And I'll bet poor Ella would love the chance to have a little fun without her for once. It's a rotten shame she has only an awful great-aunt for company.'

But Leo still looked uncertain. 'Are you sure it's a good idea for you to go to the palazzo alone?' she asked Sophie. 'What if you run into trouble?'

But Sophie shrugged this off. She was used to working by herself, and compared to half the elaborate schemes she and Lil had carried out in the past, this would be very straightforward indeed.

CHAPTER TEN

Taylor & Rose Detective Agency
Sinclair's Department Store, London

'. . . We were fairly certain that the painting was in Mr Lyle's apartment in Chelsea. But we couldn't be sure. And of course we had no way to get inside and see for ourselves. But then Sophie came up with a jolly clever idea . . .' Lil was saying.

She'd been talking to Miss Russell for over an hour. At first she'd felt apprehensive: Miss Russell kept on asking probing questions and Lil knew there was a lot she ought *not* to talk about. For one thing, she knew she mustn't reveal the details of any Taylor & Rose cases, which often concerned private matters that their clients would not want to see popping up in the pages of *The Daily Picture*. For another, she could not tell Miss Russell about the time they had narrowly prevented the assassination of the King, as it had been agreed that this shouldn't be made public knowledge. And of course she was not going to say a word to Miss Russell about her investigation into what had happened to Joe.

But as she'd begun to talk, something strange had happened. It had been like playing the part for Charlie Walters: and in acting the role of her old self, she had almost become the old Lil again. She felt as though she was emerging from a grey fog. Before long, she was cheerfully relating one story after another: explaining how she and Sophie had cleverly caught a gang of shoplifters at Sinclair's; sharing anecdotes about going undercover at high society balls and debutantes' tea parties; and now telling the dramatic tale of how they had saved the Casselli dragon paintings.

Lil knew *that* was perfectly safe to talk about. After all, when they'd recovered the stolen paintings there had been a blaze of publicity, including interviews in the newspapers orchestrated by Mr Sinclair to help promote the new detective agency Taylor & Rose. '. . . and that was how Sophie and I discovered that Mr Lyle had stolen not just one but *two* priceless paintings,' she finished with a flourish.

She was enjoying herself, Lil realised. She'd forgotten how good she was at this sort of thing: talking to people, charming them, bluffing her way through any situation. Miss Russell kept asking more questions, but Lil kept answering them – rather like playing tennis back at school, she thought, neatly hitting the ball back over the net.

'What about the rescue of the Crown Prince of Arnovia in Paris? What about the murder of Blaxland, the Professor at the Sorbonne?'

'Oh, that's really Sophie's story,' said Lil vaguely. She wasn't about to let Miss Russell know that she'd been working undercover in Arnovia, posing as governess to the young prince and princess, nor that she and Captain Forsyth had also been part of the rescue. 'But what I can tell you about is a rather peculiar mystery I once solved backstage at the theatre . . .'

Miss Russell scribbled more notes as Lil dropped a few tantalising hints about a case involving a missing pearl necklace that belonged to 'a *very* well-known actress on the West End stage' but then tapped her pencil against an old copy of *The Daily Picture* which was folded on Sophie's desk.

'What about the story in the press about German spies?' she said suddenly, indicating the headline. 'Have you ever encountered anything like that?'

For the briefest of moments, Lil hesitated. Whatever she might feel about the Secret Service Bureau, she knew she must not breathe a word about it to Miss Russell – it was a strictly confidential government operation. She smiled. '*Spies?* I must say, it all sounds rather like something from a thriller. One of those Montgomery Baxter stories, perhaps. Though I'm quite sure Sophie and I could take on a whole gang of German spies if it came to it!' She laughed gaily as if it was quite an amusing joke.

Thankfully that seemed to satisfy Miss Russell. 'Tell me a little more about Miss Taylor,' she said next. 'How did the two of you meet and begin working together?'

'Oh, well, we met at Sinclair's,' explained Lil. 'We were both working here – Sophie was a salesgirl and I was modelling frocks and so on. But we soon discovered we had rather a knack for solving mysteries . . .' She thought suddenly of the day they had first met: it seemed a very long time ago. Lil had always found it easy to make friends, but even from the first, there had been something special about Sophie. And almost at once they had been plunged into solving the mystery of the Clockwork Sparrow together. From the very beginning, they had been a team. But now she was alone, here in their office, and Sophie was far away in Venice, looking for the last dragon painting. Unexpectedly, she felt a sudden prickle of regret that they weren't hunting for it together.

'Well, I think that's more than enough,' said Miss Russell, closing her notebook with a snap. 'Thank you, Miss Rose. I must say I wish everyone I interviewed had the same kind of understanding of what our readers want to hear about as you do.'

'Shall I pop into your office to take a look at the story before it goes to press?' asked Lil, looking for another chance to get inside *The Daily Picture*.

But Miss Russell brushed this off at once. 'Oh, I

shouldn't think there'd be any need for that.' She was already putting away her notebook and getting to her feet, shrugging on her coat. 'Well, goodbye and thanks again, Miss Rose.'

She flashed Lil a quick, formal smile and then turned to leave the office, heading back towards the reception where Billy and Mei were still at the desk, talking together in low voices. Lil trailed after her, feeling a little desperate. She hadn't learned anything useful about *The Daily Picture* yet. Surely all her effort wasn't going to be for nothing?

'Wouldn't you like another cup of tea before you go? And some cake, perhaps?' she asked hurriedly. If only she could delay Miss Russell a little longer and ask her a few questions of her own!

'No thanks,' said Miss Russell, nodding to Billy and Mei at the desk.

'But I'd love to hear a little more about your work,' Lil tried. 'Being a journalist must be terribly interesting.'

Miss Russell gave her a rather surprised smile. 'Oh – er – some other time, perhaps?' she said a little awkwardly. Her hand was already on the door handle, but all at once Mei, who had been watching their exchange with a frown on her face, spoke up suddenly: 'Excuse me, Miss Russell?'

Lil glanced over at her. Mei was watching them intently but her voice sounded quite ordinary and innocent as she said: 'Before you go . . . we were wondering whether we could ask you a favour? You see Billy – er, I mean, *Mr Parker*

– well, the thing is, he *writes*. We wondered whether you might have time to have a quick look at some of his stories – to see whether any of them might be good enough to publish?' she went on. 'I know you're terribly busy, but it would be wonderful to have your opinion on them, wouldn't it, Billy?'

She gave Billy a sharp nudge in the ribs. His face was bright pink and from his mortified expression, Lil felt quite sure that this was the first he'd heard of the idea.

Roberta Russell frowned and for a moment Lil thought she was going to refuse. But then she gave Billy a sympathetic grin. 'Aha! An aspiring writer, eh?' she said in a very friendly way. She strode back towards them. 'Well, I am rather busy but I don't mind taking a quick look, if you really want an honest opinion?'

Billy was standing as if frozen, but Mei nudged him again and he reluctantly produced a neat cardboard folder. He looked rather embarrassed as he handed it to Miss Russell. 'It's just a few stories I've been working on,' he said nervously. 'Detective stories, mysteries, that kind of thing.'

There was silence for a moment as Miss Russell opened the folder, her eyes flicking over first one neatly typed page and then another. Billy was staring at her, transfixed, but Mei glanced over at Lil and gave her the smallest wink. She'd done this on purpose, Lil realised gratefully. She'd guessed Lil was trying everything she could think of to delay Miss Russell and she'd hit on the perfect way to keep her here a little longer.

But Lil glanced at the thick folder in front of Miss Russell, feeling rather taken aback. She knew Billy had always liked writing down their adventures, but she'd had no idea he'd been writing *stories*, and certainly not seriously, with the hope of becoming a published writer.

'These are all fiction?' asked Miss Russell, glancing up from the pages to look at Billy.

'Yes. I do sometimes get ideas from things that happen here at Taylor & Rose,' he admitted. 'But they're all stories that I've made up.'

'Well, you certainly seem to know what you're doing,' said Miss Russell, nodding approvingly. 'They're pacy, and you're hitting all the right notes. Intrigue, excitement, action . . . Ever had anything published before?'

Billy shook his head, his face pinker than ever.

'Come and see me at my office tomorrow morning,' said Miss Russell. 'Bring these stories and anything else you have along these lines. I rather think I've got an idea for you, but I'll have to discuss it with a couple of colleagues first.'

'*Really?*' gaped Billy.

Miss Russell grinned at him. 'I'm not promising anything, mind. But we'll see. Would ten o'clock suit?'

Billy looked as though he couldn't speak so Mei answered for him: 'That's fine. He'll be there.'

'You should come too, Miss Rose, if you can,' said Miss

Russell. 'It might be useful to run my idea past you too. Well, see you tomorrow then!'

And with that she was gone, closing the office door smartly behind her.

Left alone, the three of them turned to look at each other.

'Mei!' exclaimed Billy, half thrilled and half indignant.

Mei gave a little shrug. 'You *told* me you wanted to know if your stories were good enough to publish,' she reminded him. 'And now you do.'

'I know I did, but I never expected . . .' Billy protested.

'It's perfect!' Mei told him. 'You might get the chance to have your work published in a real newspaper! And this way Lil gets what she wants too. That *is* what you wanted, isn't it?' she added shrewdly. 'You wanted to use Miss Russell to get inside the offices of *The Daily Picture*?'

Lil flopped down in one of the easy chairs with a sigh. All of the energy that had surged through her earlier seemed to have seeped away and now she felt tired but also deeply relieved. All her efforts had not been wasted. Tomorrow she would be going inside the offices of the *Daily Picture* at last, and better still she would not be going alone.

'Mei, you're *brilliant*,' she said.

'Well, there's no need to sound so surprised about it,' said Mei indignantly.

In spite of everything, Lil laughed. It felt like the first

time she had laughed in a long time. A moment later, Billy was laughing too and Daisy thumped her tail on the floor as if she wanted to join in, and before they knew it Tilly was putting her head round the door, asking what all the racket was about.

Almost, it felt like old times. But Joe's laughter was missing and as Daisy leaned her head against her knee, Lil felt more determined than ever that once she was inside *The Daily Picture*, she was going to find the mysterious woman – and discover the truth at last.

CHAPTER ELEVEN

Venice

When Sophie drew back the rose-patterned curtains of her bedroom the next morning, she saw that a light rain was falling over the rooftops of Venice. Downstairs, in the dining room, Mrs Knight and her friends were talking of umbrellas and galoshes, but Sophie felt glad. A little rain might help provide some extra cover for her plan to get inside the Palazzo Stella.

Over breakfast, Jack and Leo invited Ella to join them on a visit to the Accademia. As Jack had predicted, Mrs Knight looked quite delighted by their invitation.

'Yes, Ella, you go,' she instructed at once. 'I shall be glad of a restful morning here at the hotel. I have a great deal of correspondence to catch up on. I *must* write to Mrs Balfour and I have been thinking that I shall send a note to Mrs Davenport too. I daresay she would welcome a visit from someone like *me*, who knows her family.'

'Perhaps she'll invite you to her party,' suggested Jack

with an innocent look on his face.

Mrs Knight said 'hmmm', as if she thought it quite likely, though Sophie could only smile at the thought of how Mrs Davenport and her glamorous New York friends would respond to a call from prim Mrs Knight.

'I'm going to stay behind too,' she said quickly. 'I think I might be coming down with a cold.'

'I'm not at all surprised to hear it in this dreadful weather!' tutted Mrs Knight. 'You may sit with me in the parlour, Miss Taylor. I am sure Signora Mancini will bring us some tea.'

'That's very kind, but I believe I will lie down in my room for a while,' said Sophie quickly.

She watched from her bedroom window as Jack and Leo set out with Ella and Dr Beagle, who had offered to accompany them and show them some of his favourite paintings. They were well wrapped up in hats and coats and carrying umbrellas and Sophie hoped that anyone watching from a distance would assume that Ella was her. Once they had disappeared over the bridge and out of sight, she blew out a little sigh and turned decisively towards her wardrobe, and to business.

Never underestimate the importance of the right clothes, Ada Pickering had taught her. When she'd posed as Celia Blaxland in Paris, Sophie had dressed like a wealthy heiress in the latest fashions; on the airfields of Europe, she'd outfitted herself like a bold young aviatrix. Now, she had to look like someone quite different – someone who would blend in on the streets of Venice. She needed to be completely unremarkable, almost invisible. She picked out her plainest dark frock and added an apron like the one she'd seen the young woman delivering flowers to the palazzo wearing the day before. She pulled on her dark overcoat and covered her head with a shawl in the same way as some of the women she'd seen at the Rialto market.

She paused and scrutinised her reflection carefully in the mirror. With her head down under her shawl, she looked quite anonymous. Deciding that she was satisfied, she put the spyglass into one pocket, and tucked the pearl-handled pistol carefully into the other.

Cautiously she opened the bedroom door a crack and peered out on to the landing. The hotel was quiet now: in spite of the weather, most of the guests had gone out for the day. However, as she went down the stairs, she could hear Mrs Knight's voice floating out of the parlour door: 'Of course it is all thanks to *my* efforts that Miss Fitzgerald is showing such a particular interest in befriending Ella. It will be a great advantage to her when she makes her début in society in the summer. And Mr Rose has been *very* attentive – no doubt he will be a most eligible dance partner for her at balls. Oh, I know he is an *art student* but art schools are very well thought of these days. Perfectly respectable. Why, the Duke of Roehampton's sister went to the Spencer, you know!'

Sophie grinned to herself as she slipped past the parlour and along the hall. There was no one to see her as she softly opened the front door and went outside into the fine rain. Adjusting the shawl to be sure it covered her head, she hurried off towards the market. At a stall she handed over a few coins in exchange for a large straw basket before ducking into a shop, where she pretended to look at some glass-bead necklaces while actually glancing through the window to check the street. Once she was confident that no one was following her, she left the shop and crossed the market square to a large old-fashioned *pasticceria*, with gilt letters across its windows reading ZANNI'S.

She'd read about this place in her mother's diaries. Alice had described it as the oldest and most famous *pasticceria* in Venice and it was just as popular today, thronged with people. As she went inside, Sophie looked around, trying to imagine she was seeing it all through her mother's eyes. She breathed in steamy warm air, rich with the scents of coffee and chocolate, caramel and spice – just as delicious as Alice had said it was. Beneath the gleaming glass counters she saw rows of pastries and cakes: sweet buns puffy with cream or glistening with sugar; biscuits studded all over with nuts; cloudy meringues in pastel colours. There were glass jars filled with sugared almonds, or sweets wrapped in gold and silver paper; and boxes of violet and rose creams topped with crystalised flower petals, cherries dipped in chocolate or glistening candied fruits.

The shop was full of tourists admiring the exquisite chocolates, local people buying paper bags of pastries and gentlemen choosing boxes of bonbons for their young ladies. It was quite easy for Sophie to slip unnoticed between them and slide to the front, where she asked for two large and extravagant boxes of chocolates, each tied with a big green bow. She paid for them, tucked them quickly into her basket, and then left, heading back towards the canal in search of a gondola.

The rain had stopped now and the sun had emerged from behind the clouds. There seemed to be more people on the twisting streets than usual and Sophie noticed for the first time that some of them were dressed in traditional carnival costumes. She glimpsed a group of gentlemen in long cloaks and tricorn hats, a lady in an old-fashioned gown, her hair curled into long ringlets and a mask partly covering her face.

Beside the water's edge, Sophie stopped, close to where a man in a colourful harlequin costume was talking to another in the white robes and tall hat of a *pierrot*. She waved to summon a nearby gondola, but as the slim black boat moved towards her, her heart sank. The gondolier was Paolo – the same young man that had taken them out the previous day. Quickly, she pulled the shawl up so it shadowed her face, hoping he would not recognise her, but to her disappointment he waved and grinned to her at once. 'Signorina Sophie! You wish to go out in the gondola again? But what is this – fancy dress?' he added, gesturing to her shawl and apron.

'Something like that,' said Sophie, forcing herself to laugh. It was unfortunate that Paolo had recognised her, but she would have to make the best of it and go ahead with the plan.

Paolo was shaking his head as he helped her aboard. 'You will need to try harder than that for Carnival, Signorina! You need a mask – I shall tell you the best shop where you can buy one. But where are your friends, Signor Jack and Signorina Leo today?'

'Oh, they're out sightseeing,' said Sophie vaguely. 'Listen, could you take me to the Palazzo Stella?'

'You wish to go past it again?' asked Paolo.

Sophie felt herself blushing. 'No, I need to stop there. I'm . . . dropping something off,' she explained.

Paolo frowned at her basket with the boxes of chocolates visible inside, tied with their distinctive green ribbons. 'You are taking chocolates from Zanni's to Signora Davenport?' he asked in surprise.

'Yes, well, the thing is – Jack and Leo and I, we would so much like to go to her party. So we thought that if we asked nicely and took her some chocolates, she might give us invitations,' Sophie improvised.

Paolo laughed as if this was tremendously funny. 'Ha! You English are always doing mad things! Well, I shall take you there, yes. You shall deliver your chocolates and we shall see what happens!'

He burst into a song as he sculled them out on to the Grand Canal amongst the boats. His eyes were twinkling and every now and again he gave Sophie a quick grin, as though he thought she was very amusing indeed. But Sophie did not smile: instead, as they grew closer to the palazzo, she sat very still with her basket in her lap, watching it grow larger. Although it looked so rich and elegant from a distance, close up she saw that the old building was beginning to crumble at the edges. There were tendrils of ivy growing along the stone walls and the statues on the waterfront terrace were cracked and broken. Just the same, there was something beautiful about it even as it began to fade and fall into ruin and Sophie wondered if it was that which had attracted the artistic Mrs Davenport.

Several other boats were already moored at the terrace and Paolo pulled up alongside them, calling out a cheerful greeting to three men unloading boxes. They nodded back, paying little attention to Sophie as she clambered aboard with her basket.

'Will you wait here for me?' Sophie asked in a low voice. Paolo nodded and winked, as though the whole trip was a very good joke, while she went swiftly up the steps, trying to look as though she knew exactly where she was going.

There were several more men at work on the terrace, hanging up strings of coloured paper lanterns, but they were far too busy to notice her as she passed by, doing her best to look unimportant. Her heart was beginning to beat faster but no one paid her the slightest bit of attention as she ducked under the crumbling old portico.

Inside, she found herself standing in a large, empty hallway of cracked marble tiles and enormous glass chandeliers. Through one archway, she caught a glimpse of an opulent salon papered in blue and gold stars, shimmering with mirrors and gilded statuary. But turning the other way, there was only a half-empty room with peeling paint and crumbling plaster. What a peculiar place! As she hesitated, wondering which way to go, she heard the approach of footsteps and darted through the archway into the room with the gold stars, watching from behind an enormous statue as two heavy-set men came striding past. Like some of the gentlemen she had seen before, they were dressed for Carnival in long black cloaks, looking rather like characters from an old fairy tale. Were they some of Mrs Davenport's guests, or perhaps the guards that Paolo had talked about, whose job it was to keep out intruders?

Either way Sophie stayed out of sight until they had passed. If she were seen and challenged, she hoped the boxes of chocolates she was holding would give her a good excuse for being there. But even so she felt nervous. She knew that anyone she spoke to would know at once that she was English and not Italian. Far better to stay out of sight altogether.

She waited a little while to be sure they had gone, and then crept onwards through a series of interlinked rooms. Most of them were empty, decorated with faded old frescoes or cracked mosaic floors. Others contained only a single velvet chair, or an enormous looking glass in a tarnished gold frame. As she tiptoed from one room to the next, Sophie thought she had never been anywhere that was at once so sumptuous and so shabby. It was hard to believe that a party was about to take place here, although every now and again she glimpsed a clue as to what was about to happen – an immense bouquet of flowers placed before a tall window or a long table covered with clean white cloths and set with crystal glasses.

In each room, she scrutinised the walls with care. Here was an old oil painting in a carved frame, there a threadbare tapestry, but she saw nothing that resembled a Benedetto Casselli dragon painting. As she came up a curving flight of stairs, where a crumbling marble statue of a horse reared up magnificently on its hind legs, she heard the sound of someone talking. Peering cautiously through a doorway hung with a heavy brocade curtain, she saw a richly furnished room where a woman was lounging back on a chaise longue, talking on a telephone. It seemed strange to see someone doing something so modern in such a peculiar old place.

The woman's back was turned to Sophie, but Sophie could see she was wearing a satin turban ornamented with feathers, and smoking a cigarette in a long holder. She was wearing what looked like a pair of loose silk pyjamas, with a fur thrown around her shoulders; long gold earrings dangled from her ears and her wrists were encircled with heavy gold bracelets. This surely must be the famous Mrs Davenport herself.

'Yes . . . it's all taken care of,' the woman was saying. Mrs Knight was right, Sophie thought – she didn't sound in the least bit American. Her voice was absolutely English, upper-class and crisp. 'The chamber is ready. We'll begin at ten, once the party is in full swing . . .'

Sophie crept past the doorway and went on, along a corridor with a black and white marble floor. At the very end of it she found a small, square room, with large, pointed windows overlooking the canal and an immense chandelier hanging from the ceiling. There was no furniture but a single painting was hanging on the wall, and at once she saw that it was *The Black Dragon*.

There could be no mistaking it. Sophie would have known Benedetto Casselli's style anywhere, although this painting was different from the others she had seen – darker and more powerful. A heavy frame enclosed the twisting image of a dragon, dark and sinuous, one leg raised and its head turned as though it was looking out of the frame, right at Sophie.

She let out a little breath. Here it was at last: the *Dragon Regardant*. She felt a strange urge to step backwards and away, although at the same time she couldn't tear her eyes from it. She took in the curving shape of the dragon, its pointed teeth, the intricate patterns of its scales, the curling tendrils of flame and smoke that swirled from its open mouth. As she looked, she saw that the shape of it was not unlike the twisting golden dragon pins worn by some of the members of the *Fraternitas Draconum*.

But there was no time to linger. Mrs Davenport was just down the corridor – she might come this way at any moment. Quickly, Sophie put down her basket and took the spyglass from her pocket. She carefully flicked the coloured lenses into place and for a few minutes she concentrated on training the spyglass over the surface of the painting, examining every inch of it. At last, there it was – in the very top corner, some faint, spidery marks. A number, written in Roman numerals – *IV*, which stood for 4, and then a symbol like a sideways triangle – <. Following it were a few words in French. *L'oeil veille sur vous.* She'd spent enough time in the schoolroom studying French with her old governess Miss Pennyfeather to be able to translate them. *The eye watches over you.*

Sophie lowered the spyglass. The dragon's eye seemed to glint in the dim light.

She'd done it, she realised. She had the last part of the code and at long last they would be able to discover the location of the secret weapon!

And yet somehow she did not feel victorious. Instead of

IV < L'Œil veille sur vous

triumph, she felt only a sudden sharp stab of unease. A shiver, as though something had brushed up against the back of her neck. It had all been too easy, she realised. Something about this wasn't right.

There was a faint sound behind her, like a whisper of breath, and then the sudden slam of a door closing. She spun around at once, shoving the spyglass deep into her pocket, a few Italian words of explanation ready on the tip of her tongue, but she saw at once that it would do no good.

Standing before her, in front of the closed door, were three tall, square-shouldered men. Each wore a hooded black cloak and a blank white mask that covered the top half of their face completely. And pinned on to each of the black cloaks was a golden pin in the shape of a twisting dragon.

As Sophie stood, poised, between the three men and *The Black Dragon*, she realised in a flash what was happening. The *Fraternitas* hadn't been following her at all. They hadn't needed to; they had already known what she had come to Venice to do. They'd been expecting her – and she'd walked right into their trap.

PART III

'. . . Today Papa took me to visit Zanni's, a wonderful patisserie (or as they say in Italian 'pasticceria'), which he tells me is the oldest and most famous in Venice. It was full of delightful smells: I could happily have spent hours there, watching the customers and tasting all the heavenly confections. Papa bought me a box of the most delicious chocolates, which I must confess I am eating as I write this . . .'

– From the diary of Alice Grayson

CHAPTER TWELVE

Venice and London

I n that first lightning-flash moment, all Sophie was sure of was that she must escape.

At last she was in possession of the secret code. After everything that she had done, she could not let the *Fraternitas* take it from her.

The way ahead was blocked by the masked men and she knew there was no way past them. She had learned martial arts and she had fought off enemies before, but she'd always relied on being quick and clever or on taking her attackers by surprise. There was no chance of that now. She was standing face to face with three large, powerful-looking men, each of whom was twice her size. She knew she could not fight them alone.

But as the men moved towards her, her fingers closed around the pistol in her pocket. With one quick movement, she drew it out and fired a shot, exactly as Brooks had taught her.

The bullet whizzed high in the air, above the heads of the men. It struck home exactly as she had intended, hitting the immense glass chandelier where it was suspended from the ceiling by a length of rusty old chain. At once the fragile chain snapped and the huge chandelier came cascading downwards in an explosion of splintering glass and crumbling plaster. The three men leaped back as clouds of dust filled the air and glass shards scattered across the floor.

It gave Sophie the few seconds she needed to reach the only escape route that was open to her.

There was no time to think about it, not a moment to hesitate. As one of the men made a dash towards her, she darted for the window and jumped straight out.

There was a fleeting moment of rushing through the air, then a sudden splash.

A moment later, the icy waters of the Grand Canal had closed above Sophie's head.

The bells of St Dunstan's and St Bride's were chiming ten precisely as Lil went up the steps and inside the offices of *The Daily Picture*.

After weeks of watching from outside, it felt very peculiar indeed to be finally passing through the big glass doors and stepping into the foyer. Lil had never been someone who was troubled much by nerves but now her stomach squirmed with tension. Somewhere in this building was the woman Joe had seen collecting secret papers from the double agent, and this was Lil's chance to find her.

Just behind her Mei was glancing around while Billy looked anxious, his portfolio of stories tucked carefully under his arm.

There had been a great deal of talking and explaining after Miss Russell had left the Taylor & Rose offices the previous day. Billy in particular had been worried about the plan.

'I'm not sure that doing an interview with Miss Russell was such a good idea,' he'd said uncertainly. 'Remember what happened in Paris? I don't know if Sophie would like her writing about us. And what about the Bureau? I mean, what will the Chief say if he sees his agents splashed across the newspapers?'

'It's not as if I told her about anything *secret*,' argued Lil. 'I'm not an *idiot*. Besides, it doesn't matter to me what the Chief thinks! This could be a real chance to find out what happened to Joe – or don't you care about that?'

Billy turned red. 'Of course!' he insisted.

'We *all* do,' Mei chimed in. 'You aren't the only one who cares about Joe, you know.'

'But we *know* the woman Joe saw wasn't Roberta Russell,' Billy went on. 'She was in St Petersburg at the time.'

'That's not the point,' said Lil, impatient but feeling more like herself. Billy might be rather aggravating, but there was something reassuring about being back here in the office, chewing over the intricacies of a mystery with the others. 'The reason I was talking to Miss Russell was to try and find a way to get inside *The Daily Picture* offices. And now thanks to Mei – and your stories – we *have* a way. We'll all go tomorrow: you two can keep Miss Russell busy talking while I scout around and see what I can find out.'

'But you can't just go snooping about,' protested Billy. 'You'll get into fearful trouble!'

'I won't,' said Lil, tossing her head. 'I'll be careful. I'm a *detective*, aren't I? Snooping around is what I *do*. Besides, I don't really care if I get into trouble,' she added. 'I'm doing this for *Joe*.'

Mei had been listening, a thoughtful frown on her face. Now, she nodded. 'We should do it,' she said decisively. 'If there's even the slightest chance we can track down the woman Joe saw, then we have to take it.'

But Billy still looked worried as a young woman in spectacles greeted them and said she would fetch Miss Russell. Lil looked at her intently: could *she* possibly be the woman Joe had seen? She was wearing a neat skirt and blouse, but Lil wouldn't have described her as especially *smart* . . .

'Stop *staring*,' Billy muttered to her in a low voice.

'I'm not!' Lil hissed back.

'Ah, you're all here,' said Miss Russell, approaching with a large stack of papers under one arm. 'Everything all right?' she added, seeing that Lil and Billy were frowning at each other.

'Just debating one of our cases,' said Mei. 'Is this your office?'

'It's this way,' said Miss Russell. Lil had an impression of a lot of stairs and passages hung with framed newspaper front pages. There was a kind of humming sound rumbling somewhere beneath them, which Miss Russell explained was the sound of the printing machines at work.

They emerged at last into a large, bustling room: glancing around, Lil took in people everywhere. There were gentlemen standing in little groups, talking intently; a long row of desks where women clattered at the keys of typewriters; boys hurrying past with packages under their arms; and telephone bells shrilling insistently. Through doors to the left and right, Lil caught sight of private offices and meetings taking place: people sitting around a table arguing about something; a group standing around a desk spread with photographs; three gentlemen in suits talking in a cloud of cigar smoke, while beside them a secretary made notes. Here and there, Lil heard fragments of conversation:

'Have it on my desk by five o'clock!'

'Good morning, *The Daily Picture*, how may I help you?'

'I say, Gordon, have you seen the lead in the *Herald* this morning?'

'Get that headline changed quick sharp – boss's orders.'

'Telegram for you, sir!'

The whole place seemed full of buzzing energy. There was a feeling of urgency hanging in the air, along with a fug of cigar smoke. And there were so many people: Lil's eyes darted from a girl going by with a tray of coffee cups to a young woman with ink-stained fingers scribbling energetically, and then to an older woman at a typewriter, who had a brooch in suffragette colours pinned to her lapel. How would she even begin to track down the woman Joe had seen?

'We'll go in here,' said Miss Russell, opening the door to one of the small rooms, where several chairs were ranged around a table. 'Emma, have some tea sent into us, would you?' she said to the bespectacled young woman who had followed them.

Miss Russell got straight to the point. 'Well, I have good news for you, Mr Parker. I've discussed it with my colleagues and we'd like to take a few of your stories. In fact, we're going to run a short series of them – the first one to be published alongside Miss Rose's interview. We'll say that they're stories written by a member of Taylor & Rose's staff, inspired by some of their exciting experiences of detective work – that's a unique angle, you see. Of course, we'll need to make a few changes – just some small edits to ensure your stories fit the space we have available and that they're right for our readers. But I think we'll start with this one,' she said, opening up Billy's portfolio and pointing to a story Billy had titled *Secrets on the Shore*. 'Spy stories are very popular at the moment. So all you have to do is sign *here*,' and she slid a piece of paper under Billy's nose.

Billy was gaping at her as if struck dumb. She handed him a pen, gesturing to the paper he was to sign and he took it as though he was in a dream.

But before he could sign it, Mei held up a hand. 'Wait a moment. What about pay?' she said suddenly.

Miss Russell laughed. 'Of course you'll be paid. What do you say to ten bob per story? We'll take five to begin with, with a view to publishing more if they are well received.'

'Ten shillings?' repeated Mei, before Billy had the chance to say anything. 'Is that all? Isn't a guinea per story your usual rate of pay?'

Billy's expression became alarmed but Miss Russell looked rather impressed. 'Well, yes, I suppose it is,' she admitted. 'However did you know that?'

'Just a little research,' said Mei crisply. 'Simply because Mr Parker is a little *younger* that your usual contributors, I'm sure you'll agree that doesn't make his stories any less valuable to you. So make it a guinea per story and he'll accept.'

Miss Russell laughed again. 'Very well,' she agreed cheerfully. 'You've got a deal!'

She reached out a hand and Billy shook it. 'Five *guineas . . .*' he mumbled under his breath, as if he could scarcely believe it.

Miss Russell had turned to Lil. 'Miss Rose, you're happy with all this are you? It will all be promotion for your agency of course.'

'It sounds wonderful,' said Lil at once. It was *perfect*, she thought. If he was writing for *The Daily Picture* on an ongoing basis, Billy was certain to be here regularly. He'd have the chance to get to know the newspaper and its staff – and then *surely* they'd be able to find the woman Joe had seen.

Just then Emma, the young woman with the spectacles, came back again, looking apologetic. 'I'm sorry to interrupt, Miss Russell. But Sir Chester is asking for you. Some urgent changes he wants to make to your piece on the Siege of Sidney Street before he leaves for Italy.'

Miss Russell looked annoyed at the interruption but got to her feet at once. Sir Chester Norton was the head of the Norton Newspapers group and evidently not a man to be kept waiting. 'Do excuse me. I'll be back in a moment,' she said to them and walked out of the room, Emma following close behind her.

'A *guinea per story!*' she heard Billy exclaim. 'Gosh! Mei, you *know* I'd have done it for ten bob!'

'Well, now you're getting paid *properly*,' said Mei. 'And just think – you'll have at least five stories printed in the newspaper, maybe more!'

But they could celebrate the good news later, Lil

thought. For now she was going to make the most of the opportunity. Miss Russell had left them alone – this was her big chance to have a look around. Through the open door she watched Miss Russell cross the room, heading towards one of the doors on the other side that must lead to Sir Chester Norton's office. She watched Miss Russell approach, but just before she reached the door it opened and a man came out, turning back to say something over his shoulder. He was a tall, middle-aged man with a bushy moustache, who at once gave the impression of being a person of importance. Perhaps it was the way he carried himself; or perhaps it was the two younger men who scuttled behind him, both carrying leather cases and looking busy and harried. He nodded courteously to Miss Russell as he passed her and she bowed very politely back to him. Evidently he was a familiar figure in this office. And he was familiar to Lil too – she was sure she'd seen him before, more than once . . .

'Good morning, Mr Lockwood, sir,' she heard one of the journalists say. *Of course* – it was Arthur Lockwood, the Prime Minister! She'd seen his picture only yesterday on the front of the newspaper on Sophie's desk. She wondered what he'd been doing here, meeting with Sir Chester Norton.

Beside her, she became dimly aware that Billy was tugging on her sleeve. 'Lil!' he was hissing. '*Lil! Look!*'

'What is it?' she said, irritated. But when she glanced

around, she saw that Billy and Mei were also staring across the room, but not in the direction of the Prime Minister. Instead, following their gaze, she saw they were looking at a woman in a trim, elegant navy-blue suit. A *smart* woman, Lil realised. She was hurrying a man in a dark raincoat discreetly through the office: as they watched, she touched her finger to her lips and gestured to another door, then murmured something into his ear in a low tone. The man in the dark raincoat nodded confidentially and slipped inside.

'It's *him*, isn't it?' whispered Mei in a shocked voice. '*That man* – the one who came into our office?'

But neither Lil nor Billy answered her. It was not even a question that really needed an answer: there could be no doubt about it, Lil realised. She had recognised the man in the dark raincoat instantly. It was Mr Brooks.

CHAPTER THIRTEEN

Venice

Down Sophie plunged. The waters of the Grand Canal swirled around her, glass-green and cold as ice.

Sophie was not afraid of a little cold water. Papa had taught her to swim and he'd said the colder the better. 'Terribly good for you!' he'd exclaim, plunging straight in, emerging red-faced and exhilarated. Not wanting to disappoint him, Sophie had plunged in bravely too, even when her teeth were chattering.

But this was different. This cold was ferocious, biting into her skin with sharp teeth. For a moment she was too shocked to do anything, and then instinct took over and she began to kick her legs frantically. She was weighed down by her skirts and petticoats, her shawl tangling around her neck, her boots heavy on her feet, dragging her downwards. Everything around her was a hazy green: above her was shimmering light and shadow, moving like ghosts on the surface. Her skirt snagged on something under the water and she kicked more furiously, trying to free herself. She stretched her arms upwards towards the surface, but then a dark shape loomed over her and she felt an instant of panic, thinking of the black-cloaked men, the white masks. There was an arm reaching towards her in the water, dragging her upwards . . .

She broke through the surface, spluttering and choking and gasping for breath. She saw that the dark shape was the black prow of Paolo's gondola – and the arm was Paolo's, reaching out to haul her up. His cheerful expression had been replaced with an expression of horror.

'*Santo cielo!* Are you mad? Are you trying to kill yourself?'

Sophie was gasping too hard to say anything. She needed all her strength to grip Paolo's arms as somehow he managed to drag her out of the water. She lay in the bottom of the gondola, coughing up water, her eyes and nose stinging.

'We have to get away. Those men . . .' she managed to splutter out, even as she felt in her pocket and found, to her relief, that the spyglass and her pistol were still there.

Paolo stared at her. 'What men?' he demanded.

'The men – in masks,' she choked out. Her mouth was full of the horrible dank taste of canal water. She thought she had never been so cold: she was shivering uncontrollably, her hair sticking to her face, her skirts clinging damply to her legs. 'Please – we're in danger – we have to *go*.'

Paolo frowned at her and then glanced back over his

shoulder at the Palazzo Stella. 'Dio mio . . . there's a man in the window looking at us. No, two of them! Signorina, did they *push* you?' He looked aghast. 'But . . . surely they would not do this, simply because you tried to bring Signora Davenport *chocolates?*' He looked baffled. 'Who are they?' he demanded.

Sophie coughed again. 'Dragons,' she said, almost without thinking. A little distance away, another gondolier called out to Paolo in Italian; she could hear the loud voices of the American tourists in his gondola exclaiming to each other. 'Say, did you see that? A girl fell right out of that window into the canal. Do you suppose she's all right?'

Paolo shouted something back to the other gondolier – Sophie couldn't understand the words but from the lightness of his tone she knew he was saying something reassuring, making a joke out of what had happened. But when he turned back to her, his face was very serious indeed. 'Dragons? Do you mean . . . the *Fraternitas Draconum?*' he whispered.

Sophie gaped back at him, still shivering. Everything about her seemed to swirl. How could Paolo possibly know about the *Fraternitas Draconum?*

But the young gondolier had already glanced back at the Palazzo Stella and picking up his oar he had begun to scull vigorously away along the Grand Canal. 'There is a rug under the seat. Put it around yourself quickly – you must keep warm. We will get you inside *pronto*. The cold is dangerous. Where are you staying – the Pension Mancini?' He gave a little snort, as if to indicate he didn't think much of the place. Sophie looked back at the Palazzo Stella – she could see a cloaked man watching them from the waterfront terrace. Was he summoning a gondola to follow them? But Paolo had already steered them deftly out into the busiest part of the Grand Canal, weaving to and fro, making sure they would be lost amongst the crowds of gondolas and rowing boats, the steam-ferries and barges.

'How do you know about the *Fraternitas*?' Sophie demanded through chattering teeth as she grabbed the blanket and pulled it around her shoulders.

Paolo shrugged. 'Everyone in Venice knows about them,' he said. Then he paused and corrected himself. 'No, not *everyone*. But the old Venetian families like mine – we remember the stories of lions and dragons.'

'The *stories* . . . ? What do you mean?'

Paolo shrugged again, as if it was all perfectly obvious. 'Long ago, all the Venetian families belonged to one or the other. The *dragons* were the followers of St Theodore, who had the dragon as their symbol. And the *Ordine dei Leoni* followed St Mark, and theirs was the winged lion.

'Once upon a time the dragons and the lions worked together: that is why you can see the two pillars side by side at San Marco, the dragon and the lion next to each other. But then there was disagreement between them. There were . . . intrigues. Plots –' Paolo broke off and shook his head, as though he couldn't find the right English words to explain himself. 'The *Dragones* became greedy and wicked and deceitful. They wanted power and wealth, and would do anything to get it. The lion families tried to stop them.'

Sophie felt dizzy. '*Lion families?*' she repeated breathlessly.

'It was a long time ago.' Paolo shrugged again. 'But some say that the *Dragones* are still at work in secret today. If they are after you, signorina, I suppose you must be a lion too.' He paused. 'You know, I ought to have guessed when I saw Signorina Leonora. Her cane, with the lion's head? I have seen one like it before. It is from here, Venice, no?'

Sophie felt dazed. The cane with the lion's head had once belonged to Grandfather Lim, who had been a member of the original Loyal Order of Lions alongside her parents. Could it really have come from Venice, she wondered? Was it really a connection back to an age-old tradition of *lion families*? How had they never known about any of this before?

'The Palazzo Stella once belonged to one of the most important dragon families,' said Paolo in a low voice. 'Perhaps it still does. Well, if you really are a lion, and the dragons are after you, then I will help you for certain. But the first thing we must do is get you indoors.'

An hour later, Sophie was warm and dry again. Paolo had insisted on bringing her right to the doors of the Pension

Mancini, where he had had a long and insistent conversation with Signora Mancini that had resulted in a fire being lit in Sophie's bedroom and hot water being brought at once for a bath. Then Paolo had gone without a word more about dragons and lions, saying only: 'Arrivederci, signorina – I will see you soon.'

When Jack and Leo returned from their morning outing, they found Sophie sitting alone in her room, wrapped in her dressing gown, sipping a steaming cup of *tisane* and drying her wet hair in front of the fire. She looked very thoughtful indeed.

'Sophie? Are you all right?' demanded Jack as the two of them hurried in, still in their coats and hats. 'What happened? Signora Mancini said something about you falling into the canal!'

Sophie motioned for them to close the door behind them. 'I didn't exactly *fall*,' she said in a low voice. 'It was more of a *jump*.'

As quickly and clearly as she could, she explained what had happened at the Palazzo Stella. 'I had no choice. It was the only way out.'

Jack looked stunned. 'But are you absolutely sure those men were from the *Fraternitas*?' he asked. 'Could they be the guards that Paolo talked about? Perhaps they saw you and thought you were a thief?'

But Sophie shook her head. 'I don't think so. I think they knew the painting was there and they were expecting me to come for it. I think they were waiting for me.' She shivered, even though it was warm beside the fire; remembering the cloaked and masked men made her feel as if she had been plunged into the cold water of the canal all over again.

Just then there came a knock at the door and they all jumped. 'Leo?' came Ella's voice. 'I've got that book – the one I was telling you about?'

Leo got up and went over to the door, opening it the merest crack. 'Er – thanks, Ella . . .' she said awkwardly. 'I'll see you downstairs in a minute.'

'Oh, all right,' said Ella, sounding a little hurt. But Leo had already closed the door and turned back to Sophie. '*Waiting* for you? What do you mean?'

'I think the *Fraternitas* know we already have the other six paintings. And they also know that to find the weapon, we need to see the seventh and final painting – *The Black Dragon*. A painting *they* have. Instead of hiding it from me, they let me find it *so that I could complete the secret code.*'

'But *why*?' asked Jack, looking baffled. 'Surely they want to stop you from getting the weapon so they can take it for themselves?'

Sophie tried to explain what she was still working out for herself. 'Why go to the trouble of stealing all six of the other paintings *and* the Professor's notebook when they could just let me do the hard work instead? They led me to *The Black Dragon*, planning to catch me there and take the secret code for themselves.' And if it hadn't been for Paolo – and the Chief's revolver – they probably would have succeeded, she realised. She felt sick at the thought. If she had been caught, she would certainly have been interrogated, and there was no doubt that the *Fraternitas* would use the most unpleasant methods to force her to reveal the secret code. After what had happened to Joe, she was more certain than ever that there was nothing they would not do.

Leo looked as though she felt rather sick herself. 'No wonder you dived into the canal,' she murmured. Sophie guessed she was remembering her own narrow escape from the *Fraternitas* – when she'd been pushed on to the tracks of the underground railway, into the path of an oncoming train.

'I was lucky to get away. I don't know if the men followed me back here, but I'm certain they'll have discovered where I'm staying, if they didn't know already,' Sophie went on. She fell abruptly silent: Venice, which had seemed enchanting, was suddenly dark and full of danger. The little room where they sat might be warm and snug, but outside the sky was the colour of slate. Rain was falling and somewhere, she knew, the masked men would be watching and waiting for her.

And it wasn't just her, she realised. The *Fraternitas* were certain to know she was travelling with Jack and Leo, which would put them in danger too. They would have to stay here at the hotel until she could come up with a plan, she thought: but even here, would they be safe? The *Fraternitas* had eyes everywhere. Anyone could be working for them: Signora Mancini or her maid, Mrs Wentworth, kindly Dr Beagle, even Ella. She couldn't afford to trust anyone.

Jack and Leo were glancing at each other anxiously. They looked rattled and out of their depth. If only Lil were here, Sophie thought with a sudden pang. Or her friend Nakamura, who was always calm and sensible and would have helped her work out what she ought to do next. Or Carruthers, who would have been certain what the Chief would say and the proper way to proceed.

The Chief. Of course – she must let him know what she had discovered. But with the threat of the *Fraternitas* watching and listening that would not be so easy. She thought for a moment and then remembered. There was a system for agents to leave a coded telephone message for the Bureau if ever they found themselves in danger. She'd never used it before – when she'd been in St Petersburg, the Chief had told her she should only communicate with the Bureau via the British Embassy and their diplomatic bag. But now she would.

She got to her feet at once. 'I need to get a message to the Bureau. Will you both help me?'

A minute or two later, the bedroom door creaked open and the three of them went downstairs, Sophie still in her dressing gown and bedroom slippers. While Jack went off towards the parlour, with instructions to keep Signora Mancini busy talking, Sophie crept towards the office. With Leo stationed outside the door as lookout, she slipped quietly inside.

The telephone stood on a table beside the window. She picked up the receiver and waited impatiently while the operator connected the call, listening out the whole time for the signal from Leo that would mean Signora Mancini was coming. After what seemed like forever, she at last heard a clipped voice, which sounded as though it was coming from very far away: 'Good afternoon, Mayfair 67. How may I assist you?'

'My name is Sophie Taylor – I'm calling with a message for Mr Clarke,' Sophie said in a low voice, desperately hoping she'd remembered the code words correctly. 'I need to let him know that *Miss Shaw is travelling overland to Salzburg.*'

There was a moment's pause, then: 'Mr Clarke?' repeated the distant voice. 'I'm sorry, miss. There's no one here by that name.'

Sophie was disconcerted. Had she got the telephone number wrong? She was sure it had been *Mayfair 67.* Or could it be that this was all part of the secret system? She had no way of being sure.

The voice wished her a crisp 'good afternoon' and then disappeared.

Sophie replaced the receiver. Would the Chief receive

her call for help – or were they all alone?

She glanced out through the rain-streaked window and then drew abruptly back behind the lace curtains.

Outside, on the other side of the canal, someone was standing, watching.

It was a man in a black cloak and a white mask.

CHAPTER FOURTEEN

Secret Service Bureau HQ, London

The door of *The Daily Picture* offices slammed behind them as Lil darted out into the street. Mei and Billy were following close at her heels but they could scarcely keep up with her as she raced up busy Fetter Lane, through the twisting back streets to Chancery Lane, across sedate squares and green lawns, and at last to the grand old buildings of the Inns of Court and the offices of the Secret Service Bureau.

As she ran, Lil's thoughts were racing too. It was Brooks! The double agent at the Bureau was Brooks. *He* was the one that Joe had seen passing secret information to the woman from *The Daily Picture* – the smart woman in the navy-blue suit. No wonder he'd been poking around at Taylor & Rose, asking difficult questions!

'Clarke & Sons!' she called to the elderly concierge, not even waiting for a reply before she went on past him, charging straight up the stairs. Billy and Mei were still behind her; she could hear the clattering of their boots. They'd never been here before – after all, only the official Bureau agents were supposed to know about the office's location, but that scarcely seemed to matter now.

She flung open the door with a bang, making Carruthers, who had been sitting at his desk poring over his paperwork, leap to his feet at once.

'Lil!' he exclaimed. For a split second, he looked delighted to see her, but then as he saw her dashing towards the Chief's door, he leaped forward and grabbed her arm. 'What do you think you're doing? The Chief's in a meeting – you can't just rush in! And what are you even doing here? You're supposed to be in Venice!'

But Lil shook him off. '*I know who it is!*' she burst out. 'The double agent! We've found him!'

'*Shh! Shh!*' Carruthers looked from Lil to Billy and Mei, neither of whom he had ever met before. His expression was aghast. 'What are you playing at?' he demanded furiously.

But Lil ignored him. She was already darting towards the door of the Chief's office, and now she threw it open without knocking. Inside, she found the Chief and Captain Forsyth deep in conversation.

'I say!' exclaimed Forsyth in astonishment as Lil charged in. 'Hullo, old girl! What are you doing here?'

'I'm sorry, sir – I couldn't stop her!' exclaimed Carruthers, rushing in behind Lil, followed by Billy and

Mei, who were certainly not going to be left out now.

'Miss Rose?' asked the Chief mildly, a little surprised but rather interested in this sudden interruption. 'I had understood you were away with Miss Taylor but I see that is not the case. Can I - er - help you with something?'

'I know who it is!' Lil exclaimed at once. She knew there was no need to be hush-hush in front of Forsyth or anyone else any longer. 'The double agent passing secrets out of the Bureau - it's *Mr Brooks!*'

There was a long pause. The Chief took off his spectacles and looked at her. 'Mr Brooks?' he repeated.

'We saw him just now! He was at the offices of *The Daily Picture*, having some sort of a secret meeting!'

The Chief frowned. 'Close the door behind you, Sam,' he instructed Carruthers sharply.

'I say - what's all this about a *double agent*?' asked Forsyth with great interest.

But no one answered him. 'Sit down, Miss Rose. And your - er - colleagues too,' said the Chief with a quick glance at Mei and Billy. 'Now, tell us what you saw. *Exactly* what you saw.'

Lil took a deep breath and tried to compose herself. She realised she was trembling. 'We were at the offices of *The Daily Picture*,' she said more slowly. 'We were there to see Miss Russell, one of the journalists. But while we were there, we saw Mr Brooks come into the office with a woman who matched the description of the woman that Joe saw collecting the information at the Embankment Gardens. She took him to a private room and they were being very stealthy, as though they didn't want anyone to see or hear them.'

The Chief glanced quickly at Carruthers, as though silently asking him a question. But Carruthers shook his head at once. 'I can't think of any reason for Brooks to be there,' he said slowly.

'Forsyth? Any reason Brooks would be at *The Daily Picture*? Anything relating to your other assignment?'

Forsyth got to his feet and strode over to the window. His voice was sombre as he replied: 'No. None at all. Golly – Brooks, a double agent? I'd never have believed it. But do you know, sir, now I think about it, I rather think it *makes sense*. I'd noticed him splashing around some extra chink lately, you know. He's never been what you'd call a particularly well-off sort of a fellow. But just lately he'd seemed to be rather *flush*. I asked him about it and he said something about having come into some money from an old uncle. I s'pose he must've been pulling the wool over my eyes the whole time.' He sighed and shook his head. 'What's he up to – selling secrets to the papers? Oh, I say, he's not working for Ziegler and the Germans, is he?'

'Worse than that, I'm afraid,' said the Chief gravely. 'We believe that Mr Brooks is in the pay of the *Fraternitas Draconum*.'

Forsyth let out a long whistle. '*Golly!*' was all he said.

The Chief drummed his pencil against his desk and then shook his head. 'Of all the people it could have been . . . Do you know, I'd always have said Brooks was as straight as an arrow,' he mused, as though talking to himself. 'But the *Fraternitas* have their ways of getting to even the most unlikely people . . .'

Lil knew that was true. Ever since they'd first encountered the *Fraternitas*, she'd seen how they could trick and manipulate all kinds of people into working for them, whether it was a wealthy art collector like Mr Lyle, or scientists, actors and even policemen.

'Did Brooks see you there, at the newspaper office?' the Chief asked now.

Lil shook her head and the Chief nodded approvingly. 'Good. He doesn't know he's been discovered then. We'll send him a message to come here at once, and we'll find out the truth. You'll be here, Miss Rose, so you can say what you saw?'

'Of course,' said Lil. What she did not say is that she knew already that she would be saying far more than *what she saw*. When she was face to face with Brooks she'd be demanding to know the truth about what had happened to Joe. Her fists clenched at the thought.

'And once Brooks has confessed, we will explain to him that he must now switch allegiances,' the Chief went on. 'At the very least, he will have useful information about the Fraternitas he can share.'

'What if he refuses?' asked Carruthers.

'I'm afraid we shall not be giving him the choice,' said the Chief in a sombre tone. 'But – before we get to that, we must also think of Miss Taylor. Whatever else is happening here, we must not leave her in the lurch.'

'Sophie?' asked Lil at once. 'Why – what's wrong?'

'Miss Taylor has sent an SOS message to say that she's in danger and needs our help,' the Chief explained briskly. 'And now I know that you are *not* in fact with her to help with the assignment in Venice, she will be even more in need of assistance.' His voice was mild but just the same Lil felt colour coming to her cheeks.

'I say, sir, ought I to go out to Venice to help her?' suggested Forsyth. 'After all, you'll need Miss Rose here to resolve this double agent business. There's a train that leaves at three o'clock – if I leave now, I should be able to catch it.'

'Thank you, Captain – that would be a great help,' said the Chief. 'Sam, you'll give him all the details, and a copy of Miss Taylor's briefing notes?'

Carruthers had already hurried out to his desk to gather the necessary papers. 'She's staying at the Pension Mancini,' he called back through the door into the Chief's office. 'I'll telephone ahead, arrange a room for you there.'

'No need for that, old fellow,' said Forsyth, who was already shrugging on his coat. 'You've got quite enough to deal with here. I'll sort things out for myself.' He flashed

Lil a quick smile. 'Cheer up, old thing – I'll see that Miss Taylor is all right and we'll be back with you here in no time. Jolly good work on finding out what Brooks is really up to. Farewell, all!' With a quick glance up at the clock, he dashed out.

The Chief settled back into his chair, placing the tips of his fingers together. 'Sam, put through a call to Brooks's office and leave a message for him, asking him to come here and report to me as soon as possible. Make it sound urgent, but don't give him any reason to be suspicious.'

Carruthers nodded at once and hurried out of the room. The Chief eyed Lil thoughtfully for a long moment and then turned to contemplate first Mei and then Billy, who had been listening to all of this, looking rather awed by finding themselves inside the headquarters of the Secret Service Bureau and face to face with the Chief, of whom they had heard so much.

'Now, Miss Rose, I rather think you should introduce me to these two young people,' said the Chief. 'Since they know so much of our sensitive and confidential business, we may now consider them official Bureau agents, I think? And as such it seems only right and proper that I know their names.'

CHAPTER FIFTEEN

Venice

'Unfortunately, Mrs Davenport was not at home when I called. But then no doubt she will be *extremely* busy with all the preparations for her party. Just the same, I expect she will return my call *very* soon . . .'

Mrs Knight's voice rose high above the tinkling of china and silverware. It was breakfast time again at the Pension Mancini, but Sophie could do little more than nibble a roll. She had even less appetite for Signora Mancini's porridge than usual. At last the rain had stopped and a pale winter sunshine was creeping in through the lace curtains, illuminating the faces of the guests: Mrs Wentworth, reading her morning newspaper; Dr Beagle, sipping his coffee; Mrs Knight, talking on and on while Ella sat looking bored at her elbow. Sophie watched them all, unable to shake the thought that any one of them could be working for the *Fraternitas*.

She'd slept badly the previous night, tossing and turning

for hours. When she'd finally drifted off to sleep, she'd dreamed about falling deep into cloudy green water. Strange visions had flickered like the pictures in a magic lantern show. Papa, in a striped bathing suit, laughing and diving into the Grand Canal; the Baron smiling coldly at her in a darkened Chelsea alleyway, before vanishing into the dark. Mrs Davenport, in her feathered turban, talking on the telephone, but this time whispering about dragons. Paolo, in his gondola, but instead of an oar he was holding Leo's lion's head cane. Amongst it all she saw the sinister figures of men in white masks and black cloaks, growing closer and closer. And then the twisting shape of the Black Dragon, watching her with its single gleaming malevolent eye.

When morning had come at last, her first thought had been of the masked man she'd seen the previous day. But when she went to the window and peered out she'd seen that carnival season had now begun in earnest. Although it was still early, the streets were already busy with people dressed in costumes: feathered hats, powdered wigs and ornate masks of every possible colour and style. Among them she saw one man after another wearing a white mask and a long black cloak. Obviously it was a favourite carnival costume. Whether any of them could be men from the Palazzo Stella, she could not possibly be sure.

She was also feeling anxious about the coded message she'd tried to send to the Chief. She had no way of knowing whether it had been received, and therefore she could not count on advice or help arriving from the Bureau. She knew too that she could not afford to sit around and do nothing while the *Fraternitas* circled closer. As the sun rose above the rooftops, she'd made up her mind: she would go ahead and find the map the Chief had told her about and use it to identify the location of the weapon.

But that only gave her more problems. She knew that the map was housed at the State Archive of Venice, but getting a look at it would not be easy. The Archive was not open to tourists or casual visitors: only scholars were allowed inside to carry out their research. And that was not her only problem. Even if Sophie could masquerade as a scholar and find a way inside, if the masked men were watching her, she'd be leading them straight to the very information they wanted most – the location of the secret weapon.

She'd have to find her way to the Archive without being seen, she told herself. She was well versed in how to 'shake off a tail', but this was not London where she knew every back alley in Seven Dials and Soho and could easily navigate her way by omnibus or underground from Camden to Clapham. Venice was unfamiliar territory: its twisting labyrinth of streets, its bridges over darkly glinting canals, its secret squares and narrow alleyways were unknown to her.

'*Scusi, signora,*' said Signora Mancini's maid, jolting

Sophie out of her thoughts. The maid had come into the room carrying a large, beautifully wrapped package with a big green bow: with a start, Sophie recognised it at once as a box of chocolates from Zanni's, exactly like the ones she'd taken to the Palazzo Stella the day before.

'This has come for you,' said the maid in heavily accented English, handing the box to Mrs Knight.

'For *me*?' said Mrs Knight in surprise. 'But I didn't order anything! I suppose it must be a present.' She took it, looking very pleased at the idea. 'Well! How *very* kind! I wonder who it can be from? Oh, but there's no label.'

'I say, Mrs Knight, perhaps you have a secret admirer?' said Jack with a grin. Ella had to hide a giggle in her napkin, but Mrs Knight was so taken with her parcel that she didn't notice.

'Do you know, I believe I know exactly who this is from – my friend Mrs Balfour!' she exclaimed. 'It *is* my birthday next week. But how *kind* of her to remember and arrange a gift for me here in Venice, especially when I know she is so *terribly* busy with preparations for the marriage of her son to Lady Cynthia Delaney. But dear Constance is always *so* thoughtful.'

She simpered and laid the box in the centre of the table, where as many people as possible would have a clear view of it and could see how large and expensive-looking it was.

'Aren't you going to open it?' asked Ella.

'Certainly not!' said Mrs Knight at once. 'Ladies do *not*

eat chocolates at breakfast time. It is extremely bad for the digestion. But I shall open them later and you may try one of course. They are from the very best *pasticceria* in Venice, you know. But you must not be *greedy* about sweet things, Ella,' she scolded. Rather ironic, Sophie thought, given that she'd noticed Mrs Knight herself had eaten no less than three cakes at teatime the day before.

Just then, Sophie saw that Dr Beagle had finished eating and was going to rise from the table. She gave Leo a quick nudge.

'Excuse me, Dr Beagle,' Leo spoke up quietly. 'Did you say that you were going to do some research at the State Archive today?'

'That's right, my dear,' said Dr Beagle, smiling at her benevolently. 'It's only a short walk away from here.'

'We've heard such a lot about the Archive and the wonderful old documents there,' Leo went on, blushing a little. 'Jack and I would like so much to see it, but we know we wouldn't be allowed inside by ourselves. I am sure you are very busy with your work, but do you suppose you could spare us a little time to show it to us? It would be so interesting to see where you research your marvellous books.'

Dr Beagle looked extremely flattered by this request. 'My dear, it should be my great pleasure! May I say how splendid it is to see young people such as yourselves with a real enthusiasm for art history? We shall go this very day.'

'Oh, thank you – we'd like that very much,' said Leo.

'Are you going on another outing, Miss Fitzgerald?' said Mrs Knight, her ears pricking up at once. 'I'm sure you would like to see this – er – Archive too, wouldn't you, Ella?'

Ella winced but Jack gave her a reassuring smile. 'Of course, why don't you join us?' he said at once, and Ella looked pleased.

'Are you sure you all want to go inside the Archive on such a fine day?' asked Mrs Wentworth from behind her newspaper. 'It may be the last one we have for a little while. It says here that a storm is forecast. We can expect high winds and a great deal of rain, perhaps even some flooding.'

'Oh dear!' twittered Mrs Knight. 'How dreadful!'

Dr Beagle smiled reassuringly. 'The Venetians are well used to flooding – *acqua alta*, they call it. It's rather a nuisance but that is all. You may perhaps wish to purchase some rubber boots to keep your feet dry.'

In the end it was agreed that they would go to the State Archive after luncheon. Mrs Wentworth and Archie would join them on the outing, though Mrs Knight said she would stay behind. 'After all, I am expecting Mrs Davenport to call,' she explained.

'She really believes Mrs Davenport is going to turn up with an invitation to the party, doesn't she?' whispered Jack to Leo, shaking his head in disbelief.

'What about you, Miss Taylor? Will you be joining us?'

asked Dr Beagle.

'I'm afraid not,' said Sophie, speaking clearly enough that anyone who might be listening would be able to hear. 'I've got some errands to do this afternoon. I'll meet you all back here at teatime.'

She felt rather nervous as she put on her hat and coat and slipped the pistol into her pocket. She knew that what she was doing was a risk, but it was too late to change her plan now. There was no time to do anything but give Jack and Leo a quick nod before she took a deep breath, turned up the collar of her coat against the cold air, and before she could think any more about it, walked out of the door.

Outside, her breath puffing out in the cold air, she tried not to show she was nervous as she walked briskly along the street and over the canal. She did not even glance at the man in the black cloak and white mask who was loitering on the other side of the canal, as though she didn't have the slightest idea that he was watching. She wanted him to feel certain she was setting off on the trail of the weapon, and to follow her in the *opposite* direction to the State Archive.

She walked quickly towards the market, being careful to keep to the busiest streets, resisting the temptation to look behind her to see if the masked man was following. She passed a stationer's; a shop selling spices; a bakery where rows of delectable cakes were laid out in the window; an accordionist playing a cheerful tune. It was not until she reached a shop selling beautiful Murano glass that she allowed herself to pause for a moment. There was an ornate mirror displayed in the window: glancing into it, she could see the reflection of the street behind her. Sure enough, there was the figure of the man in a dark cloak and white mask, lurking by a shop window as though looking to buy something. As she watched, she caught her breath, seeing a *second* cloaked and masked man join him.

She turned at once away from the shop window and walked on. Behind her, the two masked men followed briskly, their cloaks flapping like crows' wings. Sophie's heart was thumping in her chest but she knew she must not show she was anxious: she did not want them to guess she knew they were there. She went on, across the white curve of the Rialto Bridge and through the Piazza San Marco. Under cover of the crowds, she ducked quickly into the café they had visited on the first morning, but a moment or two later slipped out again, concealing herself amongst a large group of tourists who were on their way to take a guided tour of the Basilica. But once inside the grand entrance, she separated herself from them, hurrying through the church and leaving by a different door.

She picked up her pace, going a little faster, doubling back over the Rialto Bridge and pausing at the highest point to glance behind her. There was no sign of the two men in black cloaks behind her now. On the other side of the bridge she ducked quickly into a little shop displaying brightly coloured carnival masks, and emerged a few moments later with a parcel under her arm.

Next, she went to a buy a ticket for one of the steam-ferries that went up and down the Grand Canal. She only had to wait a minute or two before it arrived, and she clambered aboard amongst a crowd of people heading to the island of Murano. From the deck of the boat, she turned to scan the crowd.

She'd done it, she thought with relief as the boat pulled away from the shore. She'd lost them. But as the ferry began to chug slowly along the canal, out into the sparkling still waters of the lagoon, she froze.

They were here. On the other side of the deck, two men in matching black cloaks and white masks were making their way steadily through the crowd towards her.

CHAPTER SIXTEEN

State Archive, Venice

A few hours later, Leo was sitting outside a café in a little square beside the entrance to the State Archive of Venice. There was a feeling of celebration in the air: the café had been decorated with coloured paper streamers and a short distance away a band was playing a merry tune and a few people in carnival costumes were dancing. Leo's sketchbook lay on the table in front of her, and her pencil moved deftly as she sketched the details she could see: the curlicues of ironwork balconies; the patterns of roof tiles; the shapes of shuttered windows and ornate church spires; the twirling figures in their vivid costumes. But for once, Leo's mind was not on her drawing. She kept glancing at her watch. Sophie was supposed to have been here half an hour ago but there was still no sign of her anywhere.

Leo felt herself growing tense. She'd been excited about coming to Venice and it had been such a thrill to see it all, but increasingly she felt anxious. Sophie's mission, the paintings, the masked men from the *Fraternitas* . . . it all reminded her so much of when she'd first come to London and had got mixed up with Mr Lyle and the Casselli dragon paintings. Jack might act as though being involved in a mystery was thrilling but Leo remembered only too well just how frightening – and dangerous – it could be. She thought about what had happened to Joe and a chill swept over her.

Quickly, Leo glanced around her at the crowd but to her relief she could see no white-masked, black-cloaked men anywhere, though there was a gentleman in a red cloak and a gold mask among the dancers. As he watched, he bowed to a passing young lady who wore a mask in the shape of a cat's face and swept her up into the dance. Leo sketched them as they danced but she knew it was far from her best work.

She had to be brave, she told herself as her pencil moved across the paper. It was her duty to help Sophie and she would do it. She was a sworn member of the Loyal Order of Lions, and she had vowed to do her part to stop the *Fraternitas*. But as she checked her watch again, she saw that Sophie was now very late indeed. Was something wrong, she wondered, and if so, what on earth was she to do?

The band brought their song to an end and the dancers stopped, clapping their hands. Leo saw the young lady with the cat mask curtsy politely to her dance partner, and then to her surprise she came running lightly over to the table where Leo was sitting. The hood of her black velvet cloak fell back, revealing fair hair.

'*Sophie!* Thank goodness!'

'I'm sorry I'm so late! It took me an age to shake off those men. But I think changing into this carnival costume finally did the trick. With any luck they'll be looking for me on Murano by now.'

'Well, I certainly didn't recognise you,' said Leo, breathing out a little sigh of relief. 'Gosh, I'm glad you're all right!'

'Are Jack and Ella still with Dr Beagle?'

'Yes. He's showing them some of the old documents he's working with at the moment. I said I wanted to do some sketching, but I'm supposed to meet them in half an hour.'

'We don't have long then – we'd better hurry. Did you manage to find out where the Marino map is kept?'

Leo nodded as she quickly pocketed her sketchbook and dropped a few *lire* on the table to pay for her drink. 'It's in one of the study rooms – come this way.'

The entrance to the State Archive was just across the square, where a door beside a narrow canal had the words *ARCHIVO DI STATO* written above it. Sophie slipped the cat mask into her pocket as Leo led her inside a stone-flagged entrance hall. A serious-looking gentleman was sitting behind a desk but when Leo smiled shyly at him and murmured Dr Beagle's name, he nodded and waved them through.

Sophie had a quick impression of dimly lit corridors with echoing stone floors. Leo took her straight to a large, silent room lined with tall wooden bookcases crammed with old books. Several ladies and gentlemen were scattered about, poring studiously over old maps, documents and leather-bound books, while a row of marble busts scowled down at them from above.

Leo led Sophie to one corner. 'This is it,' she whispered, gesturing to a shelf labelled *Carta Geografica di Franco Marino*.

Sophie looked up at it in surprise. When the Chief had told her about the map, she had imagined something like the atlas she'd used in the schoolroom with Miss Pennyfeather. But the Marino map was something quite different. It was divided into a row of enormous volumes, each richly bound and elaborately decorated. With Leo's help, she eased one of the huge books from the shelf and placed it on a wooden desk with a thump that made one or two of the nearby scholars look up disapprovingly.

Conscious that time was already passing, she opened the heavy leather cover. Inside, the paper felt rough and very old beneath her fingertips. She saw page after page of images – illustrations of classical gods and goddesses, elaborate drawings of globes and intricate compass roses. There were pages of text too, written in smudgy black

173

printing, and then the maps themselves, looking quite different to any she'd seen before. They were full of intricate decorations: the oceans scattered with galleons, mermaids and ferocious-looking sea monsters; the land ornamented with trees and mountains, flags and castles. For a moment she hesitated. Where was she to begin?

Leo pushed her sketchbook and pencil into Sophie's hand. 'Write down the code!' she urged. 'We can work it out together.'

For a moment, Sophie frowned. The Chief had said it would be too dangerous to commit the code to paper, but she needed Leo's help and they were running out of time. She'd have to destroy it afterwards; that was all. She grabbed the pencil, scribbling it down in Leo's sketchbook. The six numbers – *11 5 7 18 12 155* then the number *4* and the sideways triangle she'd discovered hidden in *The Black Dragon*.

Leo ran a finger along the shelf of volumes, pointing to where the spine of each was marked with a Roman numeral. 'Perhaps the first number shows us which volume we should look at?' she whispered.

'But there isn't a volume eleven,' Sophie whispered back. 'Look – there are only ten.'

'Well then, maybe it's one one?' suggested Leo. 'That could mean *Volume 1, Page 1*.' But when they leafed through, they saw that the first few pages of Volume 1 were completely blank.

For several minutes, they frowned together over the sketchbook page, trying to work out what the number *11* might mean. Sophie began to feel anxious. All she had was a string of numbers that made no sense. The clock on the wall was ticking and she felt that at any moment, the black-cloaked figures might appear again.

'Perhaps the *triangle* is a clue,' she muttered. 'But to what?'

Leo was squinting at the paper. 'Maybe it isn't a triangle,' she said suddenly. She grabbed the sketchbook, and tapped the page with her pencil. 'We've been starting here, with the number eleven, going from *left to right*. But what if the triangle is actually an *arrow*, showing us that we should read the numbers the other way – from *right to left*, in the direction it points?' She scribbled down the numbers in reverse order, to illustrate her point.

'So . . . we'd start with volume four,' said Sophie, reaching for the book and heaving it down with an even louder thud that made one of the scholars mutter something cross. 'What's next?' Leo whispered. 'One hundred and fifty-five?'

Page 155 showed part of the map of Europe. Here was the Adriatic Sea, decorated with drawings of fearsome-looking fish. Sophie could see the long familiar shape of Italy and the island of Sicily.

'There are numbers around the edge of the map, like a grid reference,' Leo whispered excitedly. 'Look – here's number twelve!'

11 5 7 18 12 155 4 <

> 4 155 12 18 7 5 11

She followed the line marked *XII* with her fingertip. Sophie was already tracing the one marked *XVIII*, eighteen. Their fingers met in the top right-hand corner of Italy.

'But that's *Venice!*' exclaimed Leo. 'Does that mean the secret weapon is hidden somewhere *here?*'

'*Shh!*' scolded an English gentleman in a clerical collar, looking very disapproving.

But of course, Sophie thought. She'd already learned that Venice was the home of the dragons and the lions. It made perfect sense that the secret weapon was hidden somewhere here in this ancient city.

'Let's find the detailed map of Venice,' said Leo, sounding more excited by the minute. 'There's a whole volume dedicated to Italy – and it's volume *seven!* That's the next number, look!'

Moving faster now, they rifled through the pages, past Rome and Milan, Verona and Naples. At last they found the big map of Venice, with the snaking shape of the Grand Canal running through it and the sprinkling of islands that scattered the lagoon.

'Two numbers left,' whispered Sophie. 'Five and eleven – let's find them!'

Leo followed the line marked *V*, five, while Sophie found the one marked *XI*, eleven. Once again their fingers met – this time on a spot in the blue waters of the lagoon, marked with the symbol of a tiny star.

'Is that it?' Leo exclaimed in a voice trembling

with excitement.

The man in the clerical collar got to his feet. 'If you two young ladies cannot be *quiet* then you *really must leave!*' he announced.

But Sophie and Leo paid no attention. They were both staring down at the map. If their calculations were correct, then the secret weapon was barely a mile away from them. Only a little way from the shore, in the stretch of water that lay between them and the islands of Murano and Burano, was a tiny islet. Tiny curling lettering next to it read: *Mausoleo di Famiglia Casselli*.

The two girls gazed at it and then at each other. *Mausoleo* – like *mausoleum*, Sophie thought? And Casselli, as in *Benedetto Casselli*, the painter of dragons?

As she met Leo's eyes, she realised that they had both come to the same conclusion. The secret weapon was hidden on an island that housed the Casselli family tomb.

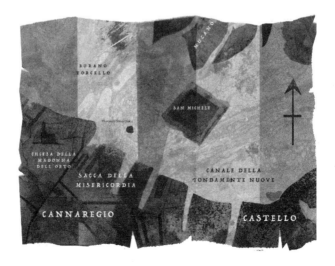

CHAPTER SEVENTEEN

London and Venice

'**B**rooks is on the approach, sir,' said Carruthers from his station by the window. 'He's coming up the steps. He'll be here in a moment.'

The Chief nodded. 'Go back to your desk. Greet him just as usual but follow him in here. I don't think he'll be fool enough to try and run for it but you never know. Mr Parker, Miss Lim, I think it would be best if you aren't here when Brooks arrives. We need to give the impression of *business as usual* – at least at first. Mr Parker, if you would just open that cupboard door over there? You will see the cupboard has a false back, leading through to an adjoining room. A little hidey-hole of mine – you never know when such things will come in useful.'

Billy stared through into the little secret room, comfortably equipped with chairs and a small table, and then looked up at the Chief with an expression of awe. 'Go through and close the door,' the Chief urged swiftly. 'You'll find you can hear everything from there quite clearly. Now, Miss Rose, are you ready?'

Lil folded her hands in her lap and nodded, trying to stay calm. In just a few moments she'd be face to face with the double agent who had betrayed Joe at last. She experienced a sudden sharp flash of dread, but before she could think about anything else there were footsteps outside and then she heard Brooks say: 'Afternoon, Carruthers. I had a message from the Chief?'

'Yes, you can go straight through,' came Carruthers' voice in response. How could he sound so ordinary? Lil felt her heart was beating so loudly that everyone else must be able to hear it, as the door opened and Brooks came into the room.

'Ah, Mr Brooks!' If Carruthers had sounded ordinary, Lil was amazed by the warmth and ease in the Chief's voice. 'Do come in.'

'Er – what's this all about, sir?' said Brooks, sounding rather tetchy. 'I've a lot to do today - and I've already wasted most of my morning. But my secretary did say it was urgent, so . . . What's *she* doing here?' he asked suddenly, noticing Lil for the first time. A suspicious frown broke across his face.

'I do appreciate you coming in,' said the Chief vaguely, waving Brooks towards the chair beside Lil. 'Apologies of course for the short notice but there is a matter of rather important business that simply couldn't wait. Miss Rose and I needed to consult with you urgently.'

'Yes – er – of course – if it's important,' said Brooks, mollified but still a little uneasy, settling down into his seat.

'Now, the thing is, Mr Brooks, I find myself faced with something of a *problem*,' the Chief began. 'It has come to my attention that one of my agents, working for me here at the Bureau, has *another employer*.'

Lil saw that he was watching Brooks keenly, studying his face for any kind of reaction. But Brooks only looked baffled. 'Another employer?' he repeated.

Just then the door opened again and Carruthers came quietly into the room. He closed the door and stood with his back against it.

'I shan't beat about the bush, Mr Brooks,' the Chief continued. 'We have discovered that this agent has another *allegiance*. And that agent is . . . *you*.'

Brooks gaped at him. 'Eh?' was all he said.

Lil could contain herself no longer. Brooks was just sitting there, pretending he didn't understand what the Chief was alluding to, and all the time he was a traitor, betraying all of them – betraying his own country. He was the one responsible for what had happened to Joe and for every miserable moment she'd spent since. 'We know everything! We saw you at the office of *The Daily Picture*, meeting with that woman!' she burst out, unable to stop herself.

'*The Daily Picture* – what? You were there too? What is

this all about?' he blustered, turning back to the Chief.

'There's no sense trying to deny it,' Lil went on. '*You're* the double agent!'

A hot red flush of anger spread across Brooks's face. He stared furiously at Lil. 'What are you talking about?'

'*You're* the one working for the *Fraternitas*! We know they've been paying you for Bureau secrets! We know you're responsible for what happened to our friend Joe – so tell us where he is!'

'How *dare* you accuse me of working for the *Fraternitas*?' Brooks got to his feet. 'I don't have to sit here and listen to this!'

He turned towards the door, but found Carruthers in front of him, barring the exit. 'Get out of my way!' he exclaimed furiously. But Carruthers didn't budge.

'Take care, Mr Brooks,' said the Chief in a quiet voice. 'Sit down and we can all discuss this sensibly.'

Brooks's red face had turned white now. 'Listen, sir, you've got this all wrong,' he said, turning back to the Chief. He pointed angrily at Lil. 'I don't know what she's told you, but this is a pack of nonsense.'

'Is it?' asked the Chief, still very calm.

Brooks wiped his sweaty forehead, looking as though he was trying hard to control himself. 'It's true, I *was* at *The Daily Picture* this morning,' he explained. 'But it was on Bureau business, I swear. We had a meeting set up with some journalist fellow. He supposedly has some information for us about the German spy ring working out of some of the restaurants and clubs in the West End – they're posing as waiters and eavesdropping on the conversations of fellows in the Army or Navy, so they can pass information back to Ziegler in Germany. Apparently, a chap at *The Daily Picture* – Smith, his name is – knows something about it.

'Forsyth and I were supposed to meet him there but Forsyth never turned up. I asked for this *Smith* and a secretary hustled me straight upstairs and into a private office – all very hush-hush, like it was a big secret. She went off to fetch him but neither of them ever came back! I waited half an hour and then came out and asked a passing fellow for Smith. He said there wasn't any journalist working there by that name! The whole thing was some sort of wild goose chase. So whatever you think you know about meetings at *The Daily Picture*, you've got the wrong end of the stick!'

The Chief was watching Brooks intently, without saying anything. It was Carruthers who spoke up: '*Forsyth* was supposed to go with you to the meeting?'

'Yes,' said Brooks, wiping his forehead again. 'He was the one who set the whole thing up.'

'But . . . he just told us he didn't know a thing about it . . .'

Brooks just gaped at him, and then to Lil's surprise the Chief began to laugh. It was not an ordinary laugh: it sounded tight and almost painful.

'I am an old fool,' he said softly to himself.

Brooks turned to look at him again. 'Listen, sir, you know I'd never turn traitor, not for any money in the world, I swear it. Someone's set me up, that's what it is,' he said earnestly, flashing Lil a dirty look. 'You have to believe me.'

'You don't have to say any more, Mr Brooks. There's no need to convince me. I fear we have done you a very grave injustice.' The Chief shook his head slowly. 'We have all been short-sighted, very short-sighted. And he was right here all the time!'

'Who?' said Brooks, looking around the room as if he expected the double agent to appear out of thin air.

'Captain Forsyth,' said the Chief quietly. 'I'm afraid he set you up, Mr Brooks.'

Lil stared at him. Forsyth was the double agent. *He* was the one working for the *Fraternitas*. He'd been so ready with that story about Brooks coming into money, and then he'd hurried off to Venice before the truth could be found out.

To Venice. Lil swallowed suddenly. Forsyth knew that Sophie was in Venice, and why she was there. They'd sent him off to *help* her. When he turned up in Venice, on the Chief's orders, she'd believe he was on her side. She'd have no idea he was the double agent.

There was a long, horrible, shocked moment where no one said anything. Then there was a sudden bang of the cupboard door as Billy and Mei emerged, looking horrorstruck, from the secret room. Already rattled, Brooks gave a little yelp of alarm and jumped to his feet again, whilst Carruthers grabbed for the telephone on the Chief's desk.

'I need to put through a call to Venice, Italy,' he barked to the operator. 'To the Pension Mancini – at once . . .'

'The three o'clock train has long since gone,' said the Chief with a sigh. 'He'll be out of the country by now.'

'Yes . . . ? Hello? Miss Sophie Taylor – *si, pronto!*' Carruthers was saying, frowning in frustration. A moment later, he banged down the receiver.

'She's not there. Out,' he explained shortly. He looked meaningfully at the Chief as he spoke.

'She may be completing the secret code even as we speak . . .' said the Chief with a sigh. 'She may well know where the weapon is already . . .'

'And we've just sent the double agent right after her,' Carruthers finished.

The light had faded when Sophie at last made her way back to the Pension Mancini. She'd left Leo to meet Dr Beagle and the others and replaced her cat mask before setting out to take a winding route back to the hotel.

All the way, she kept a sharp eye out for the men in black cloaks. She was fairly certain that she'd lost them on the ferry: she'd changed into her carnival costume in the ladies' cloakroom and then hopped ashore at the first stop.

It seemed to have done the trick, but she felt nervous just the same. It wouldn't have taken the men very long to work out she was not in Murano and there was every chance they would be lying low, waiting for her to return. The mask and cloak might not be enough to deceive them twice.

As the evening grew darker, she found herself walking a little faster. There was something creepy about Venice's streets at night – the maze of dark little alleys, lit here and there with pools of light from a window or a gas-lamp. Away from the squares and canal-sides, where people in carnival costumes were still sitting in the bright windows of cafés amongst the noise of music and voices, it felt strangely quiet. It seemed different here: the houses looked dirty and dilapidated, and a broken shutter creaked in the wind. She did not want to risk stopping to study her map, so she tried to navigate her way back to the Pension Mancini without it – yet in spite of her best efforts, she took several wrong turns, suddenly emerging in a tiny courtyard, or on the edge of a canal where the light gleamed on dark green water. The tall buildings seemed to loom over her as she hurried down an alleyway so narrow the walls seemed to almost touch one another, listening out for the pad of feet behind her. Once she heard a shriek ahead of her and almost stumbled as a black shape moved in the shadows, but then she realised to her relief it was only a cat jumping down from a garden wall.

At last she caught sight of a familiar bridge and realised

she was almost back at the Pension Mancini. She turned the last corner with relief, but then stopped short.

On the threshold of the hotel were two men in what looked like police uniforms. As she watched, another man carrying a doctor's bag came hurrying out of the door and said a few words to the policemen, shaking his head and then going on his way along the street.

What had happened? Sophie hurried towards the door, pulling off her mask. One of the policeman barred her way, saying something in Italian.

'I'm one of the guests staying here – you have to let me in!' she exclaimed. The policemen exchanged a glance and then stepped aside to let her through.

The hall was empty but in the parlour she found a few of the guests sitting in a worried little cluster – Dr Beagle, Archie Wentworth and Leo.

'What's happening?' Sophie asked at once.

'Oh, Sophie! You're back!' exclaimed Leo at once, relief flooding across her face.

But Sophie was looking around: 'Where's Jack?' she asked.

Leo shook her head, as though she could scarcely believe what was happening. 'He's upstairs with Mrs Wentworth – they're taking care of Ella.'

'Ella? Why – what's happened to her?' Sophie demanded. Her mind had immediately snapped back to when she'd suggested to Jack and Leo that they take Ella out with them so that anyone watching would think she was Sophie. What if the men in black cloaks had mistaken Ella for her? What if they had hurt her? The thought made her turn as cold as if she had once again plunged under the icy waters of the Grand Canal.

But Leo shook her head again. 'No – no – it's not Ella.' Her voice was incredulous as though she couldn't believe what she was saying. 'Sophie – you won't believe it. It's Mrs Knight. She's dead. She's been *murdered!*'

PART IV

'Yesterday I dared to venture out alone while Papa was occupied with his research at the Archive, but quickly lost my way amongst a labyrinth of winding streets and passages. Soon it grew dark and I became rather frightened, almost beginning to imagine that someone was following me. I was relieved to finally stumble upon familiar territory and make my way back to the well-known Piazza San Marco – and safety at last . . .'

– From the diary of Alice Grayson

CHAPTER EIGHTEEN

Pension Mancini, Venice

The parlour at the Pension Mancini was very quiet but for the crackling of the fire. Signora Mancini's maid, looking nervous, had crept in with a tray of tea and biscuits, but no one had touched them. As for Signora Mancini herself, she was nowhere to be seen.

'I think she's with the police,' Leo said to Sophie in a low voice. Somehow no one dared to speak above a hushed whisper.

'What *happened?*' asked Sophie. She felt stunned. Everything seemed upside down: surely there couldn't really have been a *murder* at a place as prim and sedate as the Pension Mancini?

'It happened just after we came back,' Leo explained in the same low, wary tone. 'We all had tea in the parlour. Everything seemed perfectly normal. Then Mrs Knight said she felt a little unwell. She started to cough, and then she excused herself and went upstairs to her room.'

'We could hear her going up the stairs,' said Archie Wentworth, who looked even paler than usual. He'd never spoken up much before and this was the first time Sophie had seen him without a book in his hand. 'She was coughing – and choking. Ella said she'd go up after her and see if she was all right, or if she needed anything.'

'She was only up there for a minute,' Leo continued. 'Then we heard a loud crash, and a fearful scream.'

'Signora Mancini rushed up at once, and Mother went with them. She called for me to follow, in case they needed help,' said Archie faintly. 'Mrs Knight had collapsed. She was dreadfully ill. Mother said she'd seen something like it before, out in India you know. *Dysentry*, she said. Signora Mancini telephoned the doctor at once.'

'Then he came . . . and he tried to help, but . . . it was too late,' Leo went on in a shocked voice. 'He told Signora Mancini to call the police. He said it wasn't dysentry at all – he believed Mrs Knight had been deliberately *poisoned*.'

Dr Beagle shook his head in disbelief. 'A poisoning . . . ! It is like something from Italian history. The Borgias and the Medicis, one of their schemes,' he said hoarsely.

'But what I don't understand is how Mrs Knight *could* have been poisoned,' said Leo. Her eyes were fixed on Sophie. 'She'd been here at the hotel all day and she hadn't had any visitors. At teatime, she drank the same tea out of the same pot as the rest of us. The same milk from the same milk jug. The same sugar from the same bowl. She didn't even eat any of the cakes!'

But there were dozens of ways it could have been done, Sophie thought. The poison could have been added to Mrs Knight's cup *after* the tea had been poured, it could have been in the water jug in her room, it could have been . . . but then she stopped short, realising what Leo had just said. 'Wait – she didn't eat any cakes?' Mrs Knight always ate several cakes at teatime, usually making a beeline for the largest and most delicious-looking on the plate.

'No, she didn't,' said Leo, her eyes widening as she realised the significance of what she was saying. 'She said she wasn't very hungry because she'd already eaten some of those . . .'

'. . . *chocolates*,' Sophie finished.

Out in the hallway, Sophie could see that the two uniformed policeman were still on duty beside the front door. From the office came the sound of voices: Signora Mancini's obviously distressed, and the buzz of several lower male voices talking rapidly in Italian as though they were arguing about something. The police detectives perhaps? As she began to creep up the stairs, Sophie glanced at Leo who was hovering behind her and gestured to her to follow. Outside Ella's door, she put a finger to her lips and Leo nodded. From inside, they could hear Jack's voice and then Mrs Wentworth saying something in a low, reassuring tone.

They went quietly past the door and into the room

beyond, which Sophie knew belonged to Mrs Knight. She'd guessed that the woman's body would already have been removed and sure enough the room was empty. Leo let out a little shuddering breath of relief.

Looking around, Sophie saw the room was similar to their own, though perhaps a little larger. There were the same vivid roses on the curtains and eiderdown, though the splotches of pink and crimson now seemed even brighter and more ghastly than before. It had obviously been kept very tidy: a nightgown and a pale pink satin bed jacket had been left neatly folded on the pillow, and a silver-backed hairbrush, comb and scent bottle were laid in a row on the dressing table. But in the middle of the room was the evidence of what had happened: a chair had been overturned, one of Mrs Knight's shoes was lying by itself in the middle of the floor, and beside it Sophie saw the open box of Zanni's chocolates – the green ribbon bow untied, the lid open and several chocolates spilling out.

Sophie approached cautiously with Leo following behind her, looking as though she did not quite dare to breathe. One of the chocolates had been bitten in half. Carefully, Sophie picked it up, using her handkerchief so she did not have to touch it directly. She brought it to her nose and gave it a cautious sniff.

'It could be nitrobenzene, perhaps. It would be a clever choice to poison chocolates,' she murmured.

Leo's eyes were wide. 'Why?' she asked.

'Well, the only thing that's really distinctive about it is its bitter almond smell, and you'd hardly be suspicious of that if you were eating chocolates; you'd just assume they must have almonds in them,' Sophie explained, sniffing again. 'But then again it could be arsenic. That would fit the symptoms you described and it doesn't have a noticeable smell or taste, so Mrs Knight wouldn't have noticed it when she was eating the chocolates.'

'*Arsenic?*' Leo repeated, looking horrified.

But Sophie had been a detective too long to be squeamish. Taylor & Rose Detectives didn't investigate many murders – those were usually left to the police – but even so, this was not the first time she'd encountered a case of poisoning. If only they'd been back in London, she could have taken the chocolate to Tilly, who would have carried out tests to work out exactly what poison had been used.

Leo was still staring down at the chocolate box, a frightened expression on her face. 'But how could anyone get poison inside the chocolates? Do you suppose they did it at the shop?'

Sophie shook her head. 'More likely someone bought these and then injected the poison using a syringe.' The mechanics of the murder were simple enough, but that wasn't what concerned her. Who had murdered Mrs Knight – and *why*? What possible motive could there be to kill a prim elderly woman travelling in Italy with her great-niece? Was it a coincidence that the poisoned chocolates were in exactly the same sort of Zanni's chocolate box that Sophie had left behind her at the Palazzo Stella? And then a horrible thought occurred to her. What if the poisoned chocolates had not been intended for Mrs Knight at all? What if they had been meant for Sophie?

For a moment, Sophie felt sick. She had not liked Mrs Knight much, but the thought that she might have been the victim of poison intended for her was ghastly. She forced herself to bend down and examine the box more closely, looking for a label or a name. But there was no identification anywhere to show who the box had been intended for. She looked up at Leo who was standing nervously, glancing around the room. 'We need to find out where these chocolates came from,' she said.

'It was the maid who brought them in at breakfast time,' Leo remembered.

'Yes, of course. Why don't you go and find her? Ask who brought the chocolates, and if she's sure they were meant for Mrs Knight,' Sophie said. 'I'll have a bit more of a scout around here.'

Leo nodded at once, looking relieved to have an excuse to leave the room. Left alone, Sophie looked quickly around her. She knew she did not have much time; the police would no doubt be examining the crime scene themselves and she did not want to be caught snooping. Even though she was a professional detective, she suspected that the Italian police would not take kindly to her presence here. Her thoughts were jumping anxiously, but she forced herself to stay focused as she examined the room systematically, just as she would do in any usual Taylor & Rose investigation. She must not jump to conclusions, she told herself.

She had a pair of gloves in her pocket: now she put them on to avoid leaving any fingerprints. She made a quick search of the wardrobe and drawers, but there was nothing to see but neatly arranged clothing – stockings and petticoats and nightgowns. The desk revealed only writing paper and stamps, a pen and a bottle of violet ink. Finally, from the wastepaper basket, she extracted a single sheet of paper, crumpled into a ball:

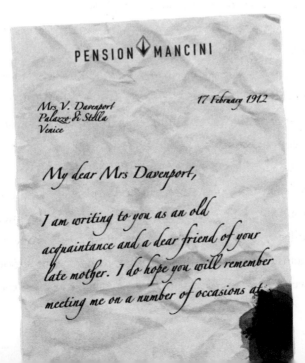

PENSION ◆ MANCINI

Mrs V. Davenport
Palazzo di Stella
Venice

17 February 1912

My dear Mrs Davenport,

I am writing to you as an old acquaintance and a dear friend of your late mother. I do hope you will remember meeting me on a number of occasions at

The Palazzo Stella again, Sophie thought. There was nothing very special about the letter and yet there was something about it that troubled her. She stared at it for a moment or two, then put it carefully into her pocket. Then she went softly out of the room, pulling the door closed behind her with her gloved hand so no one would guess that anyone had been inside.

She slipped quickly down the stairs, thinking hard. In the hall, Leo was waiting for her looking even more uneasy than before.

'I found the maid and I asked her about the chocolates!' she whispered. 'She was *sure* they were intended for Mrs Knight.'

'You're certain – absolutely certain?'

Leo nodded. 'There wasn't any doubt about it. She said the man who delivered the box specifically told her they were for Signora Knight.'

Sophie frowned. 'Who was the man? Was it someone from Zanni's? Or anyone that she recognised?'

Leo shook her head, looking even more uncomfortable. 'No. She didn't know who he was. All she said was that it was a man dressed in carnival costume. Sophie, it was a man wearing *a black cloak and a white mask!*'

CHAPTER NINETEEN

Pension Mancini, Venice

Dark clouds were gathering in the skies above Venice on the morning of Mrs Davenport's party. The wind was blowing harder now, rattling the roof tiles and shutters of the Pension Mancini. As she stood looking out of the window, Sophie thought she could hear a faint rumble – a snarling sound, like distant thunder.

But in spite of the weather, Venice was alive with colour and music. It was Shrove Tuesday and the streets were full of masked revellers; arm in arm, skirts tossed by the wind, a girl laughing and chasing after her hat before it was blown away. People stood in sociable clusters outside cafés or gathered around stalls selling roasted nuts and oranges and hot, spiced wine. Children in colourful masks feasted on *fritelle* – sugary doughnuts that were a speciality of the carnival season. On the canals, the gondoliers broke into song, while above them ladies sat on the balconies of the grand palazzos, well wrapped in furs, tossing down flowers and handfuls of bonbons to masked gentlemen below. As the afternoon drew on and the skies grew darker, the lights began to come on and soon Venice seemed to be lit with the twinkling of a thousand candles and lanterns.

The Pension Mancini seemed set apart from it all – still, silent and grave. The policemen had gone from the front door but a grim shadow still seemed to hang over everything. Several of the guests had already packed their bags and departed, for in spite of what the doctor had said and Sophie's suspicions about the box of chocolates, the official police verdict was that Mrs Knight's death had been a tragic accident, resulting from an extreme case of food poisoning.

'*Food poisoning?*' said Mrs Wentworth in shocked disbelief. 'I've never known a case of food poisoning like that!'

'Signora Mancini is most terribly distressed,' reported Dr Beagle, shaking his head dolefully. 'A death in her hotel is bad enough but a death from *food poisoning* may ruin her.'

Sophie had watched from the window of her room as the two elderly ladies who had spent much of their time with Mrs Knight had departed in a great hurry – clambering hastily into a gondola and dabbing their eyes with lacy handkerchiefs while the gondolier lifted in their bags and trunks.

She'd spent much of the morning standing there, puzzling out what had happened. There was a great deal to think about. Poisoned chocolates from Zanni's, delivered by a cloaked and masked man. A murder and what seemed suspiciously like a police cover-up. That would not be out of the ordinary if the murder was the work of the *Fraternitas*, who Sophie knew had allies everywhere, even within the police. But why would the *Fraternitas* want to murder a woman like Mrs Knight? Was it still possible that it had all been aimed at *her* in some way – a threat, intended to frighten her? But if so, why target *Mrs Knight* of all people, someone Sophie barely knew and hadn't much liked?

She found herself coming back to the crumpled note in her pocket. Everything linked back to the Palazzo Stella, she thought. The masked men, *The Black Dragon*, Mrs Davenport – and now Mrs Knight. It all led to the old palazzo, which Paolo told her had long been associated with the *Fraternitas*. All her instincts were telling her that she ought to return there and investigate further. But that wasn't what she was here to do, she reminded herself. She must keep focused on her mission: whatever else the *Fraternitas* were up to here in Venice, she had to get to the secret weapon before they did.

'Tonight I'm going to go and find the weapon,' she said at last, turning away from the window.

Jack had spent much of the morning with Ella, who was still very shaken and upset, but now the three of them were alone again in Sophie and Leo's room. 'Are you sure?' he asked.

Sophie nodded. She knew Mrs Davenport's party and

all the excitement of Carnival would provide the perfect cover for her to get out to the island without being seen by the masked men. 'I'm going to ask Paolo to take me there in his gondola. He promised he'd help.'

'Are you sure he can be trusted?' asked Leo anxiously.

Sophie paused for a moment. She'd wondered this herself: Paolo might say he was on the side of the Lions, but when it came to the *Fraternitas*, she knew she could not be too careful. It was possible he could be deliberately tricking her, only pretending they were on the same side. Yet he had helped her when she'd fallen into the canal, and got her away from the masked men, she thought. Her instincts told her he was trustworthy and they'd rarely misled her before. 'As sure as I can be,' she said. 'I'll take my pistol of course.'

'What about the storm?' asked Jack. 'Mrs Wentworth says it's supposed to blow up tonight.'

'That could be to our advantage,' said Sophie with a shrug. 'Bad weather could help us get out to the island without being seen.'

Jack and Leo exchanged a quick glance. 'Well, we've got a plan too,' announced Jack. 'We're going to go to the party at the Palazzo Stella tonight, to investigate.'

'What? But you can't!' said Sophie at once. 'They won't let you in without invitations!'

'I didn't get a chance to tell you this in all the fuss, but on our way home from the Archive, I bumped into Max

Kamensky – you know, the artist? I did some work for him, helping out in his studio a little while ago. It turns out he's staying with Mrs Davenport. Anyway, he said that I should come to the party and he gave me an invitation for myself – as well as two for my friends.' He drew three large cards out of his pocket.

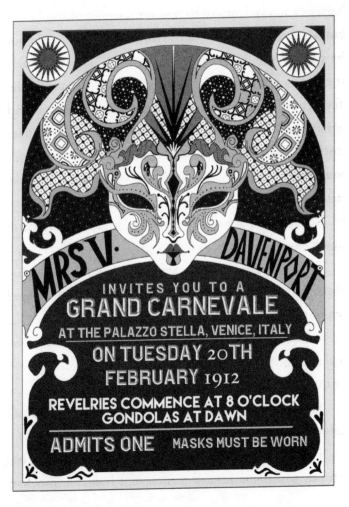

MRS V. DAVENPORT

INVITES YOU TO A
GRAND CARNEVALE
AT THE PALAZZO STELLA, VENICE, ITALY
ON TUESDAY 20TH
FEBRUARY 1912
REVELRIES COMMENCE AT 8 O'CLOCK
GONDOLAS AT DAWN
ADMITS ONE   MASKS MUST BE WORN

'No,' said Sophie shortly. 'I don't think it's a good idea. I think it could be really dangerous.'

'No more dangerous than going out to a deserted island in a storm to hunt for a secret weapon,' pointed out Leo.

'Look, once you've got this weapon we'll be going straight back to London, won't we?' added Jack. 'This might be our last chance to find out what's going on at the Palazzo Stella – the connection between the *Fraternitas* and Mrs Davenport *and* Mrs Knight's murder.'

Sophie frowned. Jack was right. She did want to fill in the gaps and take the information back with her to the Bureau. And yet she couldn't bear the idea of Jack and Leo going into danger, back to the place where she'd been cornered by the masked men. Suddenly she thought of Joe, setting off bravely on the trail of the double agent all by himself, and felt again the jagged pain that came each time she remembered he was gone.

Jack put his hand on her shoulder. 'Let us *help*,' he said quietly. 'You can't do everything by yourself. We're part of the Loyal Order of Lions too, aren't we? We swore to help stop the *Fraternitas* and we take that jolly seriously, don't we, Leo? So *let us do our part.*'

Leo had been watching her closely. 'You can't protect us from everything,' she said quietly. 'That's not your responsibility. What happened to Joe was awful, but it *wasn't your fault.*'

All at once Sophie felt tears rushing into her eyes. She

turned away, back to the window, blinking frantically so that Jack and Leo wouldn't see them. *It wasn't your fault.* But it was, wasn't it? She was the one who had got them entangled with the Baron, and the *Fraternitas Draconum*. She was the one who Lil had chased to St Petersburg, leaving Joe behind to investigate alone . . .

'Look, we're going to the party anyway,' said Jack. 'I'm not missing out on something like this. No fear! Kamensky has promised to introduce me to all his artist friends – and just imagine seeing the *Ballets Russes* perform! And if we're going, we might as well make the most of it and see what we can find out while we're there.'

Sophie dashed a hand across her eyes and turned back to face them. 'Oh, very well. But if you insist on going, please *be careful*. Watch and listen, but don't take any unnecessary risks.'

'We won't,' said Leo. 'We promise.'

'See if you can learn anything about Mrs Davenport,' Sophie suggested. 'We still don't know whether she's directly involved in any of this. You'll wear masks and costumes, I suppose?'

'Yes – we'll have to get some this afternoon. For Ella too,' said Jack.

'*Ella?*' said Sophie in surprise. Ella had barely left her room since the previous day: though she'd joined them all for breakfast, she'd looked pale and had said little. After what had happened, surely the last thing she'd want to do would be to attend a party?

Jack looked a little embarrassed. 'Er – I told her she could come with us. The thing is, well . . . I'm afraid I told her about Taylor & Rose Detectives. And I might have also said we could help investigate Mrs Knight's death.' Seeing Sophie and Leo's faces, he hurried on: 'I'm sorry! I couldn't help it! She was so upset when the police said it was all an accident . . . she's not stupid and she could see it didn't make any sense. She was awfully worried about it so I told her you were a detective and that we might be able to help. Her father is on his way here and I'm sure when he arrives he'll take charge and make sure there's a proper investigation, but for now . . . well, I think she just needs to know that *something* is being done. And she wants to help, not just be left to sit around thinking about it,' he finished.

Sophie eyed Jack knowingly, guessing how much he was enjoying being a knight in shining armour, swooping in to help a damsel in distress. She gave a long sigh. 'You'd better not have mentioned one single word about the Bureau – or the *Fraternitas*,' she said sternly.

'Of course I didn't!' said Jack at once. 'I stuck to the story – that we were here on holiday. But I didn't think it could hurt for her to know that you're a detective, and that we work with you sometimes, and that maybe we could help find out the truth about what happened . . . And surely it won't do any harm if she does come with us to the party?' he finished. 'She might be able to help!'

Sophie groaned. 'I suppose so. But you'd better make sure you take very good care of her,' she instructed. 'And meet me back here at the hotel at midnight.'

Jack nodded, looking excited. 'Right! Time to prepare our costumes!' he said to Leo.

Sophie had already turned away from them, looking out of the window once again. But this time she was looking in the direction of the islands of the lagoon, where she knew that the weapon was lying in wait for her. In just a few hours she'd be setting out on the trail of a long-buried secret – and she'd be doing it alone.

CHAPTER TWENTY

Palazzo Stella, Venice

Leo's breaths were rapid and her chest felt tight as their gondola slid along the Grand Canal, shimmering with lights. Voices called out all around her and she could hear music, the low pulsating rhythm of drums alongside the splashing of water and the rushing of the wind.

She pulled the black velvet cloak more closely around her - for reassurance as much as for warmth. She'd been just as determined as Jack that they should go to the party at the Palazzo Stella, but now they were here amongst the long string of black gondolas making their way to the waterfront terrace, she couldn't shake a sense of unease.

She fiddled with the carved lion's head of her cane, feeling the familiar shape of it beneath her fingertips. Opposite her, Jack and Ella were leaning back against the crimson cushions of the gondola seat, pointing out the brilliantly lit palazzos and people in exotic costumes, as though they were simply enjoying the spectacle. You couldn't have known that only a short while ago they'd been dealing with the aftermath of a murder.

'I know it must seem strange, going to a party at a time like this,' Ella had said earlier as Leo helped fasten her tightly laced carnival gown. 'But I know there's something peculiar about what happened to Great-aunt Caroline. If it really does have something to do with the Palazzo Stella and Mrs Davenport, then I want to know what it is.' She paused and scrutinised her reflection in the mirror, adjusting her ribbons and pinching her cheeks to make them pinker. 'It's not because we were close. I didn't know her awfully well, and I certainly didn't like her much. But she *was* my great-aunt, and the thought of her being *murdered* . . .' Ella shuddered. 'Anyway, Papa is on his way here, and I know he'll soon sweep me straight back to London and all this will be over and my life will be perfectly ordinary and respectable again. This might be my only chance to find out the truth.'

Leo could see that Ella's eyes were glinting from beneath the mask she was wearing. In her traditional *Carnevale* costume – a frilly white frock decorated with brightly coloured ribbons – she looked like a girl from a fairy tale. Beside her, Jack was certainly quite as dashing as any handsome prince in a scarlet jacket trimmed with gold brocade, worn with a black tricorn hat and a half-mask to match.

Jack had gone out to get the costumes that afternoon:

he'd brought one for Leo too, but she'd at once set aside the old-fashioned crinoline with its tight bodice and flounced skirt. Jack ought to have known better than to think she'd want to wear a frock like that, she thought. Instead, she'd decided to wear the black velvet cloak and cat mask that Sophie had used to disguise herself on the way to the State Archive. It wasn't nearly as grand, but it was far more comfortable and there were dozens of people on the streets of Venice wearing something similar, which made Leo feel anonymous and safe.

Now, as they drew closer to the waterfront terrace, she saw that it was lit with flaming torches. A retinue of servants in feathered turbans helped party guests out of their gondolas, whilst others threw flames into an enormous brazier, sending a flare up into the dark sky to the clash of a gong. Gold lights shone from the trees, their reflections glimmering in the water, and scarlet and gold flags fluttered from the windows. The palazzo was a blur of rich shimmering colour: gold and green, silver and crimson, deep violet and burnished bronze.

Leo felt a little dizzy as she clambered out of the gondola after Jack and Ella. A man in a blue satin turban scrutinised the invitation cards Jack handed him, but then waved them onwards, up the steps, where they were each handed first a sparkling drink and then a crimson rose.

Inside, she found herself standing in a quite extraordinary room. There was an immense gilt-framed looking glass hanging on the wall; beneath her feet a cracked marble floor was spread with Persian rugs; and above her head hung a Murano glass chandelier twisted into fantastical shapes. Masked women wearing shockingly scarlet lipstick lounged on velvet chairs lavishly draped in tiger skins, or danced to the honking, twanging sounds of the latest ragtime tunes, played by a band dressed in the powdered wigs and the knee breeches of the eighteenth century. It was like stepping into a piece of art, Leo thought dreamily. Perhaps a Boldoni painting, or one of Leonard Baskt's set designs for the *Ballets Russes' Scheherazade*.

Ella was staring around her. 'I think this is . . . a little different to the debutante parties I'll be going to in London this summer,' she said softly.

Leo nodded. She'd never had a London Season herself, but she'd seen enough of her older sisters to know that Ella's future held many evenings in ballrooms, drinking fruit cup and dancing quadrilles with polite young gentlemen – certainly nothing like this decadent spectacle.

'It looks like the place is simply enormous,' said Jack, who was looking around with great interest. 'I s'pose we'd better split up and explore. We'll cover more ground that way.'

Leo nodded. 'You two should stay together,' she said, glancing at Ella and remembering what Sophie had said about taking care of her. 'Let's all meet back here in an hour.'

Jack nodded. He'd tucked the red rose into his lapel and now he offered Ella his arm, looking enthusiastic about exploring these extraordinary surroundings. Their masks carefully in place, he and Ella set off in one direction while Leo went cautiously in another, heading towards a room decorated in blue and gold stars.

She couldn't stop staring at the people. Her fingers itched to draw them. They looked like figures from a dream: a lady in a gold cloak decorated with mystic symbols; a man in a sweeping fur robe, like some ancient king. A woman in jade-green velvet talking to another clad in flowing black silk, draped in ropes of pearls, and a third in what looked like rose-pink satin pyjamas. Each wore an elaborately decorated mask, richly gilded and trimmed with jewels and feathers. Leo looked closely at each of them, wondering if any might be the mysterious Mrs Davenport herself.

Here and there amongst the party guests she caught a sudden glimpse of a man in a black cloak and a white mask, stark amongst the jewel-coloured silks and satins, the rich velvets and gold brocades. Each time she saw one, her chest would constrict and she'd feel herself clutching her cane a little tighter, but then she tried to relax again. She had every right to be here, she reminded herself. She had an invitation, and even if the cloaked men *did* know she was Sophie's travelling companion, there was no reason they would recognise her in her costume. The hood and mask made her unrecognisable: even the lion's head cane that might have identified her was out of sight in the folds of her black velvet cloak.

She went onwards, through one room and then another, up a flight of stairs and along a corridor with a black and white marble floor. It was quieter here, away from the music and the people, and Leo found herself breathing more easily. She had never much liked parties and crowds: she preferred this, going along the passageway, peeping into empty rooms, admiring an old tapestry or a strange dark oil painting as she did so.

After a few minutes, she came to a square room, furnished with a long table draped with embroidered cloths in colours of green and gold, and set with heavy golden candlesticks and some old-fashioned golden goblets. It looked rather as though a grand banquet was about to take place, except that there was nothing to eat.

As she glanced around the room, she noticed something that made her stop short. Hanging on the wall above the table was a painting that she recognised at once: Benedetto Casselli's *The Black Dragon*. It made her gasp aloud.

There it was - the rare Casselli painting that everyone, even Dr Beagle, believed had been lost centuries before. She'd studied Casselli's work so closely that every brushstroke felt familiar to her, and yet there was something so different about this painting that made it stand apart from the rest. What was it? The dragon's single eye, fixed on hers, seemed to draw her closer. She stood still, studying the play of light and dark, the precise textures and colours of the dragon's scales. She forgot all about everything and stood transfixed, until the sudden sound of brisk footsteps in the corridor outside made her start suddenly.

There was a moment of panic, and then she saw the thick velvet curtains that covered the long windows and she darted behind them. Hidden from view, she peeped out through a chink between the curtains, watching as the door opened and a tall, elegant-looking woman swept into the room.

From her hiding place, Leo saw at once that unlike everyone else she had seen at the party, the woman was not wearing a mask. Instead, her face was hidden by a heavy black lace veil scattered with silver stars. She wore a dramatic gown of black velvet and long wisps of silvery silk, with a heavy beaded train that rattled as it swished across the floor. On top of her head, she wore a silver headdress in the shape of a crescent moon. Was *this* Mrs Davenport, Leo wondered?

Following her into the room came two men in black cloaks and white masks. They stood silently, one on either side of the door, while the woman paced across the room as if to check it was ready, her eyes flicking quickly over the table, the candles, the goblets. After a moment, she nodded to the two men, one of who began to light the candles, while another poured crimson wine from a golden jug into the goblets.

As Leo watched breathlessly, there came a quick tap at the door and another cloaked and masked man entered. But this man was different: unlike the others, Leo saw that his white mask had a long, sinister-looking beak. The Plague Doctor mask, she remembered.

'Well, this is all *very grand*,' said the Plague Doctor in such a hearty English voice that Leo started in surprise. 'Splendid, in fact. But rather a lot of effort to go to just for one meeting, isn't it?'

'But this isn't an ordinary meeting,' replied the woman softly. Her voice was also very English and something about it made the back of Leo's neck prickle. She could have sworn it was a voice she'd heard before: a voice she knew quite well.

'I have a great deal to prove,' the woman was saying. 'This is the first time the Society has ever formally admitted a woman. I have to show them what I can do – how useful I can be. Which is also where you come in. I trust everything went well in London?'

'*Well?* It went *beautifully*,' said the Plague Doctor smugly. 'Even better than I'd hoped. They believe they've found who they're looking for and they sent me straight here. Where's the girl? I went to her hotel but she'd already left.'

'On her way to collect the weapon as we speak. She's cleverer than you think, you know. She's worked hard to shake off my men, though not quite hard enough. She's on a gondola heading out into the lagoon, going towards the cemetery island of San Michele. I suggest you follow her there and get the weapon.'

Leo gripped the edge of the window ledge behind her to steady herself. The girl they were talking about – it was *Sophie!*

'Very well,' said the Plague Doctor. 'I'll make sure there aren't any *loose ends.*'

'Once you have the weapon, bring it straight back here – to *me*, not to any of the others, understand?' instructed the woman sharply. 'Do you hear me, Captain?'

'Of course. I'm at your service, my lady,' said the Plague Doctor with a low bow, but he sounded rather as though he was laughing. 'I'll be back as soon as I can.'

He went out of the room again. Leo felt panic rising in her chest. Sophie had a pistol and she had Paolo, but she was out on the lagoon with no idea that this man was coming after her. And there was nothing Leo could do: she was trapped here, hiding behind the curtain. If only the woman and the cloaked men would leave the room and she could get out and find Jack!

But instead, the woman turned back to the table, tweaking the drapery carefully into place, smoothing out an almost invisible wrinkle. Then she waited, and after a moment or two, the door opened again and first one man and then another entered the room. Leo saw that each was wearing a carnival costume, complete with a mask that covered his face. As they arrived, they each moved to take a place at the long table without saying a word. Leo counted eight of them in total. Finally, one more gentleman entered, wearing a gold mask. He went directly to the head of the table, nodded at the other men and began to speak:

'*Salve*, my brothers. And sister, of course,' he added, inclining his head to the woman in the veil who had taken the seat at his right hand. 'As the Gold Dragon, it is my privilege to welcome you here and to thank you for joining the international council of the *Fraternitas Draconum*. I also extend thanks to our hostess, who is responsible for this splendid occasion, and who has recently been appointed head of our New York Division. I think some of you already know her as Mrs Davenport, but we welcome her to this council under the title of the Black Dragon.'

There was a little intake of breath, as though this was a surprise to the men around the table, but their leader went on as though he had not noticed.

'There is much to be discussed. The Black Dragon will update us on developments in the search for the *Draco Almanac*, which I believe are under way as we speak. The Silver Dragon has much to tell us about progress with the political situation in the Balkans. And I would particularly like to spend some time discussing the British Division's progress with what we may like to term *spy fever*, and how this activity may usefully be extended to other nations. But before we continue any further, I think we may *unmask*. We are after all among friends here.'

As he spoke, he removed his mask. Beneath, Leo saw a surprisingly ordinary face – the face of a middle-aged, well-to-do gentleman with grey hair.

The others followed. They were all men of a similar age, though quite different in appearance. One was thin and balding with a hawk-like expression. Another was red-faced and smiling. Some were dark-skinned, others light-skinned. A man with dark hair and a pointed beard might have been Italian or Spanish; another, tall and broad-shouldered with a bushy fair moustache, had a Scandinavian look; while a slender black-haired man beside him appeared Indian. But of them all, Mrs Davenport was the only woman.

Leo watched breathlessly. An *international council?* These must be the leaders of the *Fraternitas Draconum* from all over Europe and beyond. She stared intently at each face, trying to commit it to memory, wishing she had her sketchbook and pencil. She knew this would be incredibly valuable information for Sophie and the Secret Service Bureau.

Mrs Davenport was the last to reveal her face, carefully removing her silver crescent-moon headdress before pulling back the star-spangled black veil. As she turned her face towards the light, a little gasp of surprise slipped from between Leo's lips before she could stop it.

The men around the table were completely unfamiliar to her. She'd never seen any of them before in her life. But the face of the woman in the black lace veil, the face of their hostess – New York socialite Mrs Davenport, the *Fraternitas Draconum*'s newly appointed Black Dragon – was a face she knew better than almost anyone's. A face that had once been as familiar to her as Jack's or Sophie's.

It was the face of her own godmother: Lady Tremayne. Lady Tremayne, who had turned out to be sister to the man who had called himself 'the Baron'. Lady Tremayne, who had swiftly disappeared to America more than two years ago, when the Baron's attack on Piccadilly Circus had gone so badly wrong. And now, here she was, turning towards the window where Leo was hidden.

'What was that?' she demanded sharply. 'I think I heard something!'

But one of the men was already striding towards Leo's hiding place. She backed away, feeling the cold glass of the window behind her, wondering for a split second if she could open it and jump into the canal below as Sophie had done. But Leo was no swimmer and her hand only fumbled uselessly with the window latch before the curtain was thrust back and the man was dragging her roughly out into the light, her lion's head cane slipping with a clatter to the floor.

'What's this?' said the man at the head of the table, who had called himself the Gold Dragon, surprised and faintly amused. 'Well, well! Take off her mask and let's see who has been spying on us, shall we?'

CHAPTER TWENTY-ONE

Casselli Mausoleum, Venice

The wind was growing stronger as Paolo's gondola slipped through the dark waters of the lagoon. Sophie sat upright in the stern, her hair whipping back in wind so cold it made her eyes water. She was looking ahead to the distant shape of the island of San Michele. Paolo had told her it was the cemetery island, where Venice's dead were buried. A short distance away from it, standing alone in the black water, was something that looked like a large rock but which Paolo said was the tiny island upon which stood the Casselli family tomb.

'It stands apart from the cemetery island, on an island of its own,' he'd explained as they'd sculled away into the dark. 'There are many stories about why it is there. Some say that the Casselli family were so proud that they did not wish to be buried alongside all the other Venetians. Some say that they are restless ghosts, kept separate from the others because they will not lie quiet in their graves.'

It had taken a little persuasion to get Paolo to bring her out here. He had been reluctant to leave the glittering palazzos of the Grand Canal, the music and the carnival costumes, especially as the night of Mrs Davenport's party would certainly be one of the busiest nights of the year for a gondolier. But when she'd explained that she needed his help on important lion business *and* offered him a generous fee to make up for the earnings he would lose, he'd agreed. 'But we must be quick,' he'd said, looking across the water. 'A big storm is coming and it may be dangerous to be out on the lagoon.'

Now, he paddled swiftly, the boat dipping and rising on the water as they drew closer and closer to the little island. As they came nearer, Sophie held up a lantern, the bright light glinting over the waves and illuminating the shadowy shape of the mausoleum – a square stone building with a domed roof. It stood quite alone, lost amongst the expanse of water, which lapped and splashed against the wide stone steps leading up towards the mausoleum itself.

Sophie shivered a little and then cast a quick glance back over her shoulder towards the gold and silver lights of Venice shimmering behind them. Somewhere amongst the glow, Jack, Leo and Ella would be at the Palazzo Stella amongst the grand party guests. For a moment she wished she was with them and not out here in the cold on the wind-tossed lagoon. But as the lantern illuminated stone columns and letters spelling out CASSELLI carved upon the portico, she felt a sudden thrill of excitement. She had reached the hiding place of the secret weapon at last.

As Paolo brought the gondola up to the steps, she saw that a few bunches of wilting flowers had been placed there, presumably by visitors who admired Benedetto Casselli. There were even one or two tattered picture postcards of some of his most famous paintings, beside several half-melted candles. Behind, the mausoleum loomed, dark and empty.

'You are sure you wish to go here?' asked Paolo, looking doubtfully up at it. He too cast a glance back over his shoulder at the bright lights of Carnival, and then looked back at the mausoleum again. 'This place . . .' he murmured with a little shiver, and then a shrug, as if he didn't know quite how to express how he felt.

Sophie nodded to show him she understood. She didn't believe in ghosts, but if she did, she could well imagine they would be found in a place like this. 'I have to,' she said firmly.

The rain had begun to fall again: drops pattering lightly around them, hissing on the surface of the water. Paolo frowned. 'You must hurry then,' he said as he made the gondola fast to a wooden pole evidently intended for the purpose.

Sophie clambered out on to the stone steps, shining her lantern before her. The mausoleum had once been grand but it looked old and crumbling now. At the top of the steps was a rusty iron gate, wrought into an elaborate pattern. As she studied the gate more closely, Sophie saw that at its centre was the shape of a large, five-pointed star and that grouped around it were six smaller stars. *'Seven stars . . .'* she murmured. It was the first clue and it could only mean that she had to open the gate and go *inside* the mausoleum.

The rain was falling harder as she went quickly up the steps and tested the gate experimentally. She hadn't really expected it to open, and so she was surprised when it moved back at once under her hand.

'You are going *inside? Santo cielo!* You know that is a *tomb?* Where the bodies of the dead are kept?' Paolo asked incredulously, following with his own lantern in hand.

'I have to,' Sophie said again, pushing back the creaking gate and stepping tentatively inside.

She saw that the mausoleum was simply a small, square chamber, with small, rectangular windows high up in the walls. There was not much else to see but for a plaque on the far wall, carved with the names of long-ago members of the Casselli family: *Roberto Casselli. Laura Casselli. Francesco Casselli. Maria Casselli. Benedetto Casselli.* Beneath it, on a stone plinth, stood a tarnished crucifix, watched over by two old stone statues. They had crumbled away to the extent that she could not tell what they were intended to be: angels, she thought, or gargoyles – or perhaps even dragons?

While Paolo lingered anxiously on the steps, she shone her lantern around, searching every corner for the next clue. But it was not until she looked down at her feet that she saw it. The floor of the mausoleum had been laid with a decorative mosaic: the coloured tiles were dirty and broken now, but just the same Sophie recognised the central image at once. She'd last seen it in the pages of an old book in Professor Blaxland's Paris apartment: the shape of a green lion holding the sun between its jaws. *Green lion, black sun.*

She bent down, setting the lantern on the floor beside her, and ran her fingers cautiously over the rough broken tiles. 'Can you help me?' she said over her shoulder to Paolo. 'I think this must lift up . . .'

Paolo came inside, looking around him cautiously. With the help of Sophie's pocket knife, they managed to lift up the mosaic panel and lever it carefully upwards.

Below it yawned a dark hole, giving out a dank, salty smell. Sophie shone the lantern down it, seeing the light glint on an inch or two of water at the bottom. The drop was not especially deep: probably no more than ten or twelve feet. And beneath the water she saw a rough shape had been daubed on the stone floor, just visible in the light of her lantern. It was the shape of a hand with *five fingers* outstretched.

'Do you have any rope in the gondola?' she asked.

Paolo stared at her more disbelievingly than ever. 'You

are going *down there?*'

'I'm afraid so,' said Sophie, rolling up her sleeves and pushing a few hair-pins a little more securely into place.

Paolo shook his head as he fetched a rope from the gondola. 'You know this is probably where the dead bodies have been put?' he demanded.

But dusty old bones and skeletons were not really something to fear, Sophie thought as she secured the rope and tested it to be sure it would hold. It was the people who were alive now – the men in black cloaks, the shadowy members of the *Fraternitas* – that really frightened her.

With Paolo's help, she clambered carefully over the edge of the hole, using the rope to lower herself into the dark. She felt her feet touch the surface of the water, and then the stone floor just an inch or two beneath. For a moment or two she stood, engulfed in blackness, breathing in sour-smelling damp air, feeling the water seeping into her boots and trying not to think about what might be lurking in the darkness down here. But then Paolo carefully passed one of the lamps down to her and she took it in relief, shining it around her to illuminate the dark corners.

'What do you see?' Paolo asked.

'A sort of underground room,' said Sophie, holding the lantern high. There was no sign of bodies or coffins, or anything of that sort, but she did see a few stone steps leading up out of the water to a stone archway, opening into more darkness beyond. On the wall beside the archway she could see that four twisting shapes had been roughly daubed in the same way, like the letter S repeated four times. *Four serpents.* 'I think there's a passageway. I need to go along it. Can you wait there and keep a lookout?' she called up to Paolo. 'I won't go far. Shout to me at once if you see a boat or anyone coming.'

'I will!' Paolo's voice came wavering back.

Moving cautiously, Sophie splashed through the water and then out up the steps and under the archway, her feet squelching in her soaked boots. She could hear a dim howling above her, which could have been the sound of the wind or the rain or the waves of the lagoon – or perhaps all three. Somewhere, water was gurgling and then she heard the distant rumble of thunder and made herself go a little faster.

Through the archway, she entered another small, empty stone chamber. There was a wooden door at one end of it, decorated with a faded design of what looked like a horse, standing beneath a large crescent moon and stars. As she drew closer, Sophie saw that the horse had wings. '*Winged horse and moon . . .*' she whispered aloud.

She pushed the door carefully open, feeling the old wood crumbling beneath her fingertips. Inside, she found herself in another room, but this time every wall was covered in rich gold mosaic, which reminded her at once of the magnificent ceilings they had seen at the Basilica di San Marco. There was a large stone box in the centre of the room – a sarcophagus? Was this where the remains of the Casselli family were kept?

As she shone her lamp around, illuminating the detail of the mosaics, she realised that they were made up of dozens of elaborate images of lions and dragons. She studied them intently until, high up on one wall in the far corner of the room, she found the image of a glistening golden dragon with two heads. '*Two-headed dragon* . . .' she said to herself.

Going over to look at it, she saw that just above the dragon was a small niche in the wall. Even standing on tiptoes, she could not see inside it. Clenching her teeth, she forced herself to reach up a hand and put it tentatively into the dark space, unsure what she would find there. Old bones and dust? Or something else – an unknown, deadly weapon?

Sophie realised she'd been so busy getting here that she'd scarcely had a moment to imagine what the secret weapon might actually *be*. Visions ran through her mind: the magic swords of old legends, mysterious poisons that could decimate an army, strange machines capable of wreaking terrible destruction. But her hand only closed on something that felt soft, and she realised she was touching old leather. She gripped the object and drew it out carefully.

She saw that she was holding a small, rectangular bundle. Setting her lamp in front of her on the stone sarcophagus, where it cast a round pool of yellow light, she carefully unwrapped the leather wrapping and revealed a small, very old-looking book.

For a moment, she held it in her hand. Was this it? Was this what all the trouble had been for – an old *book*? Surely that couldn't be right? But then she saw the symbol of an eye outlined in gold in the centre of the front cover. *An eye watches over you.* Somehow this book was what she had come here to find. Taking great care, she opened the cover and saw on the first page the now-familiar image of a twisting dragon – but this time beside it was the shape of a winged lion.

Sophie let out a long breath. In that moment, everything seemed to wash away: Paolo waiting in the mausoleum above, Jack and Leo at the Palazzo Stella, the masked men from the *Fraternitas*. She barely even noticed she was alone in a dark underground tomb with a storm growing louder above her.

Leaning against the old stone sarcophagus, she began eagerly turning over the pages of the book in the yellow light of her lantern. They were old and damp, stuck together in places; the text was hard to read, and in any case looked to be mostly written in Latin. She had never learned Latin but she was able to pick out a few familiar words here and there, like *draco* for dragon and *leo* for lion. And there were images she recognised too: here was the green lion shown devouring a black sun, there was the winged horse standing under the crescent moon. Here was the symbol of the hand with five fingers, and then the all-seeing eye again, at the centre of a mysterious diagram. But what did it all mean?

She turned a few pages carefully until she found a section written not in Latin, but in French, and not for the first time she felt grateful for all those hours with Miss Pennyfeather, practising her French verbs. The page was headed *LEU FEU DU CIEL*. '*Sky fire* . . .' Sophie translated and frowned, her eyes moving rapidly over the strange old black type. Beside it was an engraving of what looked like a sky full of stars, except these were not ordinary stars. They were exploding in a fiery blaze of light, so not stars after all but some kind of *fireworks*, bursting into flames that rained downwards on to outlines of rooftops and church spires. Turning the page, Sophie saw another engraving of what at first she took to be monsters, but as she looked more closely she realised to her horror that they were *people* – men and women and children, their faces contorted with screams, their clothing and hair aflame. Opposite there was a page of writing in characters that Sophie could not read but vaguely recognised. In her mind she seemed to see the faraway East End of London, the sign above the window of the Lim family's shop. Of course – *the characters were Chinese*.

Sky fire. This was the weapon, it had to be. As she stared down at the unknown shapes of the Chinese characters, something seemed to stitch itself together in her mind. She remembered the Baron's fascination with weapons. His travels in China where he'd wanted to find out the secret wisdom of the monks. His experiments with the scientist Henry Snow, using the strange minerals in Veronica's father's mines. His determination to get hold of the dragon paintings and the secrets they contained. The factory in Silvertown manufacturing *incendiaries* – chemicals that set things on fire and made them burn. His attempted attack on Piccadilly Circus, using *fireworks*.

It all made sense now, she thought. The Baron had known – or guessed – something about the lost secret weapon. He'd been experimenting, trying to replicate the information that she now realised she was holding in her hand – the secret instructions for making the deadly *sky fire* that could rain destruction and horror from the heavens.

Now the Chinese characters made sense too. The Venetians of long ago had travelled to the East, where they had visited China and learned the ancient secrets of their fireworks. They had incorporated them into their design for a terrible weapon that was intended not simply for use against armies on battlefields, but judging by the pictures at least, to attack towns, cities and villages filled with ordinary people.

From somewhere in the distance came another clap of thunder, even louder this time, but Sophie barely noticed it. Her heart was racing as she turned over the pages. Although she could not understand them, she could see that here were the detailed instructions on how the *sky fire* could be made. Whoever possessed them would have unspeakable power. At that moment, she saw very clearly that she had to keep the promise she'd made to the Count in St Petersburg. Whatever the Chief or anyone else might expect of her, she would not hand this information over to any government in the world, not even her own. It was too horrifying to think of such a weapon ever being used against anyone. She knew it must be destroyed.

Somewhere in the distance she thought she heard a thump and a little cry, and for a moment she looked up from the book, wondering if she'd imagined it – remembering where she was, in this strange chamber somewhere beneath the lagoon, lit only by flickering lantern light. 'Paolo?' she called out.

The only answer was a splash and then Sophie heard the sound of footsteps coming towards her. But as a figure appeared in the door, she realised that it was not Paolo at all.

There was a man standing before her in the doorway of the chamber. The lantern light glinted on the revolver in his hand. He wore a long black cloak and his face was covered with a white mask with a long beak.

'Hello, Miss Taylor,' he said.

CHAPTER TWENTY-TWO

Venice

'*H*ello? *Scusi?* Is anyone here?' Captain Carruthers furiously dinged the little brass bell on the reception desk at the Pension Mancini. For a hotel, it seemed peculiarly deserted, Lil thought.

The moment they'd realised Forsyth was the double agent, she'd known she had to follow him to Venice. Regardless of whether they could get a message to Sophie before Forsyth arrived, she was in danger. Sophie had sent an S.O.S. asking for help, and now she needed it more than ever.

Everything had been decided quickly in those anxious moments in the Chief's office. Lil and Carruthers would leave for Italy at once, while Mei and Billy stayed behind to assist the Chief with the ongoing investigations in London. 'Forsyth may have hoodwinked us but let us not forget we *have* learned something useful,' the Chief had said. 'We know the true identity of the double agent, but what's more we know that there is a woman at the newspaper office who is working hand-in-glove with him. Another agent of the *Fraternitas*.' He'd looked thoughtfully at Billy, and then at Mei. 'She will certainly know who Miss Rose and Miss Taylor are, but she may not yet know *you*. You have both seen this woman and now you have a unique opportunity to investigate further. As you are to be writing for *The Daily Picture*, Mr Parker, you will have good reason to visit the office, and I have no doubt Miss Lim will find occasion to come with you. I know Miss Taylor and Miss Rose think highly of your detective abilities, and of course if you need it, Mr Brooks can be on hand to lend you some assistance too.'

Brooks looked as though he was still reeling from the accusations against him, not to mention the discovery that Forsyth was a double agent. But just the same he nodded curtly whilst Billy and Mei glanced at each other, apprehensive but a little excited. There was a great deal to take in: Sophie was in danger in Venice; Forsyth was the double agent on her trail. But even as she and Carruthers made their hasty preparations to leave for Italy, Lil saw that her friends were proud to have the opportunity to take on an assignment of their own for the Chief. They'd been left behind to keep things going at Taylor & Rose for too long, she thought suddenly. They deserved to be real agents of the Secret Service Bureau.

But before Lil had the chance to say more than a hasty

goodbye to them, Carruthers had hustled her out of the office and into a motor-taxi. He'd already worked out the fastest route to Venice: 'London to Paris, Paris to Turin, and Turin to Venice,' he'd been muttering under his breath as though he was chanting a spell, all while the taxi rumbled towards the railway station.

Yet even the fastest route to Venice still felt painfully long to Lil. It didn't help that Carruthers himself was far from relaxing company. When he wasn't feverishly studying train timetables or rushing off to purchase the next set of tickets they needed, he was berating himself about how they could have been idiotic enough to fall for Forsyth's deception. 'I mean *Forsyth*! Of all people!' he'd muttered crossly to himself as damp French countryside blurred past the train window. 'It's just absolutely *ridiculous*!'

For once, Lil felt she had nothing to say in reply. As the train rattled away from Paris to Turin, her thoughts seemed to race along with it. *Forsyth* was the double agent. *Forsyth* was the man in the raincoat that Joe had seen leaving the Bureau. *Forsyth* was the man who had passed information to the woman from *The Daily Picture*.

Forsyth must have set Brooks up, she thought. Perhaps he had learned about the meeting with Roberta Russell somehow – maybe the woman from *The Daily Picture* had found out about it. Together they had arranged Brooks's appointment, staging it perfectly so that Lil would be certain to see him. Forsyth must have known she would seize at once on the idea that Brooks was the double agent. He had *used* her, Lil thought. How he must have been laughing!

She'd leaned her head against the cold glass of the rattling train window, feeling shame sweep over her. She'd got everything dreadfully *wrong*. She'd *wanted* to believe it was Brooks. After all, she'd never liked him very much. He was rude and surly and dismissive of them: it had been easy to believe he was working with the enemy. But *Forsyth?* Of course she'd found him irritating, and she'd grown heartily sick of his endless stories about his heroic exploits. But she'd always believed he could be trusted. He'd seemed so absolutely one of them. He'd been by her side in Arnovia: he'd helped her rescue Anna and Alex and get them safely away to Paris. Now, she wondered if he could have been a double agent even then. Had he been tricking them all the time, passing information from the Bureau to the *Fraternitas*, plotting against Sophie in St Petersburg, sending the Fraternitas after Joe?

She'd remembered with a sickening jolt how she'd seen him soon after Joe had gone missing. He'd clapped her on the shoulder and said 'Frightfully sorry to hear about your pal, old girl' as if he really *meant* it. She'd been completely taken in.

'Oh . . . *juggins!*' she'd said aloud. 'This is all my fault.'

Carruthers had scowled at her. 'It most certainly *is not*,' he'd said sternly. 'No more than it's mine, or the Chief's, for that matter. Forsyth pulled the wool over *all* our eyes and made us look like a jolly set of fools.' He'd shaken his head as if in disgust. 'What *does* he think he's playing at?'

He'd gone off into another long tirade about Forsyth, but Lil had only half listened. It had been a relief when they'd finally reached Venice. It had been dark when they arrived and they'd gone straight to the Pension Mancini. But now they were here, the whole place seemed oddly empty. At last, as Carruthers dinged the bell again even more insistently, an elderly gentlemen shuffled into the hall and blinked at them.

'Ah – are you looking for Signora Mancini?' he asked. 'She is lying down I believe. She is feeling unwell – it has been upsetting, most upsetting,' he added vaguely. 'But I can ring for her maid, if you wish? I daresay she can help you if you are wanting rooms?'

'We're looking for one of the other guests actually,' said Carruthers. 'Miss Taylor. Is she here?'

'Miss Taylor?' repeated the old gentleman vaguely. 'Ah. No. I believe she has gone out.'

'What about Mr Rose, or Miss Fitzgerald?' asked Lil quickly.

But the old gentleman just shook his head. 'They have gone to Mrs Davenport's party at the Palazzo Stella,' he explained.

'The Palazzo Stella?' Carruthers repeated, already hustling Lil towards the door. 'Thank you – that is a great help.

'The Palazzo Stella is where Sophie was going to look for the last dragon painting,' he explained as he hurried Lil along the street to a nearby canal, where he began trying to flag down a gondola. As first one and then another of the long, narrow boats passed them, Lil saw they were full of groups of merrymakers, dressed extravagantly in glittering masks and feathered hats. 'It's Carnival, of course,' said Carruthers crossly. 'Bother, bother! Come on – we'll be faster on foot.'

But they soon found that walking across Venice was not going to be easy either. There were crowds everywhere, as if carnival season had transformed the city into one enormous party. In every square there were dancers and musicians; every café was dazzling with bright lights; and boat after boat slid by on the canals, filled with masked people laughing and singing and calling out to one another. At last Carruthers navigated them through the twisting streets to the Palazzo Stella, which was glimmering with lights and humming with music. Two men wearing silk turbans were standing either side of the doorway that led to the street, ready to greet those guests who were arriving on foot.

'*Buonasera*, good evening,' announced one of the men, as Lil and Carruthers hurried up breathlessly. '*Invito?* Invitation?'

'Look here, we don't have invitations, but we need to go inside at once,' said Carruthers in his bossiest voice.

But the man folded his arms. 'No invitation, no entry,'

he said in Italian-accented English.

As he spoke, two ladies in extravagant velvet gowns and feathered masks appeared, each waving a large invitation card. The cloaked men at once bowed and allowed them inside, stepping quickly back into position to prevent Lil and Carruthers from following them. Carruthers looked irritated but Lil swiftly elbowed him back and stepped forward herself, giving the man her most charming smile.

'Good evening. I'm awfully sorry but we really do need to get inside,' she explained. 'We aren't here for the party. We simply need to find my friend who is in there – it's frightfully important. Would you mind if I just slip inside for a few moments to fetch her? I'll come straight out again, I promise.'

But her speech had no effect whatsoever on the man. He shook his head, his face stony.

Carruthers stepped in front of Lil and tried again. 'My name is Captain Samuel Carruthers and I'm here on behalf of the British government,' he tried, taking out his identification papers and waving them under the nose of the man. 'I have the full authority of His Majesty the King! I am here on a matter of *international importance* – do you understand? It is extremely urgent!'

'No invitation, no entry,' growled the man again, shooing them away from the entrance and back down the street.

They had no option but to walk away. Lil could feel

Carruthers bristling at her side, and she was bubbling over with frustration herself. For all they knew, Forsyth was inside the palazzo with Sophie that very minute!

'We have to get some of those invitation cards,' declared Carruthers.

But even if they did have invitations, would the guards let them in, Lil wondered? They were still rumpled and dirty from their hasty journey – they scarcely looked like guests at a grand masked ball. A group of young partygoers were making their way noisily past them along the street, and she took in their elaborate costumes and jewelled masks, which contrasted starkly with their own travelling clothes.

But as she glanced at the group, one of them – a tall, rather plump young lady, who looked magnificent in a turquoise crinoline trimmed with frills of frothy lace, lowered her mask and exclaimed: '*Lil?* My goodness, is that really you? Fancy you being here in Venice – how splendid! Are you here for Mrs Davenport's party too?'

'*Phyllis!*' exclaimed Lil, recognising at once their old friend Phyllis Devereaux. And there was her husband Hugo at her side, looking terribly debonair in dark blue velvet. 'Hullo, Lil! What a lark!' he said cheerfully.

Lil grasped Phyllis's arm. 'I don't have time to explain properly, but we need your help. We need to get inside the palazzo, but we don't have invitations.' She lowered her voice a little. 'We're here on *lion* business.'

She knew that Phyllis and Hugo would understand at once what she meant. After all, they too were sworn members of the Loyal Order of Lions, and this wasn't the first time they had helped Lil at a grand society ball.

Phyllis's round blue eyes became even rounder than usual. 'Golly!' she exclaimed. 'Of course we'll help, won't we, Hugo?'

'Didn't you say you had a couple of spare invitations, Oliver?' asked Hugo, turning to one of his companions.

The red-cheeked young man at his side nodded obligingly, fishing around in his pocket. 'Here they are! S'posed to be for my brother Rupert and a guest, you know, but the poor fellow came down with influenza and couldn't come,' he said to Lil. 'He's at home feeling simply ghastly! The old chap does seem to have the worst luck. But you're very welcome to them if you'd like, Miss . . .'

'Oh, this is Miss Rose, a marvellous friend of ours,' explained Phyllis at once. She looked curiously at Carruthers. 'And, er . . .'

'Captain Samuel Carruthers, at your service. How do you do?' explained Carruthers, stepping forward and shaking hands all round, as cordially as if they were meeting in a London drawing room instead of in a darkened street in Venice. Lil had seen this polite and amiable version of Carruthers before, but he never failed to take her by surprise. 'Thanks for these,' he was saying to Oliver now. 'We're very grateful.' He turned back to Lil.

'We'd better hurry.'

'Oh, but you'll need costumes and masks,' Phyllis said, looking them up and down. 'The dress code is very strict.' Carruthers looked harassed, but Phyllis was already taking off her jewelled mask and shrugging her velvet wrap from her shoulders. 'Here. Take these,' she said, holding them out to Lil. 'Hugo – give your mask to Captain Carruthers.'

'I say – are you sure?' said Lil, taking the mask gratefully.

'Of course,' said Phyllis at once. 'We can easily go back to one of the shops we passed in the square and buy ourselves some new masks, can't we, Hugo?' As he nodded obligingly, she went on: 'You two go inside with Oliver and the others and we'll catch you up in a few minutes.'

'Thanks most awfully,' Lil said again, quickly fastening the mask and draping Phyllis's sumptuous wrap around herself. Carruthers took her arm and a moment later they were making their way into the Palazzo Stella behind Oliver and the rest of the group, waving their invitation cards at the guard. He did not even seem to recognise them as the same couple he'd just turned away.

As they stepped through the door, a servant holding a silver tray handed them each a sparkling drink, whilst another presented them each a single rose. Carruthers took one look at the drink then discarded it immediately on a nearby table, dropping the rose beside it as though faintly disgusted with them both.

Looking around, Lil saw that they were standing in a

large room lit by shimmering chandeliers and glimmering candles. Costumed party guests were fluttering around a table heaped with delicious-looking fruit, like a cloud of richly coloured butterflies. Several masked ladies and gentlemen were engaged in painting a large mural on the wall, showing a vibrant scene of tigers and jungle foliage, whilst through an archway she caught a tantalising glimpse of exotically dressed dancers leaping barefoot to the sound of a strange discordant melody. There were people everywhere standing in little groups, sipping the sparkling drinks, and Lil glanced around at them, wondering how they should even begin to find Sophie amongst all these masked and costumed people.

'We must split up,' she told Carruthers. 'We'll cover more ground that way.'

But Carruthers was still gripping her arm. 'No fear,' he said curtly from behind his half-mask. 'If you disappear into that throng I will never find you again. We're sticking together.'

As they pushed their way hastily through the crowd of guests, Lil had to admit that Carruthers was right. It was reassuring to have him close at her side, especially as it wasn't only Sophie they were looking for. She knew there was every possibility that somewhere amongst the party guests, Forsyth was here too.

She scanned each group of people they passed for a small, fair-haired figure, but though she saw no sign of

Sophie, her eye snagged on someone else distinctly familiar. A tall, dark-haired young man dressed in a red coat with gold brocade on it was standing at the centre of a circle of people, a glass in his hand, throwing back his head as though laughing at a particularly amusing joke. At his side was a girl with blonde hair, wearing a frilly white dress, and for one wonderful moment Lil thought it might be Sophie. But then the girl turned her head, and in spite of the mask she wore Lil knew at once that she was a stranger. Her companion, on the other hand . . .

'*Jack!*' she called out, rushing towards her brother, dragging Carruthers along with her.

'Lil! I say, what are you doing here?' Jack pushed back his mask, pleased and excited. 'You decided to come after all? Gosh, Sophie will be pleased. She doesn't say much but I know she's been missing you awfully.'

'Where *is* Sophie?' Lil asked at once. 'I have to find her!'

'Oh, she's not *here*. She's gone after the – er – the *you know what*,' he said rather awkwardly, giving Carruthers – who he'd never met before – a rather uncertain look.

'The painting?'

'No – er – the other thing. She's found out it's here, in Venice.'

'By *herself?*' demanded Lil. She felt a sudden rush of temper. Surely the whole point of Jack being here in Venice was to help Sophie – so why was he enjoying himself at a party while Sophie completed her mission alone?

'No, no. She's with this fellow, Paolo. He's a gondolier. And a good sort. We can trust him.' He lowered his voice so there was no chance of the other party guests hearing anything. 'Leo and I came here to *investigate*, you see. There's been some peculiar things going on and we think this place – and the hostess, Mrs Davenport – have a connection to the *Fraternitas*.'

'Oh, to *investigate*, I see,' said Lil sarcastically. 'Because right now you look like you're doing a tremendous lot of investigating!' She felt furious with him, although really she knew she was angry with herself. Sophie had *asked* her to come and help with this mission, and she'd said she wouldn't do it, and now Sophie was alone and in danger!

'I say!' said Jack indignantly. 'I may not be a detective but I'm not totally clueless, you know. We've been talking to Max Kamensky – he introduced us to some marvellous people, including César Chevalier – and we've been asking a few questions about Mrs Davenport, and we've found out some rather interesting things.' He gestured to the girl at his side. 'This is Ella, by the way. She's been helping with the investigation. This is my sister, Lil.'

Lil shook hands with Ella but did not feel she had time for pleasantries. 'So what have you learned?' she asked at once.

'Well, that's just it,' said Jack. 'We've learned almost *nothing*.'

'What do you mean?'

It was Ella who answered. 'No one seems to really know anything much about Mrs Davenport, including the people who were invited to stay here at the palazzo. She's terribly mysterious and enigmatic. They've barely seen her. Even Mr Chevalier, who made her costume, didn't get to do a proper fitting. And when they *do* see her, she's always wearing her lace veil.'

Lil frowned. It did all sound rather odd. But she had no time to think about it now. 'Look, that's all very well, but we have to find Sophie *quickly*,' she said hurriedly. 'She's in danger.'

Jack looked alarmed. 'She's gone out to one of the islands,' he explained. 'Leo knows where it is – she and Sophie looked at the map together.'

'So where's Leo?' asked Lil impatiently.

'Oh – er – she went off to do some investigating,' Jack said, glancing about too. 'She was supposed to meet us back here – oh golly, I suppose it was half an hour ago now.' His face reddened with embarrassment. 'I suppose I rather lost track of time while we were talking.'

'I saw her a little while ago – going up those stairs,' said Ella, pointing to a spiral staircase on the other side of the room. 'She was with a woman in the most wonderful costume. Black velvet with wisps of silvery silk, and a headdress in the shape of a crescent moon.'

A man swathed in an extravagant blue and gold cloak, who was standing nearby, caught what she had said and turned to her at once. 'Ah! You have caught sight of our elusive hostess herself!' he said, speaking with a French accent. Beneath his delicate gold mask, Lil recognised him as the fashion designer César Chevalier. 'That costume is my own creation, *mademoiselle*. I am glad to hear you admire it.'

'Leo went off somewhere with *Mrs Davenport?*' gasped Jack.

'I suppose she did, if that was her costume. Should I have said something before?' asked Ella, anxiously.

Lil did not answer, but she was beginning to feel afraid. If the mysterious Mrs Davenport really was working for the *Fraternitas* and Leo had disappeared with her, then Leo could also be in danger. They had to find her – and then there was Sophie to think about, and Forsyth. '*Bother, bother . . .*' she muttered to herself.

Carruthers, who had listened to all this without saying a word, was already moving swiftly towards the spiral staircase Ella had indicated. Now, Lil grabbed Jack by the arm and dragged him in the same direction.

Ella stared after them for a moment and then said: 'Excuse us!' giving César Chevalier and the others a quick smile, before hurrying uncertainly after them.

Up the spiral staircase, they found themselves on an upper floor, where a long empty corridor stretched ahead of them, hung with old tapestries. There were several doors, but when Carruthers tested one and then another, he found they were locked.

There was no time for caution, Lil thought. They had to find Leo – and quickly.

'Leo?' she called out in a low voice.

Jack joined her. 'Leo? Are you here?'

'Jack?' came a frightened voice from behind one of the doors. 'Thank heavens!'

Jack rushed to the door and rattled the handle. 'It's me!' he exclaimed. 'And Lil's here too, believe it or not. I say – you're locked in!'

'Yes. They've locked me up in here,' came Leo's voice, wavering a little. 'But don't worry, I'm all right.'

'We'll get you out,' said Jack, who was already looking frantically around for a key. His face was rather red and Lil knew he was feeling guilty for not noticing sooner that Leo was missing.

'Leo, what happened?' she asked through the door.

'Lil? Oh, I'm so glad you're here. I think Sophie is in awful danger,' came Leo's voice. 'We all are. This *whole party* is a front for a meeting of the most important members of the *Fraternitas*! Mrs Davenport is one of them. She's the one who locked me up in here. Except – you won't believe it; I can scarcely believe it myself – Mrs Davenport is *Lady Tremayne*!'

There was a stunned silence for a moment. 'Your *godmother*?' asked Jack in astonishment. 'But . . . I thought she'd run off to America!'

'She had! I suppose she must have gone to New York and remarried there – and that's why she's now called Mrs Davenport instead of Lady Tremayne.'

'Lady Tremayne?' repeated Carruthers. 'Are you referring to Lady Viola Tremayne, born Viola Hardcastle? Sister to John Hardcastle, aka the Baron, aka the Black Dragon?' He sounded as though he was quoting from an official Bureau dossier, Lil thought.

'Yes!' said Leo through the door, her voice sounding rather muffled. 'Except *she's* the one called the Black Dragon now! I think she's taken over his title and position within the *Fraternitas*.'

Ella had been listening to everything in confused silence, but now she spoke up as though she had remembered something. '*Viola Hardcastle* . . .' she whispered. 'That's what Great-aunt Caroline *said* her name was.'

From behind the door, Leo gave a sudden gasp. '*That's it!* That's why Mrs Knight was murdered! Because she knew who Mrs Davenport really was!'

'Gosh! So *Mrs Davenport* was the one who sent the poisoned chocolates!' exclaimed Jack.

'She must have been trying to stop her real identity from being revealed,' Leo went on excitedly. 'She would have known that it was a risk coming back to Europe – that the authorities would be looking for her.'

'Is *that* why Mrs Davenport always wears a veil over her

face!' Ella wondered in amazement. 'I always supposed that she liked how mysterious and exotic it looked, but really it was because she didn't want anyone to recognise her!'

Lil had not the least idea what all this talk of murder and poisoned chocolates was about, but she did not have time to stop and ask questions now. 'So *Lady Tremayne* is hosting this party? And a meeting of the *Fraternitas?*'

'Yes! They've appointed her to their international council,' Leo explained, her words tumbling over themselves in her haste. 'She's to be head of their New York Division. I overheard part of the meeting. I was hiding, but they discovered me. Lady Tremayne recognised me straight away of course, and she brought me here and locked me up. She said she'd come back for me later, after the meeting.' In spite of her excitement, Lil could hear the tension in Leo's voice: if she had been discovered spying on the *Fraternitas*, then she was lucky that no worse had happened to her. But of course whatever else she might be mixed up in, Lady Tremayne had always had a special fondness for Leo. Now, Lil leaned against the door for a moment to reassure her. 'We'll get you out, Leo. Don't worry.'

'But Lil, listen – there's more!' Leo went on urgently. 'I think Sophie's in danger. Just before the meeting, this man turned up. He'd just arrived from London, and Lady Tremayne sent him after Sophie. She *knew* Sophie was going to get the weapon, and she knew exactly where she was headed.'

251

Lil and Carruthers exchanged a quick glance. 'Forsyth!' exclaimed Lil. 'He's a double agent, working for the *Fraternitas*,' she explained for Jack and Leo's benefit.

'Where has Sophie gone?' Carruthers demanded curtly.

'To Benedetto Casselli's tomb, on a tiny island on the lagoon,' Leo said breathlessly. 'If you head straight towards the island of San Michele, you'll come to it.'

'We'll go there now – at once,' said Lil. She turned to Jack and gave his arm a quick squeeze. 'You'll get Leo out? Phyllis and Hugo are here too, at the party – they've got friends with them and I know they'll help you. Then go straight back to your hotel and wait for us there.'

Jack nodded. 'You will find Sophie, won't you?' he asked, looking rather pale.

Carruthers' face was grave. 'Let's hope we can reach her before Forsyth does.'

CHAPTER TWENTY-THREE

Casselli Mausoleum, Venice

In the dark chamber beneath the Casselli mausoleum, Sophie stared at the man before her as he pushed back the mask with the long beak, revealing his face.

'Hullo!' he said again in a hearty voice, shrugging his wet cloak from around his shoulders. 'Gosh – this is quite a place, isn't it?'

'Captain Forsyth!' exclaimed Sophie in relief. 'Why – whatever are you doing here?'

'Ah – the Chief got your S.O.S. message and sent me to help you,' said Forsyth, glancing around him with great interest. 'So I s'pose this must be where the weapon is hidden. Have you tracked it down yet?'

The book lay beside Sophie on the stone sarcophagus but a sudden instinct made her step in front of it, blocking it from sight. Forsyth wouldn't understand why she wanted to destroy it, she thought. He'd want to deliver it straight to the Bureau, putting the deadly weapon of *sky fire* into the hands of the British government. If only she'd destroyed it before he'd arrived!

'Well, let's go on the hunt,' said Forsyth, rubbing his hands together as though he relished the task. 'I'm jolly good at this sort of thing, you know. Did I ever tell you about the time I led an expedition into Africa and we discovered a treasure trove hidden *inside* a mountain? Must tell you sometime – extraordinary yarn. Anyway, what's the secret code?'

But Sophie was frowning. There was something strange about the way Forsyth had materialised down here. It was like a magic trick: a rabbit suddenly popping out of a hat. 'How did you know I was here?' she asked.

'Oh, I ran into your chums,' said Forsyth vaguely. 'They told me where you were and I hopped in a boat and followed you out here.'

So Jack and Leo had told Forsyth where she was? That was decidedly odd, Sophie thought. Neither of them had ever met Forsyth before – how did they know he could be trusted with something as important as the location of the weapon? How had he found them at Mrs Davenport's party? And there was something else bothering her too. 'Where's Paolo?' she asked. He must have been dreadfully surprised to see Forsyth appearing out of the storm, in that sinister mask and cloak.

'Er – Paolo?' repeated Forsyth, looking baffled.

'The gondolier who brought me out here. He was

waiting up there, on lookout,' Sophie explained. Why hadn't he called out to her when he'd seen Forsyth coming?

'Oh! There wasn't anyone up there when I arrived, old girl,' said Forsyth. 'I s'pose he must've got spooked. Or perhaps he didn't want to hang about in the storm. Awfully wet out there. Either way, I'm afraid he's done a bunk!' He laughed. 'Jolly lucky for you I came along to help, what?'

Sophie frowned harder. Certainly Paolo had been nervous of the old tomb, and worried about the storm. But she felt sure he would never have just gone off and left her stranded like that – would he?

'Anyway, no time to hang about chatting! Let's find that weapon and get out of here,' Forsyth urged her. 'The storm is really blowing up and I don't know if you've noticed but the water's rising down here. The whole place is awfully old and probably not very structurally sound. It might flood for all we know!'

Sophie glanced down and saw to her alarm that Forsyth was right. The floor of the chamber had been quite dry when she'd first ventured inside, but now water was beginning to pool on the stone floor beneath her feet.

'So . . . out with it! What's the secret code?' Forsyth asked again. He was beginning to sound impatient.

But Sophie still hesitated. It felt *wrong*. And why was Forsyth still holding his revolver?

She stood looking at him for a moment and their eyes met. Suddenly, Forsyth grinned at her. He was as handsome as usual, but there was something different, something almost wolfish about that smile. She looked at him again: the black cloak, the white mask in one hand, the revolver in the other.

'It's *you*,' she whispered aloud.

Forsyth's grin got wider and more wolfish.

'*You're* the double agent. *You're* the one working for the *Fraternitas*.'

'Aha! So the game's up, is it? Guilty as charged,' guffawed Forsyth in the same ordinary, hearty voice she'd heard many times in the Bureau's office. 'Sorry for leading you up the garden path, old thing. But it had to be done. Now then, I know you've got a pistol, but I don't want you doing anything *silly*. So take out your weapon and set it down over on that bit of stone over there . . . nice and slowly, no funny business.'

Sophie knew she had no choice but to do as he asked. Brooks might have taught her to use her little pistol but she would never be faster than Forsyth, who had military training and years of shooting experience.

A desolate feeling swept over her, with the howling of the wind outside. She'd been in many seemingly impossible situations before, but this was by far the worst, she thought, as she stepped towards the stone Forsyth had indicated and placed the pistol reluctantly on it, leaving the little book exposed on the lid of the sarcophagus. She was alone here and Forsyth had her completely at his mercy.

'That's right. Good girl,' said Forsyth. 'Now, back to where you were before, in that corner.' He didn't seem to have noticed the book. Was there any way she could possibly hide it from him? *Think*, she told herself.

'What have you done with Paolo?' she asked, swallowing, trying to keep Forsyth distracted as she stepped back in front of the book.

'The young fellow on lookout? Not much good at it, I'm afraid, especially with the storm. Too busy trying to keep dry, not really keeping a sharp eye out. I crept up and gave him a jolly old whack on the head. I daresay he'll have a devil of a headache when he comes round. *If* he comes round of course,' said Forsyth with another cheerful guffaw. He had picked up Sophie's pistol and was now tossing it up and down in his hand like a toy. 'Hmmm!' he said, examining it briefly, and then threw it over his shoulder as though it was quite useless. Sophie heard a clink as it fell somewhere towards the door of the little chamber: by some miracle it did not splash into the water but she knew she'd never be able to reach it. Another great crash of thunder sounded somewhere overhead, like a clash of cymbals.

'Now, the weapon,' said Forsyth, turning back towards her.

'I'm not going to tell you anything,' said Sophie. Her voice rang out, sounding far more confident than she really felt. Paolo had been knocked out cold; Jack and Leo were at the Palazzo Stella; Lil was far away in London. There was

257

no one to help her. Forsyth had a gun and he could shoot her whenever he liked, although she knew he probably wouldn't, not while he believed she alone knew how to find the weapon. Without thinking, she shuffled forwards, shielding the book from sight, but Forsyth realised what she was doing at once.

'Aha! So you've found it already. No good trying to trick me, old thing. So that's it, is it? That *old book*? Doesn't look much like a secret weapon to me.' He leaned forward and snatched it up, flicking through it idly as though he was browsing in a bookshop. 'Hmm! Well, I daresay all the important information is in here. Not my job to decipher this gibberish, thank goodness. All I have to do is deliver it to the right people.'

'To the *Fraternitas*? You're really going to hand it over to *them*?'

'Well, I *am* one of them now, you know,' said Forsyth, puffing out his chest with pride. 'This will earn me a place at their table. Not just anyone can be a member of the *Fraternitas*! And I'm even getting a title – *The Red Dragon*. Rather splendid, don't you think? Far superior to plain old "Captain". You see, there's much better prospects for a fellow like me with the *Fraternitas* than working for the Secret Service Bureau. Of course, I'll have to be attached to one of their overseas branches for a while at least – I rather think I'll have made London too hot to hold me.' He smirked. 'But I don't care about that. You see, I've always seen myself as a traveller. An adventurer. A *man of the world*,' he said with a flourish. 'Thanks for your help with this, old girl. Now, the only thing left is to decide what to do with you. Of course I *could* shoot you, but it doesn't seem quite the thing. Not cricket to shoot a lady, what? So perhaps I'll just leave you here.' He glanced down at the water, which had now crept as high as their ankles, and Sophie realised what he was thinking. He could easily take the rope and close the panel behind him, leaving her trapped down here. If she didn't come back, Jack and Leo would certainly come looking for her, but with the water rising would they be in time to save her? And without knowing the secret code, would they even be able to find the panel leading to the underground chambers? Would they hear her down here, if she screamed?

Her legs felt weak beneath her as Forsyth went on. 'The funny thing is the Chief *did* send me here to help, you know. And poor Miss Rose, she really thought she'd solved the mystery of the double agent. She went running off to the Chief, exactly as I expected, so proud to have worked out that Brooks was the bad seed. I suppose *you* must be the brains of your little operation because she certainly isn't!' He gave another hoot of laughter. 'I daresay she's helping the Chief interrogate the poor fellow as we speak. I wonder how long it will take them before they work out they've got the wrong man?'

Sophie felt she could barely bring herself to say another

word to him, but she knew that every second she kept him talking was another second she had the chance to think. There must be something she could do, she thought desperately, some way she could get out of this. 'So it was *you* who intercepted my letters from St Petersburg,' she said. 'And it was *you* that was smuggling documents out of the Bureau to give to that woman. I suppose she works for the *Fraternitas* too?'

Forsyth sniggered. 'Oh yes. For the top man himself,' he added smugly.

'And it was *you* that went after . . . Joe . . .' Sophie went on. She could hardly bear to say his name.

'Joe?' Forsyth wrinkled up his forehead, as though he hadn't the slightest idea who she was talking about. 'Oh, of course – that young chap from your office!' he said, slapping his hands together in recollection. 'Your driver, or whoever he was.' He gave another laugh, as if the whole thing was quite a jolly jape, and Sophie felt it like a knife to her heart. 'Yes, yes, I'm afraid that was me. He was about to give the game away, you see, and I couldn't have that. So we lured him out to the East End and then . . .' He made a little motion with his fingers as though he was firing a gun.

There was a roaring in Sophie's ears. It could have been the wind and rain outside, or the crackling of distant thunder. But mostly it was simply the rage that seemed to burst out from where it had been locked deep inside her, like a volcano erupting. Forsyth had *killed Joe*, she realised.

He had killed him as though he didn't matter, as though he was playing some idiotic game of traitors and secret agents and spies.

She looked up at Forsyth as though she was suddenly seeing him clearly. He'd promised to help protect his country and its people, just as she had, but he'd thrown all that away for the money and power the *Fraternitas* could give him. He was just like the Baron, all over again. But it was too late for her to stop him now. Forsyth had a gun, and he had the book with the instructions for deadly *sky fire*. He would give it to the *Fraternitas* and they would sell it to the highest bidder, or use it themselves in their quest to spark off a war in Europe, and there would be the most horrifying consequences for innocent people. And Forsyth would shoot her, or leave her here to drown, and everything that had happened to her – her search for the paintings and the weapon, her row with Lil, Joe's death, even her papa's death – all of it would have been for nothing. Everything she had done, everything they had *all* done – Lil and Billy and Mei, the Chief, Carruthers, Jack and Leo and Tilly, Princess Anna and Crown Prince Alex, Captain Nakamura, the Count, Paolo, and Joe most of all – it would all have been for *nothing*.

Outside the storm was still raging, and inside the chamber the dark water was rising faster now, and yet Sophie felt a strange calm descend over her.

It was over, and so she had nothing left to lose.

Was this what her father had felt, when he'd run the Baron to ground in South Africa all those years ago, she wondered?

She couldn't save herself. But perhaps she could do something to take revenge on Forsyth, for Joe's sake. Perhaps there was a chance she could keep the promise she'd made to the Count – and see the book destroyed after all.

Forsyth had already lost interest in talking to her. He was flicking through the book again, turning his head from side to side as if trying to make sense of the diagrams. He wasn't even looking at her. But Sophie gritted her teeth and without a word of warning she flung herself towards him with a yell, tearing the book from his hands.

Water was splashing against the sides of the boat as Lil squinted through the rain at the black shape approaching. It was a tiny island, not much bigger than a large rock. 'I think that's it!' she called out.

Carruthers only nodded. He was rowing so hard that he could hardly speak, the rain lashing his face, fogging his spectacles, while Lil shone the electric torch ahead of them across the water. The beam flashed over a stone building surrounded by water, growing gradually larger as they came towards it through the sheeting rain.

Fastened to a wooden pole, bobbing about on the rough water, she saw a small rowing boat, not dissimilar from the one they had managed to borrow to make the journey out on to the lagoon. As they made their own boat fast behind it, Carruthers reached out to touch another length of rope tied to the pole.

'This is new rope!' he half shouted, trying to make himself heard against the noise of water and wind. He showed Lil the frayed end. 'And it's recently been cut!'

Forsyth, thought Lil. He must have followed Sophie out here, and cut the rope securing her boat, which had already drifted away on the stormy water.

Quickly, she scrambled ashore, and together she and Carruthers splashed up the stone steps. Just inside the rusty gate of the old mausoleum, they found another sign of him: the body of a young man, left slumped on the ground. In the light of the torch, Lil saw that he was wearing the striped jersey and red neckerchief of a gondolier. He was unconscious and a scarlet trickle of blood ran down one side of his face.

Carruthers bent over him. 'He's out cold, but he's breathing,' he reported. 'I think he'll be all right, but let's get him somewhere more sheltered.'

Together, they carefully lifted the young man's limp body into a corner, where it would be out of the wind and rain. As they did so, they saw that just beyond where he had been lying, a gaping hole was yawning in the floor of the mausoleum. While Carruthers held a handkerchief against the young man's head to stop the bleeding,

Lil shone her torch cautiously into it, seeing a rope snaking downwards.

'We'll have to go down,' she whispered.

Carruthers nodded. Lil knew he'd come to the same conclusions that she had: Forsyth was already there. He'd cut the rope securing Sophie's boat and knocked out the fellow who'd been helping her. He was probably with her right now, on the trail of the secret weapon. They had no time to lose.

One after another, they slipped carefully and quietly down the rope and found themselves standing knee-deep in water. They were in a kind of underground room, but a little distance away from them, Lil could hear the sound of raised voices and a gleam of light.

At once, Carruthers touched his finger to his lips and Lil extinguished her torch, plunging them into darkness. Side by side, they waded through the freezing water, feeling their way slowly up some steps. The voices grew louder. That was Forsyth, Lil thought – his voice light and cheerful. And then Sophie's – quieter but ringing with contempt.

She knows, Lil thought, feeling a rush of relief and fear and pride all at the same time. *She's worked it out.*

Carruthers touched Lil's shoulder gently, indicating she should pause. Ahead of them, they could see an open door, and through it was another small chamber, though this time the walls glistened with a rich gold mosaic. They glittered in the light from a small lantern, which was resting on what appeared to be a stone table in the centre of the room. Standing nearby, his back towards them, was Forsyth, wearing a long black cloak. He was holding a revolver in one hand and what looked like a small book in the other, and before him, backed into a corner, was Sophie.

'The funny thing is the Chief *did* send me here to help, you know,' Lil heard Forsyth's voice, reverberating around the little chamber. 'And poor Miss Rose, she really thought she'd solved the mystery of the double agent. She went running off to the Chief, exactly as I expected, so proud to have worked out that Brooks was the bad seed. I suppose *you* must be the brains of your little operation because she certainly isn't!' He gave a hoot of laughter and Lil clenched her teeth. 'I daresay she's helping the Chief interrogate the poor fellow as we speak. I wonder how long it will take them before they work out they've got the wrong man?' He sniggered again and Lil flinched, but Carruthers laid a careful hand on her arm. He was pointing to something glinting just ahead of them, on a fragment of stone poking out of the water. It was a small pistol, and as Lil watched, he quietly stretched out an arm and took it.

'So it was you who intercepted my letters from St Petersburg,' Sophie said, her voice trembling. 'And it was you that was smuggling documents out of the Bureau to give to that woman. I suppose she works for the *Fraternitas* too?'

'Oh yes. For the top man himself.'

'And it was *you* that went after . . . Joe . . .' Sophie went on, her voice cracking and breaking as she spoke.

'Joe? Oh, of course – that young chap from your office! Your driver, or whoever he was. Yes, yes, I'm afraid that was me. He was about to give the game away you see, and I couldn't have that. So we lured him out to the East End and then . . .' He made a motion with his hands, as though pantomiming a gun firing a shot.

Lil heard him laugh, and her heart shattered. He was gone: Joe was really gone. It hit her like a blow. She bent over in pain, gasping, but Carruthers was there, clenching her hand in the darkness. She gripped it back hard, grateful for its steadiness.

But at that moment, without any warning, Sophie made a leap for Forsyth, letting out a furious howl. If Lil had ever doubted that Sophie had truly cared about Joe, she knew then that she was quite wrong. It was as if Sophie had forgotten that Forsyth had a gun and she was completely unarmed. She made a desperate lunge for the little book he was holding, but he was too quick and strong and he struck back at once, sending her crashing down into the water where she lay for a moment, all the air knocked out of her.

'Oh, I say! You didn't have to do that,' he protested crossly. 'Well, now I'll jolly well *have* to shoot you.'

He directed the revolver at her as she tried to frantically scrabble to her feet.

Lil let go of Carruthers' hand. It was too late to help

Joe. He was gone; she had lost him. But she would not lose Sophie too.

In one quick move, she had seized the little pistol from Carruthers. Rushing forwards into the room, she fired.

CHAPTER TWENTY-FOUR

Casselli Mausoleum, Venice

A shot rang in Sophie's ears. It had happened. Forsyth had shot her, she thought. But she felt nothing: no pain. Perhaps she was numb.

The roaring sound had grown louder. She no longer had the slightest idea whether it was the storm outside, or the water flooding in, or simply the blood rushing in her ears.

'Sophie!' cried a voice that sounded like Lil's, but it couldn't be. Lil was hundreds of miles away in London. Lil was barely even speaking to her. She was all alone here in this ancient underground tomb.

Across from her, she saw as if in a dream that Forsyth had pitched forwards into the water. It was as if he had crumpled. He was gasping and groaning and gripping his side, which leaked something crimson on to the white shirt beneath the black cloak. He'd dropped his revolver but one hand still clutched the book.

Voices, footsteps. 'I *shot* him!' choked out a voice – that voice again. What was happening? Gripping the wet stone to steady herself, Sophie struggled to her feet.

She could scarcely believe what she was seeing. Impossible as it might seem, Lil was staggering towards her, the Chief's little pistol in her hand, and just behind her was Captain Carruthers. It *couldn't* be true, she thought, but then Lil reached her and flung her arms around her, gasping, wet and soaked to the skin.

'Is he – is he–?' Lil gasped out.

'No. It's only a flesh wound,' came Carruthers' voice from where he was bending down beside Forsyth. 'Lucky for him you're a rotten shot.' But just then he glanced up and his voice changed: 'We've got to get out of here. I think something's given way – the water's coming in fast!'

Sophie saw at once that he was right. The water was already over her knees and rising rapidly.

'Where is it – the weapon?' Carruthers yelled.

'It's there – the book!' Sophie cried back, pointing to where Forsyth was groaning, the book still clenched tight in his hand.

Carruthers quickly prised the book from between Forsyth's fingers. He gave it a cursory glance and then made as if to shove it in his pocket, but Sophie shouted out: 'No! We have to destroy it!'

For a split second there was only the sound of water rushing and Forsyth's groans. Then: '*What?*' exclaimed

Carruthers incredulously.

'I've seen what's inside it. It's – it's terrible. No one should have the chance to use a weapon like that. *No one.* I promised I'd see the weapon destroyed and I'm going to.'

'But you can't seriously mean . . . After all this —' Carruthers scoffed in disbelief.

'We can't let anyone use it. It will destroy innocent people,' Sophie said. Carruthers was still staring at her, a bewildered look on his face, and she desperately tried to find the words to make him understand. 'You can't even begin to imagine how dreadful it is. We *have* to leave it. Just let the water take it and destroy it, so *no one* can use it.'

'But – but I can't possibly do that!' Carruthers exploded.

Lil leaned over, snatched the book from his hand, and put it into Sophie's. 'Listen to her!' she urged Carruthers. 'She's right! No one else should get hurt.'

She turned to Sophie, and in that moment everything that had happened seemed to fall away and they were themselves again. Sophie and Lil. Taylor & Rose. Young lady detectives, agents of the Secret Service Bureau, and most importantly, best friends. Friends who understood each other, however different they might be.

Lil nodded to Sophie, and she opened her hand and let the book fall into the water with a splash. The gold eye disappeared under the surface. The chamber would be flooded, Sophie thought, and the book would be lost to the lagoon. That was where it belonged.

'I can't *believe* you just did that,' groaned Carruthers. But there was no time for him to say anything else: the water was surging in, gushing from between the gold mosaic panels.

He glanced down at Forsyth, who was still groaning on his knees in the water, clutching the bullet wound in his side. 'I suppose we can't really leave him down here,' he said crossly, shooting Forsyth a look of deep dislike. He reached down and heaved the captain to his feet, then flung an arm around his waist, ignoring his whimpers of pain. 'It's more than you deserve,' he muttered.

Lil and Sophie splashed after him, though it was hard-going now. Out in the passageway, the water was right up to Sophie's waist. She was the first to scramble up the rope, Lil following her, and then Carruthers fastened the rope securely around Forsyth's waist.

'You'll have to pull him up,' he called. 'And look sharp about it!'

Sophie and Lil hauled on the rope, bumping Forsyth slowly and painfully upwards. His groans and whimpers became wails. 'We can just leave you to drown if you'd rather!' came Carruthers' voice from below.

Somehow the two girls managed to drag Forsyth out of the hole, then with trembling hands Sophie untied the rope and sent it back down the hole for Carruthers.

'Hurry up!' cried Lil, shining the light down the hole, seeing the water rising even more rapidly than before. But

Carruthers was not there. '*Sam!*' she cried. But then there was a splashing sound and Carruthers appeared again at the bottom of the hole. 'All right, all right – don't fuss!' he instructed. 'I'm coming!'

Once he'd shinned up the rope, they heaved the trapdoor shut on the dark water below and then looked at each other in relief. They were all soaking wet, but the mausoleum itself was dry and sheltered from the wind, the rain drumming on the roof. Forsyth was lying limply in one corner, still groaning, whilst opposite, Paolo had come round. He was holding his head and looking around him in confusion.

'We'd better get this man to the shore,' said Carruthers.

'What about him?' asked Lil, looking uncertainly at Forsyth.

'Leave him,' said Carruthers. 'We'll never fit five of us in one boat.'

'But – but – there are two boats, aren't there?' gasped out Forsyth.

'If you think I'm trusting you in a boat by yourself – or with any of us – you've got another thing coming,' snapped Carruthers at once. 'You're staying here.' He turned to Lil. 'He's not fit to row, but take the other set of oars so he doesn't get any clever ideas about escaping.'

'But you can't just *abandon* me here!' gasped Forsyth.

'Can't we? Think yourself lucky we didn't leave you down there to drown,' Carruthers retorted. 'We'll alert the authorities and they'll come and collect you in the morning. Or perhaps your friends in the *Fraternitas* will come and save you first?' He turned away in disgust.

A moment later the rusty gate of the mausoleum had rattled shut behind them and they were out in the rain once again, while Forsyth stared after them unhappily, his face a pale blur in the dark. But already the rain seemed to be falling more gently, pattering against the surface of the water. The worst of the storm had passed.

Carruthers and Lil shared the rowing, while Sophie tried to light the way ahead with Lil's electric torch. Little by little the rain slowed, while the lights of Venice grew closer.

'*Che sta succedendo qui?* What's going on here?' muttered Paolo groggily as Sophie bandaged his head with her sodden pocket handkerchief. She opened her mouth to answer him but then closed it again. Where would she even begin?

Beside her, Lil and Carruthers were rowing hard. Intent on what they were doing, not one of them noticed that some little distance away, another boat was moving slowly across the water.

The long black gondola was decorated with gold, and inside it sat a woman in a long fur coat that reached almost to the ground, beneath which it was just possible to glimpse a dramatic gown of black and silver. A veil sprinkled with silver stars concealed her face and a servant held an umbrella above her head, shielding her from the last of the wind and rain. From the seat of the gondola, she watched the little rowing boat moving towards the shore, and then she spoke a brief word to her gondolier and her boat slid away silently into the darkness of the lagoon.

PART V

'And so we leave Venice behind and set out on our next adventure. But I feel quite sure I shall never forget it. There is something about this city that stays with you: a memory of green water and bells ringing and a winged lion looking down over it all . . .'

– From the diary of Alice Grayson

CHAPTER TWENTY-FIVE

London

I t was hard to believe London was still here, Sophie thought, as they came down the steps from the station and out into the street. And yet here it was, full of the promise of spring: the sky a pale, rain-washed blue, daffodils and crocuses in the park, a fresh breeze ruffling Leo's hair and the ribbon on Lil's hat. Here were the London omnibuses rumbling by with their colourful advertisements for Lipton's tea or Nestlé milk. Here were posters advertising a new play at the Fortune Theatre and new-season frocks and shoes displayed in the windows of the shops.

'We'll go straight to the Bureau, of course,' said Carruthers, striding forwards to hail a motor-taxi.

But Lil stopped him. 'We're going back to Taylor & Rose before we do anything else,' she said. 'Billy and Mei will be awfully worried about Sophie.'

Carruthers looked like he was about to argue, but Sophie said: 'Come with us.' He'd not spoken another word about her decision to destroy the book, for which she was very grateful. It was obvious he felt uncomfortable about what she had done; he'd been restless and on edge all the way back to London, frowning irritably, his hands continually thrust deep into the pockets of his overcoat. She knew he hated the idea of disobeying orders, and she guessed he was worrying about what he was going to say to his grandfather about the loss of the secret weapon they'd been hunting for so long.

'We'll go straight to the Bureau afterwards,' she said now. 'We can tell the Chief everything then. I'll tell him all about the book – and I'll explain that destroying it was my idea and you had nothing to do with it. But you can spare a few minutes for a cup of tea and a bun first, can't you?'

'It's what we always do, after we solve a case,' said Lil, threading her arm through Carruthers' in a chummy fashion.

'Oh, very well then, if we must,' huffed Carruthers in a voice that pretended to be annoyed but was secretly pleased to be asked.

Lil gave Sophie a quick, lopsided sort of smile. Tea and buns was an old tradition, but they both knew it would never be quite the same without Joe. Still, Sophie was glad Lil felt able to include Carruthers, and she seemed to feel that one way or another, celebrations might actually be possible once more.

Lil had sat close beside Sophie all through the long

journey back to London, sometimes leaning her head against her friend's shoulder. She'd listened to the others talking, but for once she didn't seem to have much to say herself. Though she spoke little, Sophie could feel her sadness. She guessed Lil was taking her time to think about what they'd learned in that strange underground chamber below the lagoon. Lil knew for certain now that Joe was gone and it would take a long time for her to come to terms with that, just as it would for all of them. Perhaps they never really would.

Then there was the fact that Lil had actually *shot* Forsyth, and that would take some thinking about too. Sophie and Lil had been in danger many times, but neither of them had ever done anything quite like that before. She could quite easily have killed him, Sophie thought, and after listening to him confess to Joe's murder, perhaps she had meant to. She shook her head, trying to reconcile that with the image of Lil as she'd first met her, with her infectious grin and jolly schoolgirl way of talking.

Yet in spite of it all, Sophie thought Lil now seemed somehow far more like that Lil than she'd done for a long while. Best of all, things between the two of them felt right again. As she'd talked with the others, Sophie had felt reassured by Lil's presence close by her side, where she belonged.

There had certainly been a great deal for the rest of them to talk about. Sophie had told Jack and Leo about the showdown with Forsyth in the Casselli family tomb, while Carruthers filled in the details of how they had discovered he was the double agent. In their turn, Jack and Leo had related the events of the party at the Palazzo Stella, including what Leo had heard of the secret meeting of the *Fraternitas Draconum*, and her discovery of the real identity of Mrs Davenport.

'So she was *Lady Tremayne* . . .' Sophie had sighed, making sense of it all at last. 'She must have taken on a new name and a new identity when she went to New York, but continued her association with the *Fraternitas*. She must have persuaded them to allow her to become a member and to take charge of their New York Division. She organised the party in Venice as an excuse for the most senior members of the *Fraternitas* to gather without anyone becoming suspicious. And she wore those veils and extraordinary clothes to prevent anyone from London recognising her as Lady Tremayne.'

'But someone did recognise her,' said Leo. 'Mrs Knight! She even wrote her a letter which showed she knew exactly who she was.'

'And so Lady Tremayne had one of her men deliver her a box of poisoned chocolates, to get her out of the way before she could give away the truth,' said Jack.

'The worst thing is, she *did* tell us the truth,' said Sophie with a sigh. 'We just weren't listening.'

'Tell us about what happened at the party after Lil and

I left,' demanded Carruthers, who had very little interest in Mrs Knight.

Jack shrugged. 'There isn't a great deal to tell. Ella and I hunted about for a key, but we couldn't find one anywhere. But we did find Phyllis and Hugo and some of their friends, and between us we managed to break down the door to that room. Thankfully the noise of the party was so loud by that stage, and it had all become so wild that no one paid much attention! I suppose the *Fraternitas* were still busy with their meeting and I think any of the guests that passed by thought we were up to some kind of, you know . . . *high jinks*.' Jack shrugged.

'Once they'd got me out of the room, we did exactly as you said and left the party,' said Leo, taking up the tale. 'We went straight back to the Pension Mancini. Everyone else had already gone to bed, but of course we waited until you came back.'

Sophie nodded. It had been the early hours of the morning when she, Lil and Carruthers had finally staggered into the parlour – sopping wet, freezing cold and very tired indeed. After their journey back across the lagoon, they'd taken Paolo home. They'd had to break the news to him that his beautiful gondola had been left to drift on the lagoon, where no doubt it had been smashed to pieces by the storm. Sophie had promised she would send him the money to replace it with an even finer one: if the Secret Service Bureau wouldn't pay the bill, she'd decided, then

Taylor & Rose would. They might be short of cash but she knew the gondola was Paolo's livelihood and she was going to see it was replaced.

Sophie could never have imagined she'd be so glad to see the red plush armchairs and fringed lampshades of the Pension Mancini. With the hotel so empty, there was no difficulty finding room for Lil and Carruthers and they'd all gone to bed for a few hours of much-needed sleep before the morning came and it was time to travel back to London.

It had felt very strange to be sitting around the breakfast table at the Pension Mancini one last time, with bowls of Signora Mancini's lumpy porridge in front of them. The rain had stopped, and though the canals were high with water and the streets were flooded in places, a watery sunlight now filtered through the lace curtains, illuminating the teacups and silverware.

The other guests of course had no idea what had happened and assumed that the pale faces and shadowed eyes of the younger guests were the result of a late night enjoying themselves. After Jack had introduced Lil and Carruthers, Mrs Wentworth had asked about the party.

'Oh! It was splendid – terribly magnificent, you know,' Jack had told her, but his words had come out sounding a little flat.

'I daresay you will all have headaches this morning.' Mrs Wentworth had nodded understandingly. 'A late night . . . and too much excitement.'

'Yes, it was rather – er – exciting,' Leo had said with a little laugh.

'When you are feeling better, you must tell me all about the Palazzo Stella. I know there are some most interesting paintings in the collection there,' Dr Beagle had added.

'Oh, there are!' Jack had said with feeling. Leo had opened her mouth to say something about *The Black Dragon*, but then shut it again abruptly.

'It must have been quite an experience,' Mrs Wentworth had continued conversationally. 'Archie and I went out for an early morning walk and it seems the whole of Venice is talking about Mrs Davenport's party, doesn't it, Archie?'

Archie, who had been reading at the table as usual, had only said: 'Mmmm.'

'But the biggest news is that Mrs Davenport just *disappeared* in the middle of the night,' Mrs Wentworth had explained. 'While the party was still going on, she apparently climbed aboard her gondola and *left*, with all the guests still enjoying themselves. In all that rain too! Rumour has it she's gone back to New York already. What an extraordinary woman – probably all part of her idea of creating a spectacle!'

Sophie and the others had exchanged glances. So Lady Tremayne had gone, and no doubt so had all the other senior members of the *Fraternitas Draconum*, just as soon as their meeting was over. But what had become of Forsyth? Carruthers had already telephoned the Bureau and arranged for the authorities to be notified of his whereabouts, but when they arrived, would he still be there? While the others made their preparations to depart, Sophie had persuaded another gondolier - an unknown young man in the same striped jersey and red neckerchief that Paolo had worn - to take her out on to the lagoon. Once she'd been close enough to the mausoleum, she'd taken out her field glasses and trained them on the building. It hadn't taken her long to see that Forsyth had already vanished. Had the *Fraternitas* rescued him? It was impossible to say.

'I thought I saw an interesting bird,' she'd explained to the gondolier, who was looking at her field glasses curiously. But he'd just shrugged as if he didn't much care anyway and begun trilling an opera *aria* as he'd sculled her back towards the shore.

Back at the Pension Mancini the others had been ready to leave. They'd said a warm farewell to Dr Beagle, who promised he would come and see Jack and Leo's next exhibition when he was back in London. They'd said farewell to Ella too: her father would soon arrive to take her back home, and in the meantime she'd be well looked after by Dr Beagle and Mrs Wentworth.

'Thank you for your help,' she'd said to Jack, Leo and Sophie before they left. 'I know Father will never in a thousand years believe that Great-aunt Caroline was murdered. But at least now *I* know the truth about what happened to her. She deserves that at least.'

The party at the Palazzo Stella had also had some other consequences for Ella. After her long conversation with César Chevalier, he'd given her his card and suggested that she come to see him when he was at his London *atélier* in March. 'He said he would be interested to look at my designs,' she'd explained, her cheeks flushed with excitement. 'And he said he sometimes takes on apprentices. He didn't promise anything, and goodness knows how I'd ever persuade Father, but I would *much* rather become an apprentice designer than a debutante.'

She and Jack had agreed they would keep in touch, and he'd invited her to join him at the Café Royal some evening soon. They'd lingered over their farewells, Leo and Sophie stepping away to give them a few moments alone. They'd both been rather pink-cheeked afterwards, and on the train Sophie had noticed Jack doodling pictures of Ella's face in his sketchbook. She suspected that she herself would no longer be appearing in quite so many of his portraits, but she didn't really mind. She liked Jack, and there was no denying he was dreadfully handsome and charming, but after what had happened between Lil and Joe, she felt more certain than ever that the last thing she wanted was romance.

Leo had spent most of the train journey drawing in her sketchbook too. She'd been trying to capture some of the faces she'd glimpsed at the *Fraternitas* council meeting.

Sophie had asked her to relate every detail of what she'd overheard, which had only confirmed her suspicions that the *Fraternitas* were working hard to stir up trouble and conflict in Europe. And with Lady Tremayne heading up their New York Division, their influence was reaching further afield, to America.

If only *she* had been the one behind that curtain! More than anything she wished she had been able to see the face of the man they called the Gold Dragon. She'd heard of him before, in St Petersburg, and it sounded as though he was the closest thing the *Fraternitas* had to an official leader. Leo had tried her best to draw his face. 'But it's hard!' she protested. 'There wasn't anything very distinctive about him at all!'

As she'd leaned over Leo's shoulder to look at her drawings, Sophie had noticed that in between her sketches of Venetian architecture, gondolas and masked figures, the pages of her sketchbooks were also filled with the elaborate shape of a twisting black dragon, repeated time and time again. She'd given Leo a quick, curious glance and Leo had blushed a little.

'There's just something about that painting,' she'd said. 'I can't get it out of my mind.'

Sophie had nodded. She knew what Leo meant. They might have seen the last of Benedetto Casselli's dragon paintings, but she knew neither she nor Leo would forget them any time soon.

Now, they made their way down Piccadilly in a group: Jack and Leo with their painting things and travelling bags, Lil and Carruthers with nothing more than a satchel each. Lil was walking ahead with Carruthers on one side of her and Jack on the other; behind them, Leo was looking around her as if she was seeing all the familiar London things with fresh eyes, while Sophie walked beside her, breathing in the smoky city air with a feeling of relief.

'I'm going to get some buns,' said Lil, stopping outside a baker's shop. Leo and Jack followed her into the shop to help choose, but Carruthers stood outside looking restless, his shoulders tense, one hand still fiddling with something in his pocket. Meanwhile, Sophie saw a newsboy selling papers on the corner, and she went over to him and handed over a ha'penny for the morning edition of *The Daily Picture*, just as she always did. But then something on the front page caught her eye and she let out a little gasp of surprise.

'I say, Lil – what's this?' she exclaimed as Lil came out of the shop with the bag of sticky buns in her hand, grinning over her shoulder at something Jack had said.

A few minutes later, they were all hurrying through Sinclair's department store, to the door of the Taylor & Rose office. It was after their usual opening time, but the sign on the door still read CLOSED.

Several people were standing nearby as though waiting and began whispering excitedly as they approached.

'Excuse me!' said a young gentleman to Lil. 'Are you Miss Lilian Rose?'

'Might I have your autograph?' asked another.

'Are you opening your office?' asked a young lady with roses in her hat. 'I need to make an appointment – it's urgent!'

Sophie and Lil exchanged startled glances as they quickly rushed through without answering anyone, closing the door behind them. The reception area was quite empty but in the back office they found Billy, Mei and Tilly, sitting in an anxious little huddle around the same edition of the newspaper that Sophie was holding. Daisy was sitting at their feet: as the others came in she bounded up and rushed towards Sophie and Lil, giving little yelps of excitement.

'You're back!' gasped Billy.

'We've got masses to tell you – but what's *this*?'

Billy's face turned crimson. 'It isn't what I wrote, I *promise* you it isn't!' he exclaimed at once. 'It isn't my story at all! Well, it *is* my story I suppose, but they've changed it so much. My story *was* based on one of your real assignments, but I made it about a boy detective and not about you at all! But they've rewritten it so it sounds like it's about Lil, and to make it seem like a real Taylor & Rose case!'

'This is all Roberta Russell's doing,' said Lil, scanning the page. 'She's meddled with my interview too. I didn't say *half* these things to her.'

'I should hope not!' exclaimed Tilly. 'What's all this

about your *exotic band* of helpers?' She snorted in disgust.

'You know I didn't say *any* of that rot,' said Lil. 'She's made everything sound so . . . sensational, and silly. And I certainly didn't say a word about spies.' She looked at Carruthers, who was frowning disapprovingly at the newspaper. 'I'm not that much of an idiot. She brought it up but I just laughed it off and said we'd never done anything like that!'

'It's *spy fever* . . .' murmured Sophie, sitting down slowly beside the others. 'That's what you heard them say at the *Fraternitas* meeting, wasn't it, Leo?'

Leo nodded. 'Yes. *Spy fever in Britain* . . . and something about extending it to other nations.'

The others were looking at her, puzzled, but Sophie explained: 'It's all deliberate. The news reports about German spies in Britain . . . working them into this interview with Lil . . . changing Billy's story about espionage so that instead of being fiction, it reads like the story of a real case that actually happened. They're trying to drum up fear and anxiety about spies amongst the British public. It's another tactic to help create the climate for war – building up suspicion between Britain and Germany. It's the *Fraternitas* pulling the strings.'

'But how could they be controlling the newspapers like that?' asked Jack.

'We know by now that the *Fraternitas* can control whatever they like,' said Sophie with a shrug. 'Their members are powerful and rich. And let's not forget about the woman who works there, the one we *know* is connected to them.'

'So they're trying to drum up all this about *spies* . . . and we've just *helped* them?' said Billy looking horrified.

'It's not your fault, Billy,' said Mei. 'How could you possibly have known they were going to do this? How could any of us?'

'Of course it isn't,' said Lil. 'Any more than it's my fault Miss Russell put all this nonsense about *spies* in my interview. Gosh, I wish they hadn't used that idiotic picture of me with the gun . . .' she added as if to herself.

'It's a jolly good story though,' said Jack, who had absently taken a bun from the bag and begun chewing it while he bent over the newspaper. 'I like this bit at the end, about how she works out the spy has the code book in his pocket and manages to get it away from him. Awfully clever.'

'Actually, that bit's real,' said Billy, looking slightly mollified by this.

'Except that it was Sophie who did that, not me,' said Lil, leaning over Jack's shoulder to look. 'And the fellow did give the game away rather. He kept clutching his pocket so we knew there was something important in there.' As she spoke, she turned slowly to where Carruthers was standing, hastily removing a hand from his pocket. Sophie turned to look too, and under their gaze Carruthers' face slowly turned a vivid shade of scarlet.

'What's in *your* pocket, Sam?' asked Lil suddenly, in a dangerous voice. 'You've been hanging on to something in there most of the way back from Venice.'

'Nothing!' said Carruthers crossly. 'None of your business!' But he didn't sound quite as confident as usual, and as if he couldn't help it his hand slipped back into his pocket again.

Sophie gave a little gasp. 'You've still got it, haven't you?' she asked.

Carruthers glared at her and then at Lil, looking as though he was about to erupt in a burst of temper. But then his shoulders drooped suddenly and he hung his head as if he was ashamed. He put his hand in his pocket and drew out a small book. It had obviously been soaked through: the pages were wrinkled and it looked as though the ink had smudged. But it had been carefully dried out and still looked more or less intact. The single eye on the leather cover glinted gold.

'You *took* it!' Lil cried furiously. 'You went back for it! After we'd all agreed to let it go.'

'Actually, I think you'll find I never agreed to that,' said Carruthers in a rather tetchy voice. 'You can't just destroy something like this, you know. It's old – and valuable – and besides, it's not our decision to make,' he finished pompously.

'You weren't even going to tell us, were you?' Lil

declaimed, hands on hips. 'You were just going to hand it over to your grandfather and take all the credit yourself!'

They began to argue, but Sophie wasn't listening. She was staring unhappily at the book in Carruthers' hand. It looked so small and innocent, but she knew it was not. She'd felt so relieved when it had disappeared into the water, but now here it was again, back in London. She'd promised to see it destroyed – it *had* to be destroyed, whatever anyone else said.

In the distance, she was vaguely aware that someone was hammering on the door. 'Hey, are you opening today or what?' called a voice.

Mei and Billy exchanged glances and then Mei got to her feet. Regardless of what else might be going on, they had clients waiting and appointments scheduled, and judging by the noise outside, the combination of Lil's interview and Billy's story had attracted rather a crowd. 'At least this will help us balance the books,' Mei muttered under her breath as she quickly smoothed her hair and straightened the bow at the neck of her blouse, before hurrying off to unlock the door.

A Sinclair's delivery boy in blue uniform and cap was standing on the threshold. 'Took you long enough,' he grumbled, handing her a pile of letters. 'Got your post here. What are all this lot doing out here anyway?'

Billy came to stand beside Mei and addressed the throng: 'Er – apologies for keeping you waiting. If you already have an appointment, you may come through and take a seat in the waiting room. For the rest of you, I'm afraid we have no more available appointments today, but if you will form a queue, Miss Lim will book you in for another time.'

Mei raced through to the office and handed the pile of letters to Sophie, before hurrying back to her desk and getting out the big appointment book, while Billy began marshalling the people inside. Meanwhile, Lil and Carruthers were still arguing, while Leo, Jack and Tilly had gathered round the newspaper and were reading Billy's story and eating the buns. 'It *is* very exciting,' Tilly acknowledged.

'He's a jolly good writer,' said Leo, impressed.

Without really thinking about what she was doing, Sophie began mechanically opening the letters. But as she opened the first envelope and glanced at the short note inside, she let out a sudden yelp, dropping it as though it had burned her fingers.

'Lil —' she managed to croak in a voice that sounded nothing like her own.

Lil turned to look at her, and then fell abruptly silent. She'd never seen such an extraordinary expression on Sophie's face before. 'What is it?'

'Sophie?' asked Carruthers, looking worried.

Sophie pushed the letter towards them and then covered her face with her hands. 'Just read it,' she said in the same strange voice.

Lil picked it up and Carruthers leaned over her shoulder to read it.

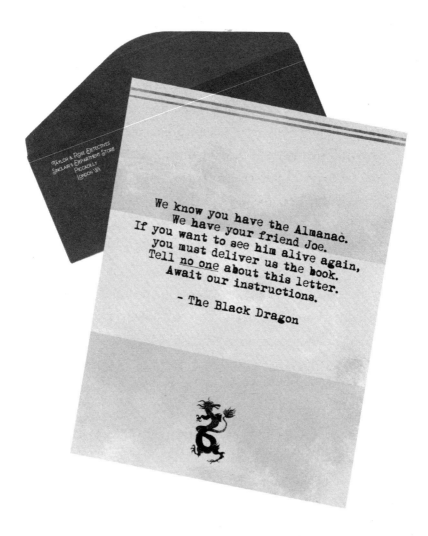

TAYLOR & ROSE DETECTIVES
SINCLAIR'S DEPARTMENT STORE
PICCADILLY
LONDON W1

We know you have the Almanac.
We have your friend Joe.
If you want to see him alive again,
you must deliver us the book.
Tell no one about this letter.
Await our instructions.

- The Black Dragon

Lil stared at Sophie, and then back at the letter. It swam before her eyes, the words seeming to form mysterious shapes, as if they were written in another language.

'*The Black Dragon!*' whispered Carruthers hoarsely.

Lil sat down very slowly in the chair beside Sophie. In that moment several things were very clear to her.

Somehow, Lady Tremayne knew that the book had not been lost to the lagoon of Venice. Somehow, she knew that they still had it, and she wanted it for herself. Somehow, she expected them to give it to her.

And somehow, Joe was still alive.

No. 2598   **A NORTON NEWSPAPER**   *One Half-Penny*

23rd February 1912

THE DAILY PICTURE

THE THRILLING EXPLOITS OF LONDON'S LEADING LADY DETECTIVE

Our reporter, Miss R. Russell meets Lilian Rose – once the darling of the West End stage, now a daring young detective.

With a selection of new portrait photographs by C. Walters

Sherlock Holmes, the great detective of fiction, may consult from his smoky rooms in Baker Street – but London's real-life young lady detective Miss Lilian Rose can be found in quite different surroundings. Amongst the exquisite gowns, Paris hats and stylish shoes of Sinclair's department store are the discreet and elegant offices of Taylor & Rose Detectives. Lovers of the theatre will recognise Miss Rose as a talented young actress, who until recently graced the London stage, but who has now turned her talents in an unexpected new direction. Like Holmes himself – Miss Rose is no stranger to the art of disguise, employing her acting skills to transform herself skilfully into anyone from a handsome young gentleman in a silk hat to an ordinary housemaid. As well as a host of disguises for every occasion, she keeps a bag ready packed close at hand for assignments that may require her to set out on a journey at short notice, whether travelling

across Europe by train on the trail of enemy spies or setting out aboard a steamer on business for one of her high society clients. In addition to her partner, Miss Sophie Taylor, Miss Rose has the support of a team of young assistants from every corner of the globe. Together with this exotic band of helpers, she is able to tackle even the most complex and baffling of mysteries that would fox the likes of Holmes himself – (continued p4)

(continued p4)

READ THE FIRST IN OUR EXCLUSIVE SERIES OF REAL LIFE CASES STARRING Miss Lilian Rose – AS WRITTEN BY Mr W. Parker OF Taylor & Rose Detectives:

SECRETS ON THE SHORE

As the train rattled towards its destination, the young detective was once more ready to embark on a dangerous mission. None of her fellow passengers in the busy train carriage could possibly have guessed that the beautiful young lady apparently headed on a seaside holiday, was in fact setting out on the trail of something dark and deadly – a ring of enemy spies (continued p7)

(continued p7)

– White Star Line's 'largest ocean steamer in the world' to undertake maiden voyage to New York – p7
– New Prime Minister appointed in Norway – p15
– Society Pages: Celebrated guests attend glamorous Carnival celebration in Venice – p28

AUTHOR'S NOTE

While this story and its characters are completely fictional, *Villains in Venice* takes some inspiration from real-life history.

In particular, the Secret Service Bureau in this story is loosely inspired by the real British Secret Service Bureau, which was established in 1909. Initially a very small operation, it soon grew, and was later divided into two separate divisions — one to deal with counter-espionage at home in Britain, and another focused on gathering intelligence abroad. Today we know these as 'MI5' and 'MI6'.

'Spy fever' was also a very real phenomenon in the years running up to the First World War, when it was widely believed that there were large numbers of German spies secretly at work in Britain, gathering information to pass back to their spymaster in Berlin. But while it's true that there may have been some German spies operating in Britain at the time, today many historians think there were not nearly as many of them as people believed. The 'spy fever' of the 1910s was partly the result of exaggerated newspaper coverage, as well as thrilling spy stories by authors like William Le Queux, which stirred up fears and anxieties about enemy agents.

The Fraternitas Draconum and the Loyal Order of Lions, are of course both completely fictional. But if you are lucky enough to visit Venice, you can look out for images of the winged lion which you'll see all over the city on flags, statues and buildings. You may also spot a few dragons — including the dragon on a tall pillar in the Piazza San Marco, which stands opposite a winged lion.

The Palazzo Stella is also imaginary, but there are many real palazzos you can see along Venice's Grand Canal. Mrs Davenport's party takes a some inspiration from the glamorous gatherings held by the Marchesa Luisa Casati at the Palazzo Venier dei Leoni - which today is a famous art gallery, home to the Peggy Guggenheim Collection.

ACKNOWLEDGEMENTS

Thank you to the wonderful team at Egmont, especially to Sarah Levison. As always, I am hugely grateful to brilliant illustrator Karl James Mountford and to designer Laura Bird, for creating such a beautiful book.

Many thanks to my agent and friend Louise Lamont, who again joined me on a research trip – this time bravely agreeing to eat cicchetti and wander the streets and canals of Venice, all the name of Taylor & Rose Secret Agents. I hope there will be more adventures in our future. And thank you to everyone who shared Venice tips and traveller's tales, including Nina Douglas and Katie Webber. Closer to home, thank you to Jen and the gang at Waterstones King Street Lancaster for their support, particularly when research books were urgently needed.

Writing a book with a baby in tow is rather challenging (who knew?!) so particular thanks go to my family, especially my mum and my husband, for keeping a certain small person entertained so I could take Sophie and Lil on this next chapter of their adventures.

Thank you as always to all the booksellers, librarians, teachers and readers of all ages who have been following Sophie and Lil's story – and who so enthusiastically clamoured to know what happened next.

And a special (bluebell-scented) thank you to Ali Dougal, who has been such a wonderful champion of Sophie and Lil from the start.

Another thrilling adventure with Sophie and Lil!

TAYLOR & ROSE
Secret Agents

SPIES IN ST. PETERSBURG

KATHERINE WOODFINE

Illustrated by Karl James Mountford

EGMONT
Books

The Sinclair's Mysteries

The Sinclair's Mysteries
THE CLOCKWORK SPARROW

KATHERINE WOODFINE

The Sinclair's Mysteries
THE JEWELLED MOTH

KATHERINE WOODFINE

oin Sophie and Lil in these exciting,
fast-paced mystery-adventures!

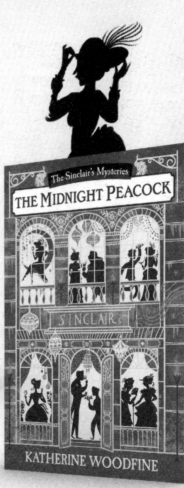